1954
M

D1013234

Spring and Fall

Also by Nicholas Delbanco

FICTION

The Vagabonds
What Remains
Old Scores
In the Name of Mercy
The Writers' Trade, & Other Stories
About My Table, & Other Stories
Stillness
Sherbrookes
Possession
Small Rain
Fathering
In the Middle Distance
News
Consider Sappho Burning
Grasse 3/23/66
The Martlet's Tale

NONFICTION

Anywhere Out of the World: Travel, Writing, Death
The Countess of Stanlein Restored: A History of the Countess
of Stanlein ex-Paganini Stradivarius Violoncello of 1707
The Lost Suitcase: Reflections on the Literary Life
Running in Place: Scenes from the South of France
The Beaux Arts Trio: A Portrait
Group Portrait: Conrad, Crane, Ford, James, & Wells

BOOKS EDITED

The Hopwood Awards: 75 Years of Prized Writing
The Sincerest Form: Writing Fiction by Imitation
The Writing Life: The Hopwood Lectures, Fifth Series
Talking Horse: Bernard Malamud on Life and Work
(with A. Cheuse)
Speaking of Writing: Selected Hopwood Lectures
Writers and Their Craft: Short Stories and Essays
on the Narrative (with L. Goldstein)
Stillness and Shadows (two novels by John Gardner)

SPRING AND FALL

A Novel

NICHOLAS DELBANCO

WARNER BOOKS

NEW YORK   BOSTON

This book is a work of fiction. Names, characters, places, and incidents are the product of the author's imagination or are used fictitiously. Any resemblance to actual events, locales, or persons, living or dead, is coincidental.

Warner Books
Hachette Book Group USA
1271 Avenue of the Americas
New York, NY 10020
Book design by Fearn Cutler da Vicq
Printed in the United States of America

First Edition: October 2006
10   9   8   7   6   5   4   3   2   1

Library of Congress Cataloging-in-Publication Data

Delbanco, Nicholas.
    Spring and fall / Nicholas Delbanco.— 1st ed.
        p. cm.
    ISBN-13: 978-0-446-57871-4
    ISBN-10: 0-446-57871-1
    1. Older people—Fiction. 2. Man-woman relationships—Fiction.
3. Domestic fiction. I. Title.
    PS3554.E442S67   2006
    813'.54—dc22   2006006561

Gail Hochman
Best of agents, best of friends

SPRING AND FALL

'Tis time; descend; be stone no more: approach . . .
WILLIAM SHAKESPEARE, *THE WINTER'S TALE*, V, iii

I

2004

THE M.S. *DIANA* SET OUT FROM THE PORT OF ROME, her destination Valetta. Powering south from Civitavecchia, she had stops planned in Sorrento and, on the coast of Sicily, Naxos, Siracusa and Porto Empedocle. Built in 1960, she had been newly refitted. The ship had a Bridge Deck, a Baltic Deck, a Mediterranean Deck, a Caribbean Deck and, just above the waterline, an Atlantic Deck. In the old days, under sail, the journey might have taken months; now the trip from Rome to Malta was scheduled for six days. In the old days, in the times of war, these waters had been treacherous; now it was late September, and a pleasure cruise.

The ship's manifest listed fifty-seven cabins and a passenger capacity of 108, not counting crew; it was 87.4 meters long and 13.2 meters wide. The M.S. *Diana*'s decor had been conceived of in the Swedish mode; she was remodeled in Gothenburg, with—so the brochure claimed—stylistic influence from

France. Her owner was American, her flag Liberian, her crew came from Croatia. Their names, it seemed to Lawrence, made a kind of music; they introduced themselves as Vinko, Darko, Marko, Ivo, Miho, Vlatka and Andrea. He tried to remember their names.

Three nights before, he had flown from Detroit and in the morning reached Rome. There he checked into the Grand Palace Hotel, on the Via Veneto, and willed himself to rest. Across the street was the American Embassy, fenced in and heavily guarded; up on the next corner loomed the Excelsior, and down the way was the Piazza Barberini, with its Bernini Fountain and cascade of loud cars. He was sixty-four years old, recovering from angioplasty, and his doctor had suggested that he take a trip.

"You're fine," he said. "You've done just fine."

"I don't feel"—Lawrence hesitated—"*ready*, really."

"The risk of stenosis is just about over. It's a statistical possibility, of course—we should wait a year to be certain—but the risk is minimal. And I'm not suggesting you go somewhere very far away. Not, I mean, some third-world country or up the slopes of Everest . . ."

"I'm not sure I'm up to it."

"Depression," said his doctor, "is a common side effect. In men our age, in fact, it's damn near unavoidable. Why don't you take a cruise?"

He knew Tommy Einhorn well. They were neighbors in Ann Arbor, and they played tennis together, and he thought of Tommy as his friend as well as doctor; the advice was kindly meant. "I'm not the cruising type," said Lawrence.

"No?"

"All that forced gaiety. The Princess Line. Calisthenics up on deck, the samba by the swimming pool; whatever it is they insist that you do . . ."

"No one's insisting on anything." Dr. Einhorn leaned back in his swivel chair and pressed his fingertips together. "It's only a suggestion. Let me repeat it: your heart's just *fine*. It's better now than it has been for years."

"Let's hope so," Lawrence said.

"And these new Cypher stents are just the ticket."

"Ticket?"

Einhorn laughed. "The ticket for the ticker, hey. Not bad. I must remember that."

So HE HAD LOOKED FOR and then booked a trip to places it seemed safe to go, first stipulating that the cruise ship must be small. By "safe," Lawrence told the travel agent, he meant not so much safety from the threat of terror as somewhere where the medicine was adequate and from which, in case of trouble, he could leave. He signed up for travel insurance. The cruise itself had begun in Marseilles, with stops in Nice and Monaco, but he elected the single-week option and flew alone to Rome.

He had not been there in years. The airport, once so brightly new, seemed faded and shopworn, a little, and the train to the *termine* reeked. Years before, he had spent time in Italy, studying Renaissance architecture, and he ventured out to his old haunts—the Spanish Steps, the Borghese Gardens, the Campidoglio and back streets of Trastevere—with a kind of dutiful inclusiveness; to have been young in the Eternal City and to come there now again as an aging tourist was bittersweet at best. He felt not so much nostalgic as aggrieved.

The traffic had increased. The streets were clogged with Vespas, buses, taxis, and the air was rank. Lawrence monitored his breathing and waited for a telltale signal from his chest. It did not come. The Pantheon was ringed by motorcycles, and the Trevi Fountain—past which he could remember wandering at night, and where Anita Ekberg laved herself in *La Dolce Vita*, gown clinging wetly to her breasts—was now a photo op. Everywhere were groups of sightseers and, waving umbrellas or pennants, their guides.

His sleep was fitful, troubled, and the room too hot. He ate by himself, poorly, expensively, and the waiters addressed him in English. The elegant Italians and the girls in their scant dresses paid him no attention; only beggars waited for him, holding out their hands. The line in front of St. Peter's was so long and daunting that he did not revisit the cathedral or its chapel but walked by the Tiber instead.

For two days Lawrence wandered the streets. He tried to recapture his old rapt excitement, the fascination of the buildings and the beauty of the hills and the Colosseum and Forum. It did not work. What he focused on instead were pigeons and the dog scat in the paving; by the time he transferred to the M.S. *Diana* he was ready—more than willing—to escape.

THE PORT OF CIVITAVECCHIA bustled with tankers at anchor. Lined up by the dock itself were cruise ships in their pastel glory, towering confections like wedding cakes on water, with names emblazoned on their bows and smokestacks: *Marco Polo, The Star Princess, Island Queen, The Attica Swan.* Last and least of this procession was the M.S. *Diana,* and this pleased him; its scale was small, its aspect self-effacing, and the driver who delivered him extracted his bags from the trunk of the taxi with something very like pity.

"Ecco, signore. Va bene?"

"Va ben," he said. *"Mille grazie,"* and tipped the driver lavishly as if to prove a point.

At the gangplank they were waiting. A man in a white uniform saluted, and a blonde in slacks and sailor's cap said, "Welcome, welcome aboard! I'm your cruise director." She produced a practiced smile; then she consulted a passenger list and checked off Lawrence's name. Inside they collected his passport and gave him a key to his cabin and, carrying his luggage, conducted him downstairs. He had a fleeting sense of brightwork, wood, an elevator in its cage and carpeting and corridors, and then the man who led him to his cabin turned and, half saluting, said in thickly accented English, "Haf a pleazant trip!"

In his room he found a set of thermal clothing and, underneath the portholes, a yellow life preserver. There was a bottle of complimentary red wine on the cabinet between twin beds and a bowl of fruit and sheet of paper asking, "Why is a ship called 'she'?"

There was a drawing of a clipper ship and, beneath it, a barbed anchor; Lawrence read the printed answer:

A ship is called a she because there is always a great deal of bustle about her; there is usually a gang of man about, she has a waist and stays; it takes a lot of paint to keep her good looking; it is not the initial expense that brakes you, it is the upkeep; she can be all decked out, but it takes an experienced man to handle her correctly; and without a man at the helm, she is absolutely uncontrollable.

She shows her topsides, hides her bottom and when coming into port always heads for the buoys.

Love her, take good care of her, and she shall take good care of you.

He unpacked his clothing first. He hung up his jackets and exercise clothes and stowed the empty suitcase underneath the bed. He arranged his medications in the bathroom and laid out his sketch pad and books on the shelf; he liked the cabin's clean enclosure, the wooden containers for stemware and bottles, the way that the cabinets locked. After the nightlong bustle of the Via Veneto this organized silence was welcome, and he lay back in his shirtsleeves and attempted to take stock.

BEFORE THE TROUBLE with his heart he took good health for granted. Lawrence watched what he ate and did not smoke and, although he could have dropped ten pounds and refused a second cocktail, did his best to stay in shape. He looked, he liked to joke, not a day past sixty-three. In truth he did seem youthful, and his students and those colleagues in architecture school who did not know his actual age would have been surprised by it; he had retained a wide-eyed and infectious pleasure in the act, the *fact* of teaching, and he paced up and down

the studio with spring in his long stride. He was more of a professor now than a practitioner—more engaged, he liked to say,
in the theory than practice of architecture. But the profession
still compelled him, and the New Urbanists still referenced his
early work. He had most of his muscle and much of his hair
and was known, in Ann Arbor, as a bit of a boulevardier; he
had three children and two ex-wives and a series of companions with whom he sometimes slept. For a long time, however,
he had lived alone.

When the symptoms of angina came he at first ignored
them, believing the bright pain in his chest was only acid re-
flux or, maybe, a pulled muscle. Lawrence went to spinning
class and worked out on the treadmill three mornings a week,
and the shortness of his breath seemed somehow a function
of hard exercise; he had always sweated easily. Now he woke
up drenched in sweat. The strange taste in his mouth increased—as though he sucked on tin, then brass—and stairs
became a problem; then the band of pain became a vise, extending from shoulder to shoulder. When he begged off from
tennis with Tommy Einhorn, Tommy asked him, "Why,
what's wrong?"

This was the start of July. In the emergency room they
asked for his symptoms and as soon as he described them
wheeled Lawrence down to the cardiac unit, where white-
coated attendants were waiting. They recorded his pulse and
blood pressure and temperature and gave him oxygen and hep-
arin and a set of EKGs. It was likely, said the attending cardiologist, he had a blockage in an artery or arteries, and they
would perform an angiogram in order to determine where the

trouble lay. This was routine procedure, nothing to be concerned about, but he had arrived just in time. An angioplasty or heart bypass might well be indicated, he was told, for he had unstable angina and should be hospitalized.

Because they did not wish to operate short-staffed on Independence Day, Lawrence waited the long holiday weekend, lying aggrieved in the hospital bed and dealing with visits from residents and interns and Dr. Einhorn's colleagues. They said that he was lucky, very lucky, and if one of his organs was slated for trouble, well, let it be the heart; we can do much less, these days, about the liver or lungs or the brain. It's a plumbing problem, mostly, and time to fix the pipes. They said he should be grateful to be alive in the twenty-first century and living in Ann Arbor, where the medical facilities were fine.

"You know the first three symptoms of heart trouble?" Tommy Einhorn asked.

"No, what?"

"Denial, denial, denial."

"Very funny."

"Very almost not funny at all, my friend. This is the riot act I'm reading you."

"All right. Okay."

"We're prepared to handle it," said Dr. Einhorn, "if you have an infarction. But now you're stable and you're being monitored; only folks in crisis get to go to the theater this weekend."

"All right."

"You have to be patient. A patient patient," Einhorn said.

"Hey, not bad. I should remember that."

. . .

THREE BELLS SOUNDED IN HIS CABIN, and a man's voice boomed from a speaker by the porthole. The purser introduced himself. "Good afternoon, ladies and gentlemen, welcome aboard," he said. "On behalf of the captain and crew of the M.S. *Diana* we wish everyone a most delightful trip." Then over the intercom system all passengers were informed that there would be a mandatory life preserver drill before they could depart. They were instructed to report to level 4 in fifteen minutes, please. Departure was scheduled for seven o'clock, and in the morning, from Sorrento, we will travel to Capri.

Lawrence roused himself. Not sorry to have been interrupted in his meditation on disease—the long wait in the hospital, the procedure itself, its aftermath—he laced on his sneakers and slipped on a jacket and found his way up to the deck. The wind was high. Passengers were milling about and awaiting instructions and laughing together and huddling in corners to hide from the wind. The man beside him on the deck was wearing bracelets on his wrist and an antinausea patch.

"Cold enough for you?" he asked.

The cruise director, smiling, nodding, said, "Everybody, your attention, please!"

Lawrence was provided with a life preserver and shown how to fasten it, then told that in the unlikely event of an emergency he should report to lifeboat station 6. He watched a demonstration of the whistle and inflatable flotation device; he was instructed what to carry with him from the cabin and what to leave behind. His concentration flagged, however, the way it drifted in an airplane when flight attendants enact their pre-flight pantomime; heart trouble happens to others, he could remember thinking, and most of the time he'd felt fine. Emergencies happen to others, he could remember thinking, and his own was in the past. The document they sent him home with began with the assertion: "Successful PCI of culprit LAD/D1 Lesion . . ."

"You've had," the cardiologist declared, "your last drink of buttermilk and your final piece of steak."

"You were lucky," Dr. Einhorn chimed in. "The left anterior descending was ninety percent occluded. But it's just like real estate—what counts is location, location. And yours was in the spot they call the widow-maker."

"I'm not married," Lawrence said.

"You were lucky," his neighbor repeated. "No joke. We caught it just in time."

His sons lived in phoenix and vail. Ten years before, their mother had remarried—a professor in the Political Science Department—but Janet stayed, it seemed to him, unbending, unforgiving. Lawrence tried to let bygones be bygones, to suggest that their marriage was far in the past and they should—for the sake of the children—be friends. The wound of his old infidelities stayed fresh with her nevertheless; if they met at a concert or the farmers' market Janet turned away and gave him, pointedly, her back. When John or Andrew brought their wives and children to town they apportioned the length of their visits and, to keep from playing favorites or offending either parent, stayed in the Campus Inn.

His daughter by his first wife was living in Chicago. As though there had been some contagion, some gene that spawned failed marriages, his daughter too had been divorced and now lived alone. In part as a result of this, Catherine was very helpful during his time in the hospital and, afterward, at home. His sons had flown to see him, and remained in touch by e-mail or the telephone, but she bore the brunt of it—the grocery shopping, the first week of driving, the details of Lawrence's medical leave. It was as though they shared again the rhythms of domestic life, and he enjoyed the way they did the crossword puzzle together, the way she matched her stride to his during their afternoon walks.

When Catherine returned to Chicago he found himself regretting it, for he had grown accustomed to her presence by his side. Therefore he invited her to join him for the trip. "You've been wonderful," said Lawrence; he wanted to show her how grateful he was and would enjoy the company. But she had used up her vacation in July and could not take another week away from work.

"My treat. I'll pay for it," he repeated.

"Daddy, that isn't the point."

"The point is," he cajoled her, "your father misses you. And you haven't ever been to see—the cruise is billed as—the 'Treasures of the Western Mediterranean.' Don't you think you need to see them? The Isle of Capri? The temples of Agrigento? Malta?"

"It's called my life, remember? And I need to get back to it."

"I *know* that, sweetheart, I do understand."

Her life, he did not say to her, was something she should try to change: a dead-end job, a bridge game every Monday night, a clutch of other single women living in Hyde Park. How had this happened, he wanted to ask, how had his golden daughter grown so plump and wan? Her husband had taken a business trip and did not return from Atlanta and, as she later discovered, had emptied out their bank account and was living with another lawyer and filing for divorce. Catherine was childless, thirty-seven, and although she tried to put her best foot forward and a brave face on things Lawrence knew that in her heart of hearts she too was disappointed; she had been so hopeful, once, such an ebullient presence. The laughter was over, the bright light had dimmed, and to the best of his ability he tried to make amends.

"How can I help?" he asked again. "You helped me so much this last summer."

"No problem."

"I *hate* that phrase, 'no problem.' It's what everybody says these days. In restaurants, at the Whole Foods checkout line, everybody's telling you, 'No problem.' What they mean, I believe, is *De nada*. You're welcome."

"*De nada,*" Catherine said.

BEFORE DINNER THEIR FIRST NIGHT on board the captain offered his passengers a champagne reception in the Elsinore Lounge. There was a bar and wicker furniture and upholstered chairs. Waiters passed trays of hors d'oeuvres. There were portraits of ladies and soldiers and amateurish hunting scenes and one of the goddess Diana covering her nudity with well-positioned boughs. She seemed beguiled by moonlight, and when Lawrence looked more closely at the painting he saw a man in the moon.

The captain was broad-shouldered, with gold braid and buttons on his coat, and close-cropped black hair. His English was not good. Holding a microphone in one hand and, with the other, his cap to his chest, he shifted on his feet and cleared his throat. The weather was *temps variable,* the captain announced, leetle rain was in the forecast and the seas are moderate high. He would do everything he could to assurance their entire comfort, and the *Diana* of course would be entire stable and safety, but he cannot guarantee conditions in the morning and if these waves continue he might have be needing to anchor in Naples. Drink up, he said, don't worry, for it is always like this on the sea, and we are very glad you joining us this voyage and in a day or three maybe the weather sure be fine.

Lawrence ate with a couple from El Paso and a widow from Des Moines. He did not catch their names. The waiter was called Darko, and he knew this because Darko wore a nameplate and, having introduced himself, served them silently, attentively. The other three had boarded in Marseilles, and they said tonight was the first time their chairs had been in locked positions on the floor; they pointed to the clips beneath each chair and table, and the fasteners attached to them; they raised and clicked their glasses, chorusing, "Anchors aweigh!" The lady from Des Moines said she wasn't the least bit concerned, she'd never been seasick a day in her life and this was her seventeenth trip. Well, only her twelfth cruise in fact but it *was* her seventeenth trip. She had been to Italy but never Sicily or Malta, and she asked Lawrence if he'd been before to any of their ports of call, and he said, Not to Malta, no, but Sicily and many years ago. She asked, How many, and he said, Oh, forty, forty-two. She said, How interesting, you can be our expert, and asked him for the salt.

The conversation trailed off. The dining room was full. The sea and sky were dark. He ate in silence—nodding at Darko, who offered more wine—imagining what Catherine would have made of his companions and how she would have handled this and whom she might have found to talk to or dance with, later on. Somewhere, a piano played. Lawrence looked around him at the room—the white-haired and the wispy-haired, the ramrod-straight or bent, all elderly—and tried not to regret his choice, this gently pitching vessel that would convey them nowhere in particular and for many thousands of dollars. The men sported striped shirts and blazers, the women wore pantsuits and pearls.

One woman at a corner table arrested his gaze briefly; she was regal-seeming, self-contained, and something in the way she held herself seemed in some way familiar. Her hair was gray. Her dress was blue. He made a mental note to try to speak to her later, when the meal was done, but the couple from El Paso were talking about immigration and the bridge to Juárez, the difficulty of border patrols, the Mexican families crossing at night, the RV they had purchased and were keeping in Las Cruces and how America was going to the Democratic dogs. "Don't get me wrong," the man announced, "you-all might just be Democrats and as long as we live in this wonderful country I'll fight for your right to have an opinion. But the opinion's *wrong*."

Lawrence drank decaffeinated coffee and a final glass of wine. He was, he recognized, exhausted, and excused himself and went on deck but saw nothing in the sky or sea and made his way down to his cabin and shrugged himself out of his clothes. What he dreamed of was a team of horses, cantering then galloping, and he awakened to the thump of his wineglass filled with water falling and breaking into splinters while the engines thrummed. He spent some minutes on his knees, carefully picking the shards from the carpet, then—when he was sure no glass fragments remained—fell asleep once more. This time he did not dream.

"You used to sing," said Catherine.

"Badly."

"Not so badly, Daddy. It was *fun*, the way we tap-danced."

"I have put off childish things," he said. "I'm an old man, sweetheart. Or haven't you noticed?"

"Not really."

"You know," he said, "last December we put on a skit—the architecture faculty puts on a skit every Christmas, lampooning each other, insulting the dean, looking consciously silly in front of the students—and I've always played a part in it and tried to steal the show. Telling jokes about Philip Johnson & Johnson or Frank Lloyd Wrong—stuff like that. Or Meier to Gehry to Graves, being Tinker to Evers to Chance . . ."

She looked at him blankly.

"Forgive me," Lawrence said. "It's a baseball joke, a joke about infielders, famous ones. And Meier and Gehry and Graves—Richard, Frank, and Michael—are the cleanup architects these days. The point is, I sang. I put on my old baseball cap and found a pair of knickers and was standing up there on the stage belting out my tune. *From Corbusier to Courvoisier, from Libeskind to Liebfraumilch, from Renzo to Piano,* fa la. And suddenly I saw myself the way the students must, an old man being idiotic, and the words just got stuck in my throat."

Catherine reached out her hand to him; he took and pressed and held it.

"There isn't that much music left is what I'm trying to say."

THE FOLLOWING MORNING DAWNED WETLY, and when Lawrence looked out of the porthole he saw that the M.S. *Diana* had been made fast to a dock. He dressed and went up to the deck. It was, the purser announced, the Bay of Naples they had sheltered in, and not the more open Sorrento, because tenders in Sorrento Harbor have proved unavailable this morning and the captain has decided not to wait until sufficient tenders for off-loading might be found. In the meantime, ladies and gentlemen, said the purser, a bus will take you to the embarkation point for the Isle of Capri, where you will see the sights. In the meantime, ladies and gentlemen, off to your left is Vesuvius and behind us the city of Naples, and we wish you all a very pleasant day.

There was a guide called Ettsio who stood at the base of the gangplank and shepherded those passengers who went ashore to a black and yellow tour bus with a driver he introduced as Giuseppe, my best friend. There was a round of applause. There was a hurtling drive past piers and storage sheds and garbage dumps to a station where they took a ferry to steep-cliffed Capri. The island loomed ahead. The sky was gray, with threats of rain, and the man beside him in the ferry said, Hey, if I wanted shitty weather I could stay home in Seattle, it would cost a whole lot less. At the Marina Grande, where they disembarked, Ettsio handed out tickets for a funicular ride to the village of Capri itself. They boarded, turn by turn, then clattered up the hill.

All this took place in a loud press of bodies, a gaggle of tourists of whom he was one. Bowing his head to the sudden hard rain, he remembered a phrase from a song by Noël Coward—a song about a widow on the Piccola Marina, drinking gin and flirting with Italians. Her name, Lawrence found himself remembering, was Mrs. Wentworth-Brewster, and "hot flushes of delight suffused her," or perhaps it had been *flashes,* hot flashes instead. Ettsio urged everyone to have a coffee, have a glass of wine, have a look please at these beautiful shops.

The tour group unfurled their umbrellas and loitered in the cobbled streets; Lawrence, however, withdrew. He felt ashamed of having joined in, of being cajoled and organized and told to report to the ferry at noon, or he would miss his lunch. What am I doing here, he asked himself, and was jostled by a German who said, *Vorsicht!* sharply, *Careful,* as he stepped back from a ditch.

There was a building on a cliff he'd read about and half

hoped to visit, a structure built by the self-styled Count Fersen underneath the Villa Jovis where Emperor Tiberio took his fatal leap. The villa on the promontory had, or so his guidebook said, a certain architectural distinction and a breathtaking view. But the rain was heavy and the site too far away; he contented himself with a grappa and the promise never ever again to join a guided tour. "We then crossed into DI with PT graphix wire and performed kissing balloon inflations with 3.0 x 15 balloon in LAD and 2.5 x 15 balloon in DI."

ONCE MORE THAT NIGHT AT DINNER he found himself at table with loquacious strangers—this time from Las Vegas and Stamford. The man from Las Vegas had never been out of the country before, and he announced this with pride; I always say, he said, you should see America first. We've been to all the fifty states and every single presidential library and figured we'd give Italy a try—but so far, I have to tell you, it's nothing to write home about. Nancy here has relatives who come from Sicily, Palermo, a village near Palermo, and we'll spend a week together when this trip is done.

Darko glided past them noiselessly, and Lawrence asked for wine. Again he scanned the dining room and saw the gray-haired woman sitting where she sat the night before. Although she was part of a table of six she seemed to be eating alone. This time he caught the woman's eye and this time she half smiled at him; she understood, she seemed to say, how little he enjoyed his meal or suffered such company gladly. She seemed at ease with, complicit in silence, and once more her features looked somehow familiar. Again he tried to place her: had they met before, he asked himself, and if so when and where?

The snatch of song returned to him—*But who knows where and when?*—and he found himself humming the chorus; the man from Stamford said, "Name that tune," and his wife said, "Don't mind Dicky, he's just jealous, he never could carry a tune."

Then she talked about the musical they'd seen last month on Broadway, a lollapalooza of a show called *Wicked,* whose whole idea was based on *Oz,* that wicked witch who used to live in Stamford, which is why the two of them bought tickets in the first place. He, Lawrence, might not remember the actress who played—in the movie now, I mean to say, the woman said, *The Wizard of Oz* with Ray Bolger and Bert Lahr as the cowardly lion and poor unhappy Judy Garland—but who we're talking about is the Wicked Witch of the West, that skinny and pointy-nosed actress by the name of—what was her name, Dicky?—*Margaret,* that's right, that's it, Auntie Em and the Wicked Witch of the West were *both* the actress Margaret Hamilton, and her life was made, well, miserable by neighborhood children all shrieking every time they saw her and some of them soaping her windows or worse come Mischief Night; she's dead, of course, and this happened long ago, but both of them assured him how Miss Hamilton was nice as nice could be and yet tormented, *tormented* by neighborhood kids and not excluding theirs.

"More wine, sir?" Darko asked, and Lawrence nodded yes. When the meal was over he stood again, exhausted; the dining room was nearly empty and the Elsinore Lounge had a sad clutch of drinkers and he stepped out on deck to see nothing: the dock, the lights of Naples winking, the cranes and trucks off-loading in the middle distance. In his cabin he did fifty push-ups and tried to read and sleep.

AT NINE HE HAD BEEN VERY ILL, first with a cold and then strep throat; the fever would not go away and became rheumatic fever. Dr. Purvis listened to his heart and informed the family that he heard a murmur, endocarditis of the right mitral valve; the pediatrician looked grave. Larry would have to stay in bed and not even go to the bathroom alone—but Dr. Purvis was optimistic, because a recently available antibiotic could treat and then prevent a recurrence of infection. Bed rest will work wonders, predicted the doctor, and gave him penicillin. It came in a bottle, strawberry-flavored, and he drank it three times a day.

The ceiling spun; the radiator hissed, and he tried to decipher the water pipes or crows in the tall trees outside. Lawrence lay in bed for weeks. His mother watched over him; so did the maid; so did his father on weekends, and friends, but what he saw and could not shake were figures in the furniture, the walls careening madly, the radio beside his bed expanding and contracting. The engines of the M.S. *Diana,* pulsing underneath him now, brought all this flooding back again: the way his body *was* and was *not* present, *there* and *not* there in its envelope of skin. He had asked his doctors if angina and rheumatic fever might have been connected, but they told him no.

He slept. Near dawn he dreamed of heedless health and early love; a woman was a statue and the statue was marmoreal but warmed to his hot touch. When Lawrence woke he was aroused but there was grief in it also: what had he done or failed to do that left him here alone? What was he dreaming, had he dreamed, that brought him to this pass?

Again the passengers descended and were herded to a tour bus and, at ten o'clock in the morning, conducted to Pompeii. This morning the tour guide was called Gabriela, who spoke English with a German accent; when someone asked how long she'd lived in Naples she said seven months. But she was pursuing, she told them, a doctorate in archaeology, and she knew more by now than ever she could possibly have imagined or, *wirklich, veramente* wished to know about the business of excavation and the procedures involved. Gabriela had red, spiky hair and tattoos on both arms. She said, Those of you who wish to be alone should meet me at the kiosk by this entryway at one o'clock for lunch; those of you who wish to listen come along. We have a special lunch and it has been ordered already so I see you later on. It is, she said, bureaucracy, these Italians are in love, enraptured with bureaucracy, and it is of course the case that everything of any value is in the museum in Naples, but you must imagine what it felt like for the people of the city to look up and watch Vesuvius erupt; it is not so much, she told the group, the popular conception that they were caught by lava as they died because of smoke; it is smoke inhalation, said Gabriela, it's, how do you call it, asphyxiation that makes Pompeii a special place, and nowhere to run to because of the sea which would be in any case boiling. They could not land the ships. But in every cloud there is, *come se dice*, how do you call it, a silver lining also. Because perfect preservation was enabled by the accident—people sitting, people baking bread, people chained to their workplace because they were slaves—and dogs and mosaics discovered intact beneath fifteen meters of ash. You will want to see a rich man's house and also the place of the baths; you will want to see a wine shop and what we call the Luparium or brothel and also, naturally, the marketplace; there is more than it is possible in one single visit to see.

Lawrence set out on his own. He studied temple columns and those excavation sites where the work continued: young people with shovels and pails. He wandered for an hour in the increasing sun, consulting his guidebook and looking at the trees and ruins and the ruts in stone where chariots had driven. He thought about Vesuvius, its fecund slopes and lethal ash and how the tethered slaves would have watched death approaching. In a side alley stood a tour guide with a group of tourists, and he stopped to listen. The guide was enjoying himself.

"Signs," he was explaining, "you have, how you say, McDonald's, and everybody knows what they can order when they see the golden arch; there are pictures showing everybody what McDonald's serves. So you point to *this* one, say, a Big Mac, or *that* one, say, a salad and a coffee, and the people who are serving know what item you prefer." For effect, the tour guide paused. "You don't need to speak the Latin, *spikka da langwich, parler la langue*; you can be, for example, a sailor from a foreign place just off a ship. Well, this building, very popular, very im-

portant in Pompeii, is called the Luparium—because women when they were not busy would come out to the corner and howl in the street to make known they were available, though not of course for free. So it is called Luparium, the place of wolves—and they have pictures, you will see, explaining what to order. On the *outside* of their rooms is a kind of advertisement, gentlemen and ladies, for what goes on *inside*. The oldest profession, correct? One has such and such a specialty, one has another instead."

There were appreciative titters; people shifted their weight on their feet. The tour guide relished the attention, clearly, and fanned his cheek with his cap. "I will not embarrass you, ladies, by describing what the pictures show but if you look at them carefully carefully you of course can see who prefers to be on top and who is on whose knees. If you were, how do you call it, a bigwig, a very special customer, you go upstairs and spend the night but mostly this is, how do you call it, a quickie in and out. And so because this is so popular a place to visit we must take our turn like customers"—he smiled—"ten at a time. Therefore everybody will have space: enjoy, enjoy. And when you will have had your fill of looking at the pictures"—again he paused, theatrical—"next person has a chance."

Lawrence waited for his turn to enter; then he stepped inside. The Luparium, by contrast with the noontime heat, felt cold. Above the doorless door frames and the entrances to empty rooms he could indeed see pictures—ancient, faded, but intact—of prostitutes: some lying down, some standing, sitting, others on all fours or leaning openmouthed above priapic men.

He felt not so much excited as bereft. It made a sad display.

For centuries, for thousands of years these same arrangements had been or were being enacted; nothing had changed or would change. Immobile, the plump painted figures nonetheless aped motion, and someone in the bedroom next to him said, "Hey, baby, look at *that*."

Lawrence stepped outside. His companion in the dark enclosure touched his sleeve. "Hello."

"Hello."

It was the woman he had noticed in the dining room, then failed to find. "You don't recognize me."

"Excuse me?"

"You don't know me, do you?"

He looked at her. The Luparium had been enshadowed, and the light out here was bright.

His eyes adjusted. "Good Christ."

"No, not exactly." She smiled her widemouthed smile at him. "Hel-*lo!*"

"Hello yourself. You haven't changed."

"Oh yes I have. How *are* you?"

Self-deprecating, dismissive, she made a motion with her hands. "How long has it been?"

"Forty years. Well, forty-two."

"And counting." She put on her dark glasses.

"I *thought* I saw you. Knew you. But you kept disappearing . . ."

"It's not the perfect way to meet again."

"What . . ."

"Here, I mean." She tilted her head to the building behind. "But we're on the *Diana* together. I'm not sure I believe it . . ."

"Good Christ," he repeated.

"No."

"No?"

"Only Hermia," she said.

II

1962

W HEN HE SAW HER THE FIRST TIME, SHE STOOD
in the hallway, her book bag slung over her shoulder.
She was talking to another girl, the one he would learn came
from Chile, and the way she extracted her hair from the green
strap it was snagged by caused her to wriggle, a little. The book
bag slid down to the floor. When she saw him the first time she
noticed him watching, his locker half-open, a key in his hand.
The Fogg Art Museum had a library he studied in; Lawrence
picked up her satchel, then handed it back.

"Thanks," said Hermia, and turned and walked down the
hall. They would remember this later. He said, "You dropped
it on purpose," and she said, "Don't flatter yourself."

It was mid-March 1962, and he was a senior at Harvard.
He had been driving his mother's Impala, the gray convertible she'd loaned him for use in his final semester; he had a

friend on Irving Street with a parking space. On weekends he and Will would drive together to the Cape or Walden Pond or Newport or to L. L. Bean's in Maine. There had been a thaw that week, and they took the top down and turned on the heater and the radio full blast. Monday morning, returning from Truro, Lawrence had ordered a hot dog for breakfast, and Will respected this. "It's all about freedom," he said.

Hermia was black-haired, tall, and already late for class. The class was on the origins and flowering and decline of the Baroque, and it made no difference that she would be late. Her art history professor stood on a raised platform in front of the screen, using a flashlight as pointer and talking about the meticulous brushwork of a woman's necklace or a soldier's beard. He was an expert on Rubens, and much of the term was devoted to Rubens, whom he labeled "a prince among painters"; he said nobody before or since took such pure pleasure in flesh. "You can practically *feel* it," said the professor, trailing his beam up the nude's outstretched leg. "Just look at the articulation of this ankle and the way the knee enters the sheets."

They met again that afternoon, at Elsie's Sandwich Shop. Lawrence was waiting for his order, the one he always ordered—an Elsie's Special, heavy on the dressing—when she came through the Mount Auburn Street entrance and took a vacant stool. "Aren't you the one with the book bag?" he asked, and she gazed at him unblinkingly and said, Yes, hello. "How was your class?" he asked her, and she told him, Dull. Well, not exactly, not really *dull*, but on a spring day like this she just hadn't wanted to *be* in the room, she just couldn't wait to be out in the light, and he said he'd felt that way also and had driven in that morning from the Cape.

"Oh, where?"

"Truro, you know it? The dunes?"

Hermia nodded. "I do."

She asked herself, and could remember wondering, if she wanted this back-and-forth to continue or the conversation to stop. Did she need to tell him, for instance, that her family had been vacationing in Truro for what seemed like forever, and since 1951 had owned a house by Ballston Beach? She loved it there—the weathered shingles and climbing roses by the fence, the path to the sea she could see down the hill—and it was her secret space, the place she prized most in the world. Did she need to tell him her father the painter had had a show in Provincetown of dunes in every season, every weather, every time of day, and yes she did know Truro and had explored each hummock of the beach . . .

"I'm Lawrence," he told her.

"Hermia."

"Art history—is that what you're majoring in?"

"No. English."

"I thought so," he said. "Well, I didn't know it was English but I did think it wasn't art history."

"Because?"

"Because that's *my* major," said Lawrence. "And I would have noticed."

Her roommate Silvana arrived. Silvana came from Valparaiso but had gone to boarding school in Switzerland and her English was formal, precise. The girls spoke about the weather and the group they were part of to memorize slides: two hundred paintings by Peter Paul Rubens they needed to learn for the hour exam.

"He didn't do a lot of them," said Lawrence.

"Are you kidding? Hundreds. *Thousands.*"

"Except his studio apprentices would rough in the sky and the clouds. Or the background figures, often, or the occasional horse."

"Are you a painter?" asked Silvana.

"No."

"Her father's a painter," she said.

Hermia stood. "Well, we've got to start our study group; we memorize them all. We each take forty images and tell the others what to look for. Venus and Adonis. Actaeon and the hunting dogs. The one where he gazes on Artemis—or would Rubens have called her Diana?—and hey presto our great hunter turns into a stag."

"What kind of painter?" asked Lawrence. He received his roast beef sandwich and paid his fifty-five cents.

"A good one," said Silvana. "You'd have heard of him."

The girls left.

THE THIRD TIME WAS THAT THURSDAY, and again unplanned. He saw her walk down Hilliard Street and recognized her loose-limbed gait, the way she stepped out from the side entrance to the Loeb Drama Center and strode long-legged, the swing of her hips, and how she held her head down. She was wearing a green cape and knee-high polished leather boots and a knitted cap. There was slush in the gutters and snow shoveled in piles at the edge of the pavement; the afternoon was dark.

He followed and caught up to her. Her eyes were a deep brown.

"Hey," Lawrence said, "hello."

Tires screeching, a delivery van rounded the corner from Brattle Street. They stepped back from the spray.

"Strange, isn't it?" said Hermia. "Three times this week."

"They're trying to tell us something."

"Who?"

"The gods of coincidence. What were you doing at the Loeb?"

"*The Flies,*" she said. "The play by Jean-Paul Sartre?"

"Rehearsing?"

Hermia shook her head. "Stage-managing," she said. "Silvana—you remember her—is playing the part of Electra. I go along for the ride."

"Can I buy you a coffee?"

Her gaze was frank, assessing him. What else was he asking, she wondered, what else would he offer and should she accept? A fine snow fell. In time to come he would remember standing there, the silence between them extending, expanding, and how the pause before she answered made it seem a kind of verdict: "Yes."

They went to Casablanca and drank café au lait. He told her that he planned to be an architect, an urban designer maybe, because he believed in design; a sense of the shape of the whole, he said, is what this country needs more of, *consciousness, coherence,* and not the higgledy-piggledy every-which-way arrangement of the marketplace. He was going, he assured her, to make trains run on time.

"You're joking, right?"

"Right," Lawrence said, and lit her Pall Mall, and stared at the rise of her breasts.

CASABLANCA WAS A COFFEE SHOP beneath the Brattle Theater; it displayed framed posters of the movie *Casablanca* and wall-size photographs of Humphrey Bogart and Ingrid Bergman and Claude Rains. The space at that hour was dimly lit, empty, and the man behind the bar was setting out glasses in rows. Above them hung a poster of Rick's American Café and one of the sheet music for "As Time Goes By."

Upstairs they were showing *L'Avventura* and Lawrence asked if she had seen it, and what she thought of Antonioni; he himself had seen *La Dolce Vita* twice. He thought the final sequence on the beach was astonishing, remarkable, and the scene at Trevi Fountain with Anita Ekberg splashing in the water and summoning Marcello was a hoot.

"But that's Fellini, isn't it?"—Hermia corrected him. "Not Antonioni."

He asked if she had sisters or brothers and if they all had such names.

She shook her head.

"An only child?"

"Yes." She stubbed out her cigarette. "At least it's not

Hermione. That's what my father wanted." Her fingernails were bitten, and her fingers long.

"Your father . . ."

Consciously she changed the subject. "And you, are you an only child?"

He shook his head. "A brother and a sister."

"Oh?"

"But I'm the oldest, so for three years I *was* an only child. Or felt like one . . ."

She looked away, looked at the door.

"Tell me about *The Flies*," he said.

She did. She said *The Flies* was fun to do; apparently the Germans never understood it as a protest play but allowed Sartre to mount it in occupied Paris. They thought it an update of the *Oresteia*, which on the surface it was, but more importantly it's an attack on fascist rule. The collaborator Aegisthus is a figure out of Vichy and a version of the Nazi stooge *Le Maréchal* Pétain or maybe Pierre Laval. Hermia liked stage-managing and the experimental theater, the small black box with risers that they called the Ex. The lighting designer was a friend, and she didn't mind the detail work, the lists of "To Do" and lists of "Done," but the director was a horse's ass and always putting a move on the dancers; we open next Thursday, she told him, and do you want to come?

He was twenty-one, she twenty, and both of them pretending to a worldliness they had not earned; she had traveled with her family to Italy and France. He had been to Mexico the previous summer and ingested peyotl buttons and been violently ill; the mushrooms were bitter and strong. His hallucinations were multicolored, and the cactus he had focused on seemed ten feet tall. She had had three lovers and he five.

Her first had been in high school. Timmy wanted to be an airplane pilot, then a fighter pilot, and now that JFK established a space program he would want to be an astronaut. They slept together twice, the week of graduation, and when she thought about him now she thought mostly about the blood on the couch of his family room, how she had rubbed and scrubbed at it while Timmy said, "Oh, shit." Her next had been in Italy, a gallery owner exhibiting her father's work who took her on a tour of Rome, then back to his apartment, where he seduced her efficiently, saying, *"Bella, que bella, bellisima,"* while they undressed. The next afternoon, however, when she went with her family to the gallery beneath the Spanish Steps, it was as though nothing had happened, as though they were polite strangers, and she never saw Giovanni again.

Her third affair was serious, and it had lasted all fall. Though Hermia had gotten over it, was getting over it, she sometimes thought that she and Bill were taking a break from each other, a not-so-romantic vacation, and would date again and marry down the line. Bill was in law school; they'd met at a mixer, and he drove an Austin-Healey and had reddish, curly hair she liked to run her fingers through; at Thanksgiving he had introduced her to his parents and said, "Mom, this is the real deal." After two or three years in his father's law firm, he explained, he was planning a career in politics; he would make a run for the statehouse, and was sure he'd be elected, and she'd make an excellent wife.

He had it all planned out. He had no doubts at all. He had attended Exeter, and his family came from New Hampshire, and there was a seat in the statehouse that was going to be vacant; with a pedigree like his—his uncle had been governor—and a photogenic Radcliffe woman at his side it would be a lead-pipe cinch. That was his phrase, a "lead-pipe cinch," and Hermia respected his impermeable self-assurance but distrusted it also, disliked it, and when she told him so he said well I may have made a mistake, it's possible I'm wrong.

"About getting elected?"

"No. You."

He announced this in his apartment. She felt herself go cold all over, rigid with the shock of it, and got out of bed and walked to the window and covered herself with his blue button-down Oxford and stood looking out. There was snow on Boylston Street, and a red light changing to green; a man across the street was walking two dogs at once. He stopped beneath a streetlight while the larger dog—a German shepherd, a husky?—lifted his leg at the pole; then the small one took his turn.

"Come back to bed," said Bill. "You must be freezing, baby."

"No."

"No you won't come back to me, or no you aren't freezing your ass off?"

"The good citizens of New Hampshire," she said, "expect their elected officials to marry a virgin and not to say 'ass.' We both of us made a mistake."

. . .

Now LAWRENCE WAS SAYING yes to *The Flies,* he'd like to see the production next week, and what house did she live in? She told him, Cabot Hall. Should I meet you there, he asked, and Hermia said, No, I'll leave a ticket because I'm at the theater *hours* before curtain time and I'll see you after the show. He talked about the dean of architecture at MIT, an Italian called Pietro Belluschi, and how he was more interesting—so Lawrence said—than the dean at Harvard, José Luis Sert. He talked about the aesthetics of Belluschi and Sert, how they differed and were similar, and what it would mean to study at Princeton instead. The best of them all was probably Yale, but he just wasn't up for New Haven and in any case, he told her, he was planning on apprentice work, he wanted some experience in the professional world. He needed to be sure of architecture as a profession before committing himself to the course of study; he was tired, *tired,* sick to death of school. There were architecture firms in New York or Chicago or even San Francisco where he could just do office work; he needed a year or two off.

She studied him. His eyes were blue, his mouth was full-lipped, mobile, and his cheekbones were pronounced. He had a way of talking—rapid, allusive—she liked. He was trying to impress her, and though she was unimpressed she liked how hard he tried. The coffee shop was filling up; music played—"As Time Goes By"—and Hermia felt happy to be sitting at a table with this boy-man in a black turtleneck sweater and brown Harris Tweed. She picked at her croissant. She had not had a date since Bill—"Bill the pill," Silvana called him—but that was three months ago and the mournful self-pity had passed.

Looking at her watch, she saw she had an hour left until the cast was scheduled for costume fittings at the Loeb. The costumes were either leotards or togas, black or white, and the actors moved a large red crown from head to head when power was transferred. She had been planning to go to her room and maybe get some reading done, or stop in at the Agassiz and check out a monograph she needed for an essay for her soc. rel. section. But this coffee together was pleasant, this Lawrence whose last name she realized she did not know was talking about architects, designers, interior designers, advertising and technology and the city of the future while she shifted in her seat, adrift, and looked at the length of his hair.

"So how did it go?" he asked.

"What?"

"That test of yours. The one on Rubens."

"We haven't got it back," she said. "I did know *Venus and Adonis*."

He smiled at her. "And Actaeon?"

"You *were* paying attention."

"I was," he said, and smiled again, showing a gap in his teeth.

THE LOEB DRAMA CENTER, newly built, housed a main stage and experimental theater; *The Flies*, as a student production, had been allocated to the smaller downstairs space. The set was stark, with rocks suggesting both the fields of Argos and its palace. Rock piles had been built out of canvas and wood, then covered with papier-mâché. The director was a senior; he had spent the previous summer in Paris, researching Sartre, Artaud, and agitprop theater, and he smoked Gauloises. On opening night Orestes came down with laryngitis, and so the actor used a bullhorn, but everyone agreed the bullhorn was appropriate, a kind of threatful magnifier that made his speech, "People of Argos," seem more totalitarian and demagogic-fascist when he incited the mob.

It was the beginning of spring: March 21. The snow gave way to sleet. After the performance, at the cast party in an apartment down the street from Cronin's, the director passed a pipe. It came straight from Jamaica, he said, and on Sunday when the run was done and after they had struck the set, he'd pull out all the chemical stops, they'd have an existential no-holds-barred and flat-out celebration, but tonight they all needed to just loosen up and not worry about what the *Crimson* might say. The reviewer from the *Crimson* had given him a thumbs-up sign, and that was a good omen, but as far as he himself was concerned what mattered was how each of them had played their parts, since—here he mimicked Jaques's speech in *As You Like It*, lisping—"All the world'th a thtage."

But seriously, gang, the director continued, I'm proud of you, how *everyone* stood and was counted and we've—now he raised the ponytail of the dancer he was sleeping with—given our damnedest, our *all*. He balanced on a DR stool, holding a bottle of Mateus rosé and slipping into a Southern accent. *"Dang,"* he said, "I'm jes so dang *proud* of y'all!"; then he declared himself impressed by how they'd pulled together, pulled it off, and the director was, as the French say, if he said so himself, *bouleversé, épouvanté.*

"The only other title I know by Sartre," said Lawrence, "is *La Nausée.*"

Hermia laughed. "Well, what about *No Exit?*"

"Is that an exit line?"

"It is." She slipped her arm through his.

Parietal hours were over, and they could not go to Cabot Hall or Lawrence's room, a single in Claverly Hall. In any case, she told him, it felt too soon, too sudden, but she pressed against him when they kissed and, disengaging, stared at him wide-eyed; he had an erection she grazed with her palm.

"Maybe we could see each other on Saturday? Sunday?" asked Lawrence, and she told him, "Yes."

The moon was high, the stars emerged, and that promise stayed with him as he walked back to his room. He spent the next day on his thesis, a chapter on Palladio and his influence in Newport, the English manor house and French château adapted to the gentry of America, their ideal of country living by the bay. Will called and said, "We heading out tomorrow?" and Lawrence told him, "No."

THEY BECAME LOVERS that weekend and stayed together all spring. He lived alone in Claverly, in a wood-paneled sitting room with a sleeping alcove, on the building's second floor. His windows gave out on an alley, and the light was poor. But Lawrence loved the privacy, the illusion of self-sufficiency, and when he brought Hermia up to his room he hoped she would approve of it: the reproductions of van Gogh and the Mexican bark paintings he had acquired in San Miguel de Allende, the serape on his bed and bookcases he had fashioned out of shelving and glass bricks.

When he thought of it, years later, he thought of it in pictures: a silent movie played out without language, in scenes. He saw the cowl-neck red sweater she wore, and the brown woolen skirt with the slit to the knee; he saw the mascara and lipstick he smudged and the way that her bra strap had frayed. He saw the two of them embracing by the wooden desk. In her leather boots she was taller than he, and when she bent to remove them he watched the blue vein at her ankle, the curve of her calf and then thigh. He had, and was embarrassed by, pimples on his back. He had a box of condoms in his bedside table, and when the time arrived to open it he was clumsy, fumbling, and her hair cascaded darkly when she bent across him to help.

They talked; they must have spoken, but what he remembered was silence and the bright whites of her eyes. His pillows were yellow, his blanket was green, and the rug on the floor was a full-size flokati his mother had given him: long, tufted lamb's wool dyed blue. He remembered the lamplight, the shadows it cast, and how he turned off the light. He remembered how Hermia paused, emerging from the bathroom, the tilt of her head when she moved to his side, the stretch marks at her hip, the scar along her knee. He remembered in detail the shape of her breasts—the left was a little bit larger—and how her eyes closed when she sat on him, pumping, and the coils of pubic hair and how her neck arched when she came.

The following Sunday they drove to the Cape, and she took

him to her parents' house—still closed down for the winter—
and walked the path to Ballston Beach. The wind was blustery,
the waves were high, and they sat together in the dunes while
sand whipped past them, eddying.

"It's beautiful."

"I love it here," said Hermia. "I *love* it," and the word
echoed between them; she had not used it before.

Gulls rose and circled, then settled again, and white foam
unfurled from the waves. She found the hidden house key
where her parents kept it, on the crossbeam of the overhang
where the woodpile had been stacked. They opened the door
to the kitchen—its hanging pots and candles in wine bottles, its
dried bunches of herbs tied to nails in the beam. The living
room was long and low; she led him past couches in sheets.
Bookcases were stuffed with old leather-bound books, and the
fireplace had logs laid in it crosswise and ready for burning.
Paintings by her father's friends covered all the walls. Lawrence
recognized, or thought he did, a set of prints by Motherwell, a
Kenneth Noland target painting and a Hans Hofmann oil.
There was a landscape that looked like a Hopper—a yellow
house athwart a green and ocher cliff—and later he would understand the value of the art he'd seen so casually displayed,
unheated, unprotected, but Hermia was leading him to her
small bedroom by the porch. He pulled down his pants and she
pulled off her panties and they came together standing up. It
was quick and sharp and fierce and in the sudden aftermath
she rested her head on his shoulder.

"I've never been with anyone here before," she said. "Not
anyone."

On the wall of her room, by the west-facing eave, hung a life-size portrait of Hermia herself when young: her skirt spread wide, her black hair splayed about her face, and playing with a golden retriever puppy on her lap. The picture had been painted with authority; it was, he guessed, her father's work. The girl on the wall had grown up. Yet the smile on her face then was how she smiled now: a proprietary, ease-filled gaze, a dallying.

"It isn't too cold in here, is it?" she asked, and he told her, "No."

"Remember how you'd been to Truro that first morning when we met?"

" 'You *were* paying attention . . .' "

"Mi casa es su casa."

Wooden shutters with a heart cut out had been fastened at the windows, and through the heart-shaped apertures Lawrence saw the sky. They kissed. He felt, and would remember feeling, as though he had been singled out: so fortunate, luck's shining child, this beauty in his arms.

AT FIRST THE TWO OF THEM WERE CAREFUL, spacing their encounters, but once a week gave way to twice and then to three meetings or four. By the end of April they met each other daily, drinking coffee at Hayes-Bick, walking along the Charles River or down Mass Ave for Chinese food and going to movies at night. They saw Bergman and Antonioni and Alfred Hitchcock films, and he told her she looked like Monica Vitti when Monica Vitti wore a black wig. Lawrence completed his thesis on time, and she continued to go to her classes: Social Relations 10, the Baroque, the English Novel and Shakespeare: The Late Plays. All through the month of May Hermia left letters in his mailbox, or underneath his pillow, and if they did not see each other at night or over the weekend—if she visited her family or he went on a field trip with his art history seminar— they called.

On the telephone he told her he missed her, he couldn't stop thinking about her. The scent of her perfume remained in his room, the smell of their sex on his hands. In May, and with her mother's approval, she was fitted for a diaphragm; they had a joke about "Most Happy Fella" and called it her Big D. She liked to imagine the child they would have, the way their children would look. Other companions fell away, and Hermia and Lawrence talked about the future: this summer when he would be graduated, the trips they hoped to take and how they would manage to do so and where he planned to live.

She spoke about her father, the way he drank and unwound with his buddies at cards, playing high-stakes poker the whole night long and smoking cigars, and how he swore and terrified her as a child. The golden retriever, Tigger, became her pet the year she had an operation on her knee and couldn't ride a bike. The knee was fine, completely fixed, but that explained the scar he'd noticed and was tracing with his tongue.

She talked about her father's art, his fame, and how he demanded attention, admiration, ceaselessly, so everything about dear Dad was *me, me, me, me, me*. Their apartment in Brooklyn was a disaster, with hot water only sometimes when the landlord fixed the plumbing, and a bathtub in the kitchen and nobody bothering to make the beds or take the garbage out. Still, it had an upstairs studio with a world-class view of Manhattan, and Hermia's mother seemed content to live in what once had been a warehouse, drinking Campari and soda and posing for her artist friends and being written about in the *New York Times* and being called everyone's Muse.

Lawrence talked about *his* mother, the rigid propriety of his family home and how the suburbs seemed the absolute opposite of what she described, Brooklyn Heights. *His* father, a banker, had been a hushed presence all through the years of his childhood, an absence with martinis and the *Wall Street Journal* in the TV room. His father wore bow ties and button-down shirts and was unfailingly polite to strangers, at ease on the golf course and tennis court and the club car in the train. The hedges by their house were clipped, the stones that lined the driveway painted white.

But then his father left when Lawrence turned eighteen. One Friday evening in October he did not return from work, and that was the end of it. There was nothing to do or to say. His father took an apartment on Gramercy Park, filling the closets with his suits and setting out his photographs on the table in the foyer. There was a silver-framed photograph of Lawrence at his high school graduation, a photograph of the three children in their tennis whites, and a series of sepia portraits of parents and grandparents standing with horses or at their ease in evening clothes or poised on a ski slope, with skis.

He became his mother's confidant, the child to whom she complained. His brother and sister were too young, but he was old enough to listen over Thanksgiving or Christmas vacation while she raged on and on about unfairness and that s.o.b., excuse me, who used to call this place home. Their father, it turned out, was having affairs, and one of the girls in the office got pregnant and wouldn't have an abortion, and his father did the right and honorable thing—which is what, dripping with sarcasm, his mother chose to call it; the honorable s.o.b. left his wife and children to marry a teller instead. Well, maybe she wasn't a teller, maybe a branch manager or executive vice president, but Lawrence's mother had been certain she worked her way up the corporate ladder by spreading her legs, lying down.

So the family remained in Scarsdale, in the mock-Tudor gabled house, but all the king's horses and all the king's men—the cash and property transfer and alimony payments—couldn't put them together again. His brother applied to Reed College, going as far away as possible, putting the whole continent between himself and Westchester. His sister, Allie, turned sixteen and didn't need a plane to leave; she lay all day long in her canopy bed, so busy with the telephone she couldn't really tell you if it was afternoon or evening or when midnight came. The lights switched on or off, the music played, and downstairs in the kitchen his mother beat at scrambled eggs or pounded a veal cutlet flat and scrubbed the kitchen counters in a kind of vengeful fury . . .

They agreed they came from different worlds but not so far apart the distance was unbridgeable; besides, said Hermia, it's too much fun doing the bridging. He laughed. She had a sense of humor that took him by surprise; she was sly and slantways in her wit, and she liked to tease him. She signed her nightly letters "Huntley/Brinkley" when sending him the day's report;

one of the notes she left in his bed was a folded page of paper. On the top half she had written, *I love to suck your great big hard beautiful sweet-tasting* and, on the inside fold, *ear.*

That season at Harvard, two teachers—Timothy Leary and Richard Alpert—were distributing psilocybin and instructing students to keep journals of their sensations and thoughts and perceptions while high. "The Doors of Perception," as Aldous Huxley called them, had opened wide, and LSD became the drug of choice. At Club 47 on Mount Auburn Street, Joan Baez and Tom Rush and curly-headed Bob Dylan sang folk songs alone or together. The world was young, or so it seemed, the world was theirs to conquer, although conquering was not the point, and neither Hermia nor Lawrence wanted to divide and conquer but only to remain together and lie down together in bed.

IN YEARS TO COME they were not certain what went wrong between them. There was no single reason that they broke apart. He was twenty-one, she twenty, and they were not ready for marriage and could not live together in the fall. Lawrence grew restless; he wanted more of the world, he told himself, than the chill insularity of Cambridge. He wanted, he told her, to travel—to look at great examples of civilization's great buildings—and Hermia would not respect it if he just stayed around. "I'll wait for you," he promised. "Except we're so parochial, so proud of our Tea Party and bad sherry at the Signet and the people who never leave Boston. It's time to move on, move along . . ."

His friend Will who lived on Irving Street was fat and had a high-pitched voice and a cheap guitar. He played the instrument well, however, and at night in his dark basement sang, "I'm going away, for to stay, a little while. But I'm coming back, if I go ten thousand miles . . ." He closed his eyes while singing, and rocked back and forth on the chorus while they all joined in. Will was twenty-five, and famous for his parties, and one night after playing threw a pass at Hermia. "Hey, pretty lady, little darlin'," he said, "that first tune was for *you!*"

She was going to be a senior, and could not leave Cambridge, and though she and Lawrence promised each other they would stay together and it would make no difference it did make a difference. He found himself wondering where else to go and what else to do; Will said he was pussy-whipped and *ought* to hit the road. At a party in a carriage barn behind a red brick mansion on Fayerweather Street, he got drunk on bad sangría and found himself in a bedroom kissing a girl called Charette, a girl with whom he'd studied the Italian Renaissance, and when he pulled away from her she said, "Don't stop; why stop?"

Thick-tongued, he explained to her, or tried to, that he was at the party with his girlfriend Hermia, downstairs, and Charette said, "Why does that matter?" and was stepping out of her Indian print skirt when Hermia appeared. "You can join us if you want to," said Charette, and Lawrence was so shocked he laughed, and that was what, said Hermia, she couldn't forgive: his complicit drunken laughter and the way she felt, oh, not so much insulted as dismissed.

To make him jealous, therefore, or at least to demonstrate

what it was like, she called Bill to congratulate him on having finished law school, and Bill said, "Hey, baby, I was *thinking* about you, this is great."

"Great?" she asked him. "Why, what's so great?" but was flattered, nevertheless, that he was thinking about her, or bothered to lie, and when he asked, "Are you busy, are you free tonight, I've just tuned up the growler and was planning on a spin," she said, "All right, okay."

He arrived in twenty minutes, in the Austin-Healey, looking well, and she got in the passenger seat with the ease of habit and a sense of, if not vindication, relief. She pulled back and tied up her hair. She had been reading *Othello,* and she knew that Shakespeare meant the Moor to love "not wisely but too well," and that the Moor of Venice had been driven half-insane. " 'Beware, my lord, of jealousy,' " she found herself reciting, " 'it is the green-eyed monster.' " Except jealousy was not the point and she wasn't playing Iago, or the part of Desdemona; she was being driven fast down Storrow Drive, in a convertible with an old boyfriend, catching up . . .

Fidelity meant faithfulness; it meant wanting only one thing. It meant there was no difference between what you had and what you wanted, no space between the space you occupied and where you hoped to be. But nothing was ever so simple, she knew; what would happen, for example, if you desired more than one person or thing? This became a problem; this was something she and Silvana discussed; they were living in, said Silvana's professor of European history, the "Age of Anxiety," and one of the anxieties engendered by freedom is the problem of multiple choice.

She had planned to be faithful forever; she had wanted to love only Lawrence. But he never did say that he loved her, he never could quite get around to the words, and she was tired not so much of waiting as of his closemouthed caution, his timidity. When she thought about the bedroom on Fayerweather Street, him laughing with that girl upstairs—her eyes like pinwheels and skirt down around her ankles—she thought she could never forgive him, and so she drove away with Bill to the North End for dinner and made herself forget. Hermia's father was a famous man, her mother a great beauty, and she herself was finishing her junior year at Radcliffe. She was tired of multiple choice. Integrity meant oneness; it meant staying faithful and true to yourself, and she would return, she told herself, though she went ten thousand miles.

III

HERMIA GRADUATED FROM RADCLIFFE MAGNA cum laude, and she moved back to New York. Her thesis, "Romance: The Fools of Time in Shakespeare," was difficult to write but, in the end, rewarding; her senior year had been a sad one, and she was ready to leave. If she thought about *The Flies* or, the following fall, the production of *Blood Wedding*, she felt a little embarrassed and even, a little, ashamed. They all had been so *serious*, so convinced of their importance at the Loeb. With the Cuban Missile Crisis, things came into perspective; the world was dark and difficult, and it seemed beside the point to arrange for props and costume fittings and check lighting cues. Stage-managing was a diversion, and the diversion passed.

Silvana too said good-bye to the stage; she had played the bride in Lorca's play but put off, as they called it, childish things. Instead she got engaged to the son of the ex-ambassador from Chile and returned to Valparaiso and in her letters every month complained about the difficulties the wedding planners

were making and how much fuss and trouble a formal marriage can be.

At the suggestion of her senior tutor, who knew the man-
aging editor, Hermia applied for and was offered a job in publishing. The job was entry-level, at Harry N. Abrams,
Publishers, but it paid the rent. As editorial assistant, she had
schedules to comply with and deadlines to meet and decisions
to participate in and books about art to produce. Attempting to
comply with them, she came to admire the exacting standards
of the man she worked for, his pedantry and fussiness as to the
quality of paper and the quality of color in the plates. He wore
striped shirts with white collars and a monogram on the pocket
and horn-rimmed glasses he wiped on his sleeve. His name was
Jack, and he took her out to lunch and, over his second mar-
tini, confessed he was infatuated—had been hopelessly in love,
in *lust,* for what felt like *forever,* and had to tell *someone* about it—
with the editor in chief.

This was, she came to understand, a speech he made to all
the young women who worked at Harry Abrams; it was no secret to the interns or staff and had not been news for years.
The editor in chief had no interest in Jack, or at least no romantic interest; instead there was an office pool as to which
new female arrival the editor in chief would proposition next.
Hermia wore miniskirts and white boots by Courrèges. When
she herself was propositioned it was easy to refuse; she lied that
she was flattered, very flattered, but had just gotten engaged.
He said, "Congratulations, he's a lucky man," and made a
mark in his desk calendar and said, "Excuse me a minute, but
I have to take a call."

Office politics were fun because she had no stake in them; this would not be a career. She knew she was just marking time; nevertheless, she worked hard. In truth she did enjoy the job and the parties afterward, the art world's ornamental fringe where she was welcome because of her father, his more and more prominent name. Hermia lived alone, on Riverside Drive and Eighty-seventh Street, and made friends with the doormen and liked to walk downtown.

HER PARENTS SPENT THEIR SUMMERS ON THE CAPE. After her second promotion at Abrams, she earned three weeks vacation, and Hermia rented a car and drove by herself to Bar Harbor, where a weekend with a lawyer turned out to be a mistake. He was recently divorced and obsessed about his Rhodes 19, its rigging and performance, and in bed inert. When they said good-bye she didn't bother to pretend they would meet or date again; instead she drove to see her family in Truro.

That July, on his fifty-fifth birthday, her father threw a party, and it was a large one: collectors and curators and critics—so her father said, emphasizing the c—all had been invited, the whole catastrophe of hangers-on, and even a few of his friends. There was a reception up in Provincetown, and then a dinner at the house and fireworks down by the beach.

Her father's black cluster of curls had gone gray, and his beard was white. Lately he had seemed subdued, favoring his left leg when walking, and complaining of migraines and gout. But on that night he had, again, the manic celebratory energy she remembered from the binges in her childhood, and he sweated profusely and insisted on dancing and made the guests assemble while he tried to do the Charleston. "I used to perform the kazatsky," he mourned, "I used to be a champ." By eleven o'clock he was so drunk—irrevocably, irrecoverably drunk—he passed out on the living room couch.

Her mother stood above him, still dismissive and seductive and aloof. "Will you look at that," she said. "That's the great man his very self, the birthday boy. My hero, our hero, *everyone's* hero. Asleep."

Then she stubbed out her cigarette in the ashtray by Picasso, one of the series of plates and bowls they had bought that year in Vallauris, and turned to Clement Greenberg and said, "Dreadful sorry, oh my darling Clem, but may I have this dance?"

"Are you all right, Dad?" Hermia asked.

He did not move.

"Can you hear me?"

Softly, laboringly, his chest rose and faltered and fell.

"Daddy, it's your *party!*"

"Fuck off."

She was shocked not so much by his language—*fuck* was a word he used often—or that he would swear at her, as by the lack of recognition in his wide-eyed stare. Glaring at Hermia he said it again, "Fuck off, fuck off, fuck *all* of you off," and built himself back to his feet and jostled his way to the porch. Outside, Roman candles exploded. Enfolded in a dancer's arms, her mother was swaying, her slim back arched, ignoring or refusing to acknowledge her husband's bad behavior. The celebration went on.

Then Hermia heard, or thought she did, a truck door slam, an engine roar. "What was *that?*" she asked the room, but nobody replied. "Did anyone hear anything?" she asked. She saw a set of lights ignite and wheel away and veer down the driveway and disappear. "Where's Dad? He shouldn't be driving," she said, but a bodybuilder had asked her to dance, and the music was infectious, and all this had happened before . . .

She heard—she would swear it—the crash. She sensed the collision before she could hear it, felt it reverberate up through her throat. Then Hermia closed her eyes and *saw* it, saw her father's truck, accelerating, making for the stand of pine before the fork at Pamet Road as though itself enraged . . .

At first she tried to tell herself that what she heard were fireworks: some partygoers out on the beach setting off Catherine wheels.

Her partner asked, "What's wrong, is something wrong?"

She turned from him, turned to the door.

Years later, she would remember how they learned the news—the gallery owner from Wellfleet who stumbled back to the party, saying *Help,* saying *Call the police*—and the crumpled, smoking wreckage, her father slumped over the wheel. She ran to where he crashed. He had negotiated the driveway but missed the second left turn. She would remember the steam from the engine, the shards of glass, a white pine bent double above the smashed hood as though protective, pitying, and how they could not open the pickup's driver-side door.

. . .

He did not die in the truck. He was a tough man, limp from drink, and had somehow remembered to fasten his seat belt; the Rescue Squad arrived and, using the Jaws of Life, extracted him and drove him down Route 6 to the Cape Cod Hospital. It took him three days to die. Hermia spent the entire time in Hyannis, waiting with her mother and listening to doctors and visiting the ICU and, when permitted, sitting at the side of this object attached to machinery, this arrangement of tubing and bottles and monitors with numbers flashing on a screen and lights that went green and then red.

A little, in the waiting room, she slept. Once, at a nurse's urging, she went for a walk off the hospital grounds. In a nearby sandwich shop she bought a cup of clam chowder and a lobster roll. She could not swallow the sandwich, however, and left it for the gulls.

Her mother was inconsolable; she cried and cried and blamed herself, saying, "I knew it, I should have known it, I should have hidden the keys," and hoping for a miracle, or so she told the reporters. Our life together has been astonishing, her mother said, miraculous from the first time we met, the very beginning, he's such a wonderful painter, and she repeated she couldn't believe that this stupid avoidable once-in-a-blue-moon accident would be their story's end.

There were police and journalists and friends. There were many telegrams and telephone calls of support and more bouquets of flowers than the hospital could handle. In any case, the nurse explained, on account of how it wrecks the oxygen we don't want no bunches of flowers in the ICU. Men and women with mops and laundry and meal carts were polite to Hermia but made her feel in the way. Doctors and technicians bustled past. As always, she felt herself excluded from the melodramatic spectacle of her father's life, the privacy to which she had no access and the large public display. She had watched all through her childhood and her adolescence and now she was a spectator while her father died. It was as though he ruled some distant seagirt kingdom, but had been deposed. His eyes were shut. He opened them; she watched him try to rise or shift position in the bed—imperceptibly, inwardly, silently—and then again he shut his staring eyes. The monitors registered this; the line of light above his head pulsated, blinked, and went flat.

HER MOTHER FOUND CONSOLATION. She had always looked her best in black, and the grief was its own kind of diet; in the three months after the funeral, her mother lost ten pounds. The great quantity of work unfinished in the house in Truro and the studio in Brooklyn Heights became a retrospective; Last Paintings proved both a critical and commercial success, an "event of the first importance," a "high-water mark of the abruptly terminated career." Olitski, Diebenkorn, De Kooning—all these were evoked by way of comparison, as were such modern masters as Rothko, Gottlieb, Kokoschka—and the range of reference suggested, in and of itself, the wide variety and restless questing of her father's work. In his early years he had been called "derivative," in his middle period, "eclectic";

now he was hailed as an American original, a jack-of-all-painterly-trades. "No other artist of the last decade has tried his hand so daringly at so many forms of expression," wrote one reviewer of the show, "and we can only begin to imagine what he would have undertaken next."

At Harry Abrams they asked Hermia if she would consider introducing a book about her father's art and career, a personal accounting of the painter's life. When she declined, they commissioned a writer called G. Edson Lattimer to produce the text. G. Edson Lattimer was British-born, raised in Paris and Vienna, and his clothes were perfectly tailored and his bald head gleamed. He invited the widow and daughter to lunch at Lutèce, and appeared to know the owner, referring to him as André, and returning—there was something wrong with the cork, then the ullage—two bottles of wine. His manners were impeccable, he was courteous during the interview, and though Hermia distrusted him her mother found him charming.

All along there had been "players," as her parents called them—the assistants and other artists and other people's wives or husbands with whom her parents "played." But this was different, somehow, this seemed too soon, a violation, and when her mother invited the writer to the studio next morning Hermia felt betrayed. Although she would have been welcome, she did not join the two of them—not in Brooklyn Heights or, the following night, at Quo Vadis—and when Lattimer asked that Saturday what it felt like, in the early years, to sit for her father's sketches and portraits, she said, "I loved it, *loved* it, it was how I got Daddy's attention."

"Undivided," said her mother.

"Right. He used to call me 'Princess.' And then 'Herm the worm.' "

Lattimer laughed.

"The best portrait of all," said her mother, "is the one with Tigger, the dog we gave her when she was—what were you, darling, seven?—six? Up in Truro. You should see it."

"Absolutely," Lattimer agreed.

Therefore for the sake of completeness and to provide him with, as he put it, a better sense of "local habitation and a name," her mother took the critic for a weekend to the Cape. The house in Truro, after all, would be crucial to the monograph, a quintessential locus of the late artist's art. It was the start of December and time to drain the pipes and put the Adirondack chairs and picnic table away. Her mother said she didn't want to, couldn't *bear* to do the job alone and would be grateful for some company; while she shut the house for winter her guest could examine the walls.

"Don't you think," she asked Hermia, returning, "he's a charming man?"

"Not really, no."

"*I* do," she said. "He has such a sense of decorum. He knows all the right questions to ask."

"Like what exactly? Like what was Daddy drinking? Like what happened at the party?"

"Of course not, no. That's not what he's been asking."

"Oh?"

"This is an essay on *painting*, Herm. And not your father's personal habits."

"What was he like in bed?"

"Who?"

"G. Edson Lattimer." Even in the asking, she knew she'd crossed a line. It was not the act itself but the question that seemed indiscreet, a mark of bad behavior that would not be erased. Her mother turned away. But all the anger Hermia was harboring—the shock and loss and guilt and sorrow—made her implacable. "How could you *do* it?" she asked. "How could you value Dad so little, how could you be such, such a, so . . ."

"Say it!"

"*Cheap!*"

"Expensive," said her mother. "We'll be married in the spring."

SHE RESIGNED FROM HARRY ABRAMS in a kind of silent protest at the book; she did not want her father's art to grace the coffee tables or the bookshelves of the rich. At her farewell party—champagne in plastic cups and a wedge of cheese and bagels with smoked salmon—the editor in chief put his hand on her shoulder and, squeezing it, asked, "Are we still, you know, otherwise engaged?"

"Excuse me?"

"Weren't you, aren't you?"

"No," she said. "I never was."

He frowned and turned away. Then Jack, who had been watching, raised his glass and said, "My beautiful assistant. What will I do without you? How will I ever manage, how will *we?*"

Hermia found a job at Random House, but her heart was

no longer in it; it was 1968. The world of art and publishing now seemed as self-indulgent to her as had been the stage. The war had gotten serious, and there were marches to march in and demonstrations to join. She stopped using makeup and wearing a bra, but it made no difference; it was a fashion statement like the other fashion statements, and men hit on her anyhow in parties or at bars. She turned twenty-six years old. The "business as usual" attitude of editors and agents seemed corrupt to her, co-opted, and the last best hope of the last best hope of mankind was the Protest Movement; if Amerika did not withdraw from Vietnam she might have to leave it, and when she was teargassed while marching on the Pentagon she thought the time had come.

The Pentagon was ringed with troops, smug and dangerous and hateful, and she could not advance past the bridge. Hermia retreated in a press of bodies, and though their presence was a comfort it felt alarming also; she feared she might be crushed. Her throat was raw, her eyes were streaming; all around her there was screaming and a chorus of "Pigs, pigs!" She did not go to Chicago and the Democratic Convention, but friends of hers did go and get beaten and arrested, and when they were in New York again they talked about establishing a safe house in Nova Scotia. One of the men she had slept with that year owned property in Cape Breton; his name was Joe Arnoldi and he said it was the place to go to, a throwback to the old days and ways, with more sheep than police.

She and two other women traveled north. They had trouble at the border but did have valid passports and were let through, finally; the long drive through New Brunswick past the Bay of Fundy and through the empty Maritimes was fun. They drove a VW Bus. Hermia and her companions—a film-maker, a dancer—had become political, because everything was political, and you were either a part of the problem or part of the solution. This was a mantra and slogan, of course, but also political fact. It was only a question of whether or not you acknowledged the fact or instead chose to ignore it.

For years they *had* ignored it, taking privilege for granted, taking wealth and position for granted, and using their sex as a marker in the game of capital: a board game of money and sex. In Monopoly you bought hotels, you acquired Boardwalk and Park Place, and when you had everyone's money and everyone else had gone bankrupt you put the game away. But the soldiers standing at attention with their rifles and their gas masks had been serious, not playing or playacting, because power gets enabled and reality established by the barrel of a gun . . .

Each afternoon, it rained. When they reached Cape Breton, however, the skies turned a bright blue. This seemed like a good omen, a reason to continue, and there was never any trouble finding rooms with three beds in motels. The dancer's name was Sally and the filmmaker's Marian, and they liked to sign the hotel or the motel register together: S&M. Whatever else the movement had accomplished in Amerika—and this was not nothing, this was by definition something—it had changed forever the currency of sex. Sex was not a case of ownership, not a commodity to barter for a mortgage and two cars in the garage.

Sally wore a bracelet made of shrapnel and a dead soldier's

dog tag; Marian wore a locket with the photograph of Che. The friends talked about what it would mean to go underground and not to make any telephone calls or leave a signature trail. Alexander Dubcek had failed to stop the Soviets, and Czechoslovakia had been invaded just as Hungary had been before; it's so much easier, said Sally, to feel authentic in Europe—just think about those men and women in Prague who performed a pas de deux in front of tanks.

I can't imagine, Sally said, I just can't get my mind around it: all that training, all those centuries of culture and then the storm troopers, the pigs. Get used to it, said Hermia, it's just around the corner and it can happen here.

Don't be dramatic, objected Marian, who had been part of a camera crew the year before in a documentary on Birmingham, and Hermia said, I wasn't being dramatic, I was quoting Sinclair Lewis. " '*Can't* happen here,' is what he wrote," said Marian, and they agreed that in this case the two phrases were the same and "can't" is its dialectical antithesis, "can."

THEY WANDERED THROUGH ANTIGONISH and Ingonish and along the Cabot Trail. They visited a town called Dingwall and, at the outer edge of Cape Breton, a village called Meat Cove. After a week they drove to Inverness, where Joe Arnoldi was living in a trailer, and the friends took turns taking showers in the warm-water shower stall he had rigged outside. He was renting out his pastureland to the neighboring sheep farmer, or not so much renting it out as bartering for help with the house that he was building—he pointed to a wooden frame and pile of lumber down the hill—and smoking this terrific dope; he had hand-lettered posters on the trailer walls: *Turn On, Tune In, Drop Out* and *Make Love, Not War.* Did they know that Richard Alpert was no longer teaching at Harvard and had become Baba Ram Dass?

They bought lobsters for a dollar each and that night prepared a feast. Joe had grown a mustache he was proud of, brown and luxuriant, and he kept smoothing it and saying, "Dynamite you guys are here, it's dynamite you came to see me, what a gas!" He and Hermia had slept together twice, and she remembered how his balls were hairless and his cock seemed to bend to the left.

Now, however, he had other plans; he had his hand on Sally's knee and was beating out a rhythm on her thigh. Watching, drinking a glass of white wine, Hermia felt not so much rejected as relieved. She was into abstinence, had been into abstinence for weeks, and she hadn't wanted to sing for their supper by making it with Joe, their host; she ate a second lobster and sopped up the butter with bread.

That night she lay outside. Marian was sleeping on the air mattress in the camper, and Sally and Joe used the trailer, so she took a bedroll and stretched out beneath a tree. Except for the others up here on the hill, there was nobody who knew her who knew where she was lying, and Hermia could not decide if this made her happy or sad. She would call her mother in the morning, she decided; she did not belong in a Volkswagen Bus or on a hill in Cape Breton, and her mother ought to know that she was well and safe. She was not in political exile and not among *The Wretched of the Earth.* Above her, in the pines, a screech owl screeched.

Then again there was silence. She felt her heart beat. To calm herself she inhaled to the count of eight and held her breath and, to the count of eight, exhaled. Hermia thought about her father's death, the way the orange truck had seemed somehow volitional, hurtling down the driveway: an engine of destruction she foresaw but failed to stop. She repeated her breathing, exhaling, trying to think about nothing at all until she did feel calm. Faintly, from the trailer, she heard bedsprings, Sally's cries.

And then she too was crying, feeling sorry for herself. She had a sudden memory of lying down with Lawrence in his bed in Claverly; they both had been so young, so tender with each other, but that was very long ago and she did not feel young or tender. Where has it gone, she asked herself, where has it disappeared to?—love, my love.

YEARS PASSED. G. Edson Lattimer and her mother settled into a routine; they bought a pied-à-terre in Manhattan and spent half the year in England, returning to Lattimer's cottage in Kent every spring. She visited them sometimes, liking her stepfather better each visit and driving his Jaguar, sleeping in the oasthouse they'd converted to a guesthouse and dating the sons of Hunt Club neighbors or musicians on the rise. She and her mother made a truce of sorts, agreeing not to disagree, and profiting together from her father's legacy. The year that she turned thirty Hermia was given, by the trust established in her father's will, the house and land in Truro and, with the exception of her father's paintings in storage, its contents; its contents were evaluated—"Surprise, surprise!" her mother said—at two million dollars' worth of art. She sold the Noland and Hopper and the Motherwells at auction, in order to pay the inheritance tax, and now that she was well enough off not to need to earn a living lived as she chose, as she pleased.

Edson Lattimer had been married previously, and one winter night in New York she met his son. Paul Lattimer was thirty-four, a correspondent for Reuters on assignment at the U.N. To Hermia he seemed a younger version of his father, with thinning sandy hair and a pronounced nose and slight stammer she found endearing. They were introduced at dinner and had, as Paul told her, something in common. "What's that?" she inquired, and he said, "I wasn't any h-h-happier than *you* were when they married." He said this as though he had known her reaction, and she wondered if he had been informed of it or simply had guessed how she felt. In either case she liked his declarative clarity, his way of taking for granted that they would get along.

That evening they discussed Islam, the growing fundamentalism of the Muslim nations, and she was impressed by Paul's knowledge and his prediction that the Third World War would be fought over water and faith. He was in Manhattan on a six-month stint, and leaving soon, and regretted it had taken them this long to meet. At evening's end they shared a taxi and, as he dropped her off at her building, he asked, "Would you permit me to see you again?" Again she was impressed by his propriety and courtliness, and she answered, Yes.

At thirty-two she had grown conscious of the way her eye-lid drooped, the way her breasts were dropping and the added inches at her waist. She discovered and began to pluck gray hairs above her ear. Men still said she was beautiful, but that was a code word for single, and rich, and she had long since lost the illusion that someone she was seeing would say what he was thinking or tell her the literal truth. She was tired of hypocrisy; she was sick to death of vanity, and how men had to be flattered, and did not like or want to think the same held true for her. So when Paul Lattimer confessed he'd been reluc-tant to meet her, had seen and studied her photo in Kent and thought her a glamorous woman, too much so to be intelligent or anything except a model, or possibly an actress, she did not believe him.

"In person you're even more l-l-lovely," he said, "remark-able," and she said, "Stop it, please."

"I mean it," said Paul. "I never say what I d-d-don't mean."

Their courtship was brief. Hermia liked his cultivated stam-mer, his beak of a nose, the small mound of his belly and his erudition and wit. She was surprised by her own urgency, her sudden sense that this made sense and was what she'd waited for; she had been jagged-edged before but now the edges fit. At dinner the next week she felt a wave of *rightness, comfort,* and she and Paul Lattimer talked and talked as though they had all night to chat.

They had, they discovered, a great deal in common; they both liked Brussels sprouts, for instance, and detested purple; they both liked Ella Fitzgerald and disliked Frank Sinatra. His mother had died in a plane crash, a single-engine seaplane in foul weather off the Isle of Mull, and this represented another bond between them; each had lost a parent, and then their parents met. It was as though she'd found a brother, a long-lost relation, except that she could sleep with him and there was no taboo. They were happy together in bed. Paul joked that he and Hermia were "sexual relations," enjoying all the advantages of incest and none of the blood taint.

He had traveled widely, spending years in Thailand and Hong Kong, and he told her stories of being in Alaska and chased by a Kodiak bear. He liked the work at the U.N. and liked his work for Reuters, but lately he had wondered if he shouldn't settle down. He announced this to her carefully, and carefully she asked him, "Where?" and he said, "It doesn't matter, really, where would you p-prefer?"

They were married without ceremony, by a justice of the peace, and that evening the groom's father gave a dinner at his club. Photographs of expeditions and explorers and old, fabled ships and shipwrecks and big-game hunting parties lined the walls. They drank champagne.

Hermia felt buoyant, giddy, and she told Paul when he asked her, "Aren't you g-g-glad you waited?" that she wasn't only glad, she was *delighted, elated,* and it was worth the wait. It had all been worth the wait. He raised and kissed her hand where the diamond sparkled; he kissed her wedding ring.

"May you be as fortunate in your marriage," said G. Edson Lattimer, "as I am in mine."

"We hope to be, Papa," said Paul. "We f-follow where you lead."

"Which one of you is Alphonse, and which Gaston?" asked

her mother—a flash of her old arrogant impatience visible again. "What's that thing they're always saying, Alphonse and Gaston, 'After you'?"

"*Après moi,*" said her stepfather, "*le déluge.*"

"More wine, sir?" asked the waiter. They ordered a third bottle and drank a toast to absent friends and agreed that the mousse was too sweet.

Hermia was married now, and thirty-three, but it was as though the whole thing happened when she hadn't quite been watching; one fine day she had a husband and had become a wife. The whole was a bright blur. She was surprised by how little she'd noticed, how the details of the planning and the details of the wedding passed her by. She remembered the orchids he gave her, a stuffed bear on the stairwell of the Explorers' Club and how her mother was crying, how the blue garter she borrowed came undone while the two of them danced. That night Paul fell asleep inside her, and her first reaction was to wake him, shake him, but she had had her orgasm and did not require another and felt a wave of warm proud tenderness for this sleeping almost-stranger in her arms.

THEN SHE DISCOVERED SHE WAS PREGNANT. It might have happened the week of her wedding, or the week before, or after; her period had been irregular for years. She did not understand, at first, the way her body felt—the sleeplessness, the queasiness. She had not in particular wanted a child, had certainly not planned for one or thought it would happen so soon. And because she was no longer young, Hermia worried that the baby—her baby, their baby, *the* baby—might not come to term. But throughout her pregnancy—the difficult first trimester and then the easy one and then the final waiting months, the way her body changed and everything was re-arranged—she felt that same sense of *rightness,* of *comfort;* this was the way things should be.

Paul was solicitous and told her he adored her, she was his sacred vessel, and he could not bear it if she felt discomfort or pain.

She felt no pain. It was as though her whole previous life— the pointless jobs and pointless men, the work and play and politics—had been only preparation, only a way of waiting for a child to call her own. She had been idling and now was in gear; she had been lost and was found. When the baby came—a daughter, seven pounds six ounces, and perfectly beautiful, perfectly formed—they named her Patricia, after Paul's mother, and brought her back from Mount Sinai in a taxicab festooned with flowers. She was healthy and bright-eyed and, from the beginning, good-humored; she had ten toes and fingers and those enchanting rolls of baby fat and enormous eyes.

It was brilliant, said Paul, it was bliss.

But something had been happening, something not blissful or brilliant. Again she'd failed to notice and had not quite been watching and, as with her wedding, the details passed her by. She could not put a date to it or say, It *used* to be this way, it *used* to be different and better. There was no single thing to re-member and say, Here, *here's* where the trouble began. But the familiar man she married was becoming unfamiliar; the almost-brother who liked Brussels sprouts and Ella Fitzgerald and oral sex was not someone she could predict.

Paul changed. He added a police lock to the apartment's service door and, for good measure—although they lived on the tenth floor—iron grilles on all the windows. In their bedroom he kept the blinds drawn. When he was finished with his stint at the U.N., the management of Reuters asked him to consider a job as bureau chief in Tokyo, and he told them no. They had sufficient money so he had no need to work and instead took a "sabbatical, a time to s-s-s-sit down and think." He was doing research for a book, he said, but sat for hours in the living room, staring at the window, not reading or writing anything. He took amphetamines to stay awake and sleeping pills to sleep; he swallowed tabs of acid in order, he explained, to clarify his thinking on the project he was planning—and sat at his desk humming, rocking, cradling his head in his hands.

Paul grew jealous of the baby, aggrieved at the amount of time Hermia was spending with their child. When she got out of bed at night, to nurse or comfort Pat-a-Cake, he tried to keep her lying down and said, "It's g-g-good for her, good for the lungs." When she and Patricia went for a walk—using the baby carriage, and then with the Snugli or stroller—her husband stalked beside them as if he were their hired guard, as if he thought a passerby might threaten or make off with them instead of ignore them or smile. Once Hermia lost weight again and her breasts stayed full from nursing, he grew even more protective and jealous and suspicious—as though the men in elevators or behind a desk in galleries or idling at a traffic light might have been or would become her lovers, as though their friends were more than friends and she couldn't be trusted with men.

It was irrational, of course, it made no sense at all. But when she tried to talk to him he would not discuss it, saying only that he had his reasons, that he hadn't been born yesterday and was nobody's fool. "I've l-lost one Pat Lattimer already," he said, "and it w-won't happen again."

His face was red, his eyes were wild, and she thought he might be drinking though he did not smell of drink. "But I *love* you," Hermia protested, "I don't love anybody else."

"What about P-Patricia?"

"That's different, that doesn't count."

"Who's c-c-counting here?"

"*I'm* not."

"What, eleven, t-twelve, thirteen, how many men have you b-been with since our pretty b-b-baby was born?"

She began to be afraid of him, to fear for the child's safety, and when he started breaking things—a frying-pan handle, a set of Limoges they'd received for the wedding—she tried to find some help. Her mother was in England, and she called the house in Kent, but neither her mother nor stepfather would quite believe what she was saying. It was difficult to tell G. Edson Lattimer about his son's behavior, and Hermia could not convince them she needed their support. "Aren't you, are you exaggerating just a little, Herm?" her mother asked. Her friend Silvana came to New York twice a year for shopping, yet when she told Silvana she was frightened of her husband, her old roommate shrugged: "In Chile we are used to it," she said.

. . .

P<small>AT-A-CAKE</small> <small>WAS</small> <small>ALMOST</small> <small>TWO</small> when Paul fell completely
apart. She smiled and clapped her hands and learned to speak
and walk, but every time she smiled at a stranger he grew
more dark, more difficult. So too with Hermia; if she said
hello to the doorman he ordered her to stop it; when she
talked with other mothers in the playground about clothes or
weather or how their children were maturing, he warned
her—for Paul would accompany them always, standing by the
slide or swing, sitting cross-legged on the next bench down,
pretending to read the *New York Times* while he glared at
men out walking dogs, or tending daughters of their own—to
"S-s-s-stuff it, s-stop it, my last d-duchess, or I'll hang you on
the wall."

"Please don't," she said. "Please don't be jealous."

"It isn't jealousy," he said.

"What is it, then?"

"It's making sure what's mine is m-mine."

"We *are*," she said. "We completely are."

"Remember when you said," he said, "that you were
g-g-glad you waited?"

"Yes."

"Remember when I said," he said, "I thought you were an
actress. Too b-beautiful to be an actual person? A model, my
d-duchess. Unreal,"

"I'm *not*," she said.

"What?"

"Unfaithful."

"Don't lie to m-me," said her husband. "I s-s-swear I'll make you regret it."

"What? Regret what?"

"If I ever c-c-catch you . . ."

"What? Doing *what?*"

"You know," he said. "And I c-certainly know."

So that evening when he came at her—the wild glint in his eye again, the kitchen knife outthrust—she was ready with a can of Mace and blasted him full force. It had been in her handbag for weeks. She had had her suitcase packed, and her daughter's, and while Paul was groaning, collapsed upon the kitchen counter, covering his face and carving patterns in the air, cursing, trying to find water, she picked up Patricia and left.

IV

1962

WHEN LAWRENCE LEFT COLLEGE HE DROVE HOME alone, using his mother's Impala. The week of graduation was a week of parties, and he did what he could to enjoy them, drinking and discussing the future of the planet and sleeping with Charette. His parents attended commencement but would not speak to each other. They took turns having meals with him and telling him how proud they were and how they knew the end of school was only a beginning. The completion of your studies, said his father over breakfast, is the start of what's to come.

First he returned to Scarsdale, having packed his books and clothes and radio, feeling sentimental but excited to leave Cambridge behind. On his final day in Claverly Hall he surveyed his empty room and found, beneath the mattress, a piece of paper wedged there. It was in Hermia's handwriting, her blue pen and her open scrawl; he unfolded it and read: "I *adore* you. Adore you. *Love.* Love." The note was undated, on yellow lined paper, and he folded and kissed it and threw it away.

In Scarsdale things had changed. His mother was seeing a doctor, a widower across the street with a prizewinning Pekinese who was, she told him, the reason they'd met; she'd noticed the two of them—Robert and Sam—out walking every morning and again at night. Then one night at nearly midnight she heard the Pekinese barking, barking madly at a tree. She put on her bathrobe and opened the door to see what was happening, what had gone wrong, but the streetlight showed her nothing and so she went down to the street. Across the hedge the Peke was going *yap-yap-yap*, having cornered a raccoon, and up there on the branch the animal was hissing, spitting, terrified, a pair of eyeballs gleaming from a body twice Sam's size. And there had been something so, so *ridiculous* about it, said his mother, she just had to laugh.

"Can you hold the leash?" her neighbor asked. She could; she held the dog. He hunted for and found a rock and flipped it up sidearm precisely, and although it fell short of the target it caused the raccoon to shrink back. "I think you hit him," she declared, and he said, "Think I missed." Then they introduced themselves—she conscious of her bathrobe and he apologizing for the noise, for having disturbed her, for the racket Sam was making and how late it was. "Do you always walk this late?" she asked, and he said no, it had been a long day, a difficult procedure at the hospital, and they wished each other good night.

That first conversation had led to another, a third, a meal, and now she and the doctor were friends. This was how she described it: "good friends." Her neighbor was, she told Lawrence, an excellent surgeon and father—he had two grown sons in San Diego, both in commercial real estate—and Robert was a decent man, a man who wouldn't lie to you or live a secret life. That was what mattered most to her, his mother said: Robert's cards were on the table and everything up front and out in the open—how much he missed his dead wife, for example, was a subject they often discussed. She expected Lawrence to like her new companion and be pleased for her, a little, or at least try to be pleased.

He was not so much pleased as relieved. His mother did seem happy, taking pains with her appearance and going to the opera and, before it closed, to *My Fair Lady,* because they'd each enjoyed the show the first time they'd seen it on Broadway, and wanted to see it together. In the kitchen his mother hummed snatches of song—"I Could Have Danced All Night" or "On the Street Where You Live"—and busied herself preparing complicated dishes when Robert came over to eat. She was girlish in the surgeon's presence, laughing at his jokes and making sure that Lawrence got the punch line, making sure he understood how carefree she could be.

His sister too seemed happier, caught up in being a Racquet Club lifeguard and asking for advice about which college to apply to, since she would be a senior in September. Allie's hair was sun-bleached; she had been working on a tan, and when he looked at her he saw a golden girl with braces, his kid sister growing up. She and a clique of girlfriends were always in her bedroom, cackling together and using the phone and playing the stereo loudly and practicing the twist. His brother was in Oregon, his father on Long Island—remarried now, and with a three-year-old—so Lawrence lazed about the house with a sense of earned inertia, sleeping late and lying shirtless in the hammock, reading books.

At the induction center he was classified 4F. He had had to register, but it was 1962 and there was little pressure on the draft. On the appointed day he showed up for his physical with letters from his doctors attesting to rheumatic fever, a murmur of the mitral valve contracted during childhood. His mother made him breakfast and drove him to the train. "Don't let's worry, darling." She stubbed out her cigarette. "Robert is certain they won't take the risk."

"What risk?"

"The army doctors will reject you. It's the 'cloud's silver lining,' he says. They won't want to deal with medical trouble—not a precondition anyhow—when you wear a uniform."

This proved to be the case. Lawrence waited in a white high-ceilinged room for his turn to be examined, while a soldier with a clipboard paced up and down the line. There were names of diseases called out. There were "cancer" and "epilepsy" and "flat feet" and a long list of medical conditions; when they reached "rheumatic fever," he stepped forward from the line. He was wearing only underpants, and cold. A doctor with crew-cut red hair told him to do fifty push-ups and then listened to his heart, saying, "Breathe," and "Hold," and "Breathe deeply, hold," and then he folded his stethoscope and said, "You're out of here, kid." They were in a cubicle, with a drawn blue curtain, and Lawrence dressed himself again and collected his papers and left.

THAT EVENING HE HAD DINNER with his father. They ate at an Italian restaurant, and his father drank dry martinis and over wine confessed he sometimes worried he'd made a mistake: he'd been not so much *railroaded* as *steered*, not so much *forced* as *lured* into being a banker, and sometimes—today was one of them—it felt like his career at work had been only an attempt to meet other people's expectations and other people's needs. It was water way under the bridge, said his father, milk spilled so long ago there was no point crying about it, but he didn't want his oldest child to wake up thirty years from now with the same sense of, not so much *failure* as, well, yes, the word was *regret*. He wanted Larry to take some time off, to not get caught up in the rat race, and now that he had finished school and the army wasn't an issue he should travel a little and see the wide world. His graduation gift—he must have noticed, hadn't he, how he'd received nothing at the commencement ceremony up in Cambridge?—was an open-ended ticket and blank check.

His father smiled. The circles underneath his eyes were deeper now, and darker, and though his hair had been carefully barbered it was thin and gray. Don't think I mean *blank* check exactly, he said, it's not, I mean, a bottomless well, but there's enough for you to travel with and we'll start with five thousand dollars; that should get you out of here and let you see the world. Don't tell your mother but I sometimes think if the two

of us had had some time together that was off the beaten track
we'd still be happy together . . .

"I'm grateful, Dad."

"Don't mention it."

"No, I *want* to mention it. I'm very grateful to you."

His father's face was pale. "Have some dessert?"

"No."

"Zabaglione. *Zuppa inglese.* Everything that starts with *z*.
You're a growing boy."

"I'm fine. I'm full."

"Well then, the check." He gestured at the waiter, and the
waiter came. "I want you to be happy," said his father solemnly,
and wiped his mouth with his napkin. "It's the only thing I
want."

So HE WAS TWENTY-TWO, and free, intending to be an architect but not this year, not yet. He went to parties in New York
and talked to friends from Harvard and one of them insisted
the best way to join the profession was not to think about it but
to absorb the way that people live. What does that mean,
Lawrence asked, and his host, Dick Silver, plucked a sandwich
from the sandwich tray and swallowed an olive and said,
"When you travel you take yourself with you. Except a roof in
Africa is a very different thing from one in Greenland or
Nepal."

"Excuse me?"

Dick Silver repeated himself. It was his birthday party; they
had been drinking Singapore Slings. Dick himself was working

on Wall Street and had no desire to travel. But nevertheless, if he said so himself, he had a fondness for adventure, intellectual adventure, and if he said so himself he was as intellectually venturesome as any of those armchair travelers their professors at Harvard had been. You can explore the world in a hammock just as much as on a camel's back or with a canoe or dugout or, what do they call it, caïque . . .

They drank. The *idea* of roof is various, Dick Silver continued, and its function varies greatly, and you have to have some sense of where the variables come from and what different people think of as a "roof." If he himself had hoped to be an architect he'd work on the distinction between and the comparative construction in a structure made of, for example, thatch or slate. Satch and thlate . . .

They were at the Players' Club, of which Dick Silver's father was a member. Wearing a double-breasted suit and handlebar mustache, he greeted them in the foyer. "Glad you could join us, gentlemen," he said. "Can you believe this boy of mine is twenty-four? That must mean I'm over thirty." Then Dick Silver's father joined his own friends in another room, under oil paintings of actors, saying, "Order whatever you want."

"We were discussing architecture. Food, clothing and shelter," pronounced their host. He raised his glass, inclusive.

"And of those three," said Roger, "our Larry here intends to focus on shelter. The last shall not be least."

"The bare necessities. The *bare* necessities," repeated Dick. With both hands he shaped an hourglass, then whistled. "It's what I myself would study in—it's what they *wear* there—St. Tropez."

"The best preparation is looking around," said Allan Silverwhistle. "Just seeing what's out there to see . . ."

This seemed a good idea. Lawrence excused himself and went to the bathroom and stared at himself in the Players' Club mirror: long-haired, blue-eyed, strong-nosed, drunk. One of his teachers used to say that there are builders and breakers; there are those who worship icons and those who strike them down. In the future, gentlemen, you will decide which party is the one to which you pledge allegiance—you must cast your lot with nave or knave and not be in between. There's the temple or the wrecking ball and you will have to choose.

His teacher quoted Samuel Beckett:

Spend the years of learning squandering
Courage for the years of wandering

And when he finished the lecture—this had been famous at Harvard, a ritual performance—he would fold his papers at the podium and place them in his briefcase and put on his raincoat and, completing the quatrain, lean into the microphone:

Through the world devoutly turning
From the loutishness of learning.

And exit to applause.

As a dog urinates, not completely, but in stages and to establish dominion, so Lawrence shifted towns. He flew from Idlewild to Orly but was saving himself for Paris and did not enter the capital but took a train to Versailles. There he spent the evening with an ambulance driver's family; he had stopped the ambulance driver to inquire as to hotels, and the man had a cousin in Boston and invited him to dinner. At the hotel he met a man from Glasgow who recited limericks and went "tum-de-tum-de-tum-tum" when he could not remember the words. The man said Glasgow was an awful place, unimaginably horrible, and Lawrence, if he hoped to preserve his sanity, should never go to Glasgow or, for that matter, Edinburgh. "Being impecunious," he said, "you won't have servants there."

He visited the palace. In the hall of mirrors he tried to track the sight lines and the effects of perspective; he admired the balconies and stairwells and the long *allées*. He had read about the Sun King's lush extravagance and the queen who played at being a milkmaid, pretending to work on a farm. Yet Versailles astonished him: the scale of it, the delicate grandeur. He saw the chairs and tapestries reflected in the mirrors, and the way each object was by its own image paired. When he reached to touch a window, the guard said, *"Défendu.* It is forbidden, *m'sieur."*

Next morning he proceeded from Versailles to Clermont-Ferrand. Lawrence found a cheap hotel behind the railway station, where a woman in the restaurant said, *"Tiens, les yeux d'un poète."* She sat down at his table and smiled. She was, he came to understand, a prostitute, and she took him to her room and washed his penis carefully and, arousing him, patted it dry. He paid her for an hour but she let him stay two hours and he flattered himself that she meant it when she said "the eyes of a poet"; he liked Clermont-Ferrand, its Romanesque cathedral and the shadows cast by plane trees in the streets.

After two days in that city, however, Lawrence took a night

train east and north. He made a special pilgrimage to Le Corbusier's Ronchamp. The complicated structure in celebration of simplicity, the way the building both belonged to and stood separate from landscape, the proportions and materials and upward-striving thrust of it: all these enthralled him. The chapel seemed a marriage of the ancient and the modern in a way that honored both; he studied the shape of the roof.

Next he spent a week near Marseilles. Lawrence moved from town to town without purpose, with no sense of obligation or hurry, convinced he would profit from travel. He ate and drank and viewed the sights—Arles, Avignon, St. Rémy— with diligence, taking pleasure in the trip; he was often alone but not often lonely and he kept a notebook, noting buildings that he saw. His first focus was cathedrals—Gothic, Baroque— and the structural components of their downspout gargoyles and stained-glass windows and flying buttresses and the carved stone saints. These he drew.

From Aix-en-Provence he took a train to Cannes, where he met a pair of English girls on what they called their hols. When he asked them what they meant by hols they said, Don't be so thick, it's *holiday*, and the three of them went to a wine bar. They were big-breasted and exuberant, with white skin and red cheeks. They said the Riviera was smashing, they had been here for a week already and having a rattling good time. One of the girls, Valerie, confided that her friend Estelle quite fancied him, and Estelle took him aside and said Valerie was frus-*trat*-ed, so he paid for a bottle of *vin rosé* and proposed they empty it together as a threesome in his room. "No thanks," they said, "not bloody likely," and linked arms and left.

Spring and Fall

. . .

FROM NICE HE TOOK A TRAIN to Rome and stayed in the city two weeks. He walked the hills and narrow streets of Trastevere, admiring the monuments and merchandise in shops. He studied work by Brunelleschi and Bernini and decided that his favorite of the "three Bs" in Rome was Borromini; he filled a notebook with the work of Borromini, his use of perspective, his windows and ceilings and domes.

At the American Express office in the Piazza di Spagna he found letters from his parents saying everything was fine and sending him their love. He sent his parents postcards of the Trevi Fountain and the Spanish Steps. He went to museums and churches and the Vatican and drew several versions of the Pantheon. Again he found a prostitute, this one from Morocco, and relieved himself inside her while she made encouraging noises and swiveled her thin hips.

Lawrence stayed near the Villa Borghese. The Porta Pinciana was crowded with cars, and men on Vespas hurtled past, but he liked to dawdle with a glass of mineral water and a half-carafe of wine in the cafés. There he watched the busy traffic on the Via Veneto; he visited the Colosseum and bookstalls by the Tiber and the Baths of Caracalla. From his window in the Pensione Villa Borghese he could see the Villa Borghese itself, and in the morning when he walked the garden paths there were prophylactics everywhere. It was December now, and growing cold, and there were fewer tourists; he went south.

First he took a train to Naples and saw the peak of Mount Vesuvius, but it looked bleak, its flanks littered with trash, and he decided he would rather climb Mount Etna than Vesuvius. He stayed in Naples two nights. An Italian lawyer bought him dinner at a restaurant by the water, plying him with wine, but when Lawrence rejected the suggestion that they go to his apartment the lawyer slapped him twice, not lightly. "You have been playing with me, *ragazzo*," said the lawyer, "a game it can be dangerous to play."

Although he was not frightened he left Naples the next morning. Carrying a duffel bag and knapsack he reveled in his freedom, the way he could elect to leave a town or stay. Lawrence crossed the Strait of Messina and went to Siracusa and Taormina but found himself disliking Taormina. There were tour buses and curio shops, a self-important quaintness that felt false. He bought a pair of hiking boots and commenced to climb Mount Etna but was turned back before the peak, because Etna was erupting; the brochure discussed Empedocles and the Titans. It rained. His hotel in Catania cost the equivalent in lire of eight dollars and he stayed there for six nights, admiring the black volcanic rock of the buildings of the city.

The proprietor of the hotel served a white acidic wine and called it the wine of the Cyclops; if you drink one liter for lunch and another in the evening, he declared, you lose an eye. According to our legend, the Cyclops's cave, he said, is very near this part of town and when Odysseus blinded the Cyclops he threw a boulder at the ship and it landed here, just here . . .

After two weeks on the island Lawrence had enough of Sicily and took the ferry to Piraeus; in Athens he stayed in a hotel beneath the Plaka, and from his window saw a section of the Parthenon itself. Spotlit, it floated on air. At the American Express office in Syndagma Square he collected mail and found letters from his parents and one from Allan Silverwhistle, saying life in the city was dishwater-dull. Wish I were there, Allan wrote. His father wrote to tell him that the fall had been spectacular, leaf season a real pleasure on Long Island, and his mother wrote she missed him very much, most of all during holiday season, and Allie and Robert sent love.

"I couldn't help but notice," said the man behind him in the mail line, "you know somebody in Scarsdale. And the return address is just around the corner from where I used to live."

This seemed sufficient reason for a drink. Anthony Palamis was of Greek extraction, but he confided that his Greek was less than stellar; winking, he confessed—when Lawrence asked him the name of a dish in the menu they were reading—"Oh, it's Greek to me." Anthony wore horn-rimmed glasses and a black elastic band securing them around his neck; he was, he said, a poet and he greatly admired the poetry of Constantine Cavafy, but poetry won't let a person eat. A person must put bread on the table, a person can't subsist on air and odes and therefore he was working at a travel agency just down the street.

Anthony was thirty-six, a year past Dante's age at the start of the *Commedia*, and he said Syndagma Square was scarcely an Inferno but the office in the summertime could be infernally hot. He was working on a sonnet sequence about the Elgin Marbles, and it was more than a little discouraging—dis*piriting* would be the word—to know most people still believe that "marbles" is a game to play, not something quarried in Carrara or Ferrara. And who *was* Elgin anyhow, he asked, how much does anyone remember about a fellow called Lord Elgin, and why he purchased those marbles and when he shipped them back?

Lawrence bought a new notebook for Greece. He studied the distinctions between Doric and Ionic and Corinthian and drew the base of columns and then their capitals. On the Acropolis he studied the details of the temples—how the columns gently fattened in the middle, and how they angled perceptibly inward but appeared from the ground to be straight.

After ten days in Athens and at Anthony's suggestion, he booked passage on a tour boat through the islands. The ship was called *Kalliope* and had scheduled ports of call in Mykonos, Delos, Corfu, Crete, and Rhodes. It flew the Liberian flag. Because he did not wish to seem too obviously a tourist, he avoided other passengers—the women in seersucker jumpsuits, the men with their hands in their pockets and wearing striped shirts and shorts. But Lawrence was befriended by the cook, a man from Pittsburgh called George Psacharopolous; they shared cigars on deck. He was welcome in the galley and sat there in the afternoons while the cook washed plates and cutlery, then rubbed down the cast-iron pots. Crusts and lettuce leaves floated in the galley sink; when George had finished washing dishes he would rinse his arms. The other members of the crew pronounced his name as *Iorgo*, always saying, *"Iasu, Iorgo,"* and chattering in Greek. George owned a record by Nana Mouskouri and one by Perry Como and several records of Django Reinhardt and Mikis Theodorakis and one of Flatt & Scruggs. He played the records during dinner, and sometimes while he prepared the dinner, and always afterward.

The cabin Lawrence slept in had three other passenger berths. Two of them were occupied, although the bed beneath his own was empty; he preferred the upper berth. His two companions came from Conway, Massachusetts, but had lived in Barcelona for the past three years. "We just love Barthelona," they said, pronouncing the *c* as *th*. They were lovers, and secretive at the beginning of the trip, but not secretive by the third day. They clambered into bed together and, when the stabilizer equalizers failed and the ship tilted, lost their balance noisily and giggled and complained.

LAWRENCE SPENT THE WINTER on the islands, staying in Rhodes for four months. He acquired a taste for retsina wine, its bitter-edged flavor and the way it was served in open tin tankards; nightly in the tavernas he ordered *taramousalata* and artichokes and fish. He liked the fort and seawalls and olive trees and lemon groves and the narrow, steep-pitched streets. He liked the people, their bluff warmth, but could not understand them and contented himself with smiling, nodding, speaking pidgin French and English and drinking quantities of coffee in brightly colored cups. He climbed Monte Smith. In February he contracted what would later on be diagnosed as amebic dysentery and lay immobile for weeks, unable to keep down the tea and toast and brandy that the mustachioed doctor prescribed. An English tourist passing through said, "These should help," and handed him a set of pills called Enterovio-form; "They're for holiday tummy," he said.

But the pills did not help either. Lawrence rented a room near the harbor, reading *Incidents of Travel in the Yucatán* and a guidebook with an appendix of useful phrases in Greek. In a bookshop with a newspaper stall he found a pamphlet by C. A. Doxiadis, called "Dynapolis: The City of the Future," and this he read with attention. There was no telephone and the electric light was fitful and he felt both sick and homesick, re-membering his own clean bed and the abundant food and spotless bathrooms at home. He was very far from Scarsdale now and lay by the water adrift; he tried to remember what he had done for each of the days and weeks and months of his trip, and why he had traveled and what he had wanted to see.

There had been—he was sure of it—snow. The ceiling above him had intricate tiling, and he tried to make sense of the pattern and where the tiles were stained. Dick Silver's face emerged from the floor, making pronouncements about shelter and what his birthday party guests should notice around them in the whirling world, but nothing he said was in English and none of it made sense. Lawrence sweated and shivered and rocked. In his dreams he dreamed of Scarsdale and, wakeful, thought of Truro and his times with Hermia there.

The men of the island were kind. Wearing colored hats and jackets lined with wool, they smoked and played board games with dice and tiles and smiled and nodded at him while he drank his tea or lemon soup and tried to decide what to do. He still had his passport and six hundred dollars folded double in his money belt and in the zippered pocket of his boots. In March he purchased a book on the Bauhaus and the role of Walter Gropius. On the same shelf he found an English-language pamphlet on Le Corbusier and the role of the builder, the technological and social determinants that constitute "New Objectivity" as proclaimed by J. J. P. Oud.

Our purpose, he read in the preface, is "to change the mild course of modern fashion architecture into a struggle for a revolution in the architectural world." The ideal of personal license must be replaced by objective limits—or so the pamphlet's author wrote—and the collective value of a structure outstrips its private signature. When Mies declared, famously, "Less is more," he ignored or failed to acknowledge—as has been often noted—that less can also be less. The conscious application of design, the writer concluded, means function yoked to form in a way that neither leads nor follows: two halves of a unified whole.

The spring, when it came, was a gift. Fruit trees burst into blossom, and the bougainvillea and bright oleander bloomed. Lawrence had lost weight; his clothes hung on him loosely, but his hallucinations faded and he began to improve. He drew elevations of the harbor and the forts built by Crusaders and imagined versions of the Colossus of Rhodes. He had been, he told himself, aimless for a reason, and his thumbprint on the window showed the whorled striations of a cypress tree or flowers by van Gogh. By the time that he felt strong enough to travel he had memorized Doxiadis and read *Incidents of Travel in the Yucatán* three times.

At the end of April, and with the last of his traveler's checks, he bought a ticket home. On the airplane he took stock. He had spent his father's money and traveled through parts of Europe and Greece looking at cities and buildings and learning, a little, to be by himself. He had, or so he assured himself, strengthened his sense of vocation; he was much more certain now he hoped to be an architect. He had visited great structures—Versailles, the chapel at Ronchamp, St. Peter's, the Parthenon—and been moved by them; he had filled notebooks with sketches of windows and floor plans and façades. During the flight he read Doxiadis's *Ekistics: New Problems and New Solutions in Human Settlements* and fell asleep fitfully, sweating. He had fallen sick and was well.

ON ARRIVAL HE INFORMED HIS MOTHER—who collected him at the airport, driving Robert's black Mercedes—that in his months of wandering he'd learned a little history; societies are shaped in part by the shape of their cities. It makes a difference, for example, if the common space sits on a hilltop or instead down by the water. And the great thing about architects, Lawrence maintained, is they build a better mousetrap for the landscape of the future and by conscious decision influence the habitat of generations to come . . .

She told him she was getting married. Next month she and Robert were tying the knot—that was the phrase she used, "tying the knot"—and she didn't want to feel like a burden to her children. "There's nothing worse," his mother said, "than a fifty-year-old by herself in the world, and I'm not lonely anymore, you know that, don't you, darling?"

"Congratulations, Mom."

"Your sister too, she's happy for me."

"How's Allie doing?"

"Fine, she's fine."

"And Tim? Still in Portland?"

His mother talked about her wedding plans—well, not so much the *wedding* as the honeymoon thereafter, because all her life she'd wanted to visit New Zealand and the Fiji islands, and she and Robert would travel for two weeks. "It's the most he's been away for *all* his career, the longest they could spare him"—she giggled—"from the hospital. 'Youth is wasted on the young.' I know you don't believe that, really, I know it's a foolish expression. But these months you've been in Europe were—what's the word I want?—*remarkable*, a privilege, and I hope you don't take it for granted . . ."

Her voice trailed off. They were crossing the Bronx-Whitestone Bridge. Co-op City loomed ahead, and he asked himself what he had in fact learned during the course of his time away, if his talk about landscape and cities made sense, and where he would go next. Had he wasted or made use of youth; what had he decided to do?

Lawrence closed his eyes. On the screen of his shut eyelids the book on the Bauhaus appeared. It was rectangular, thin, white. There were diagrams and photographs and scale models of buildings and illustrated charts. The image of Walter Gropius—in the photograph the architect was surrounded by disciples, and pointing with his spectacles at drawings on a blackboard—remained. They made the turn to the Hutchinson River Parkway, then Weaver Street, then home.

· · ·

THE NEXT DAY, in Manhattan, he met his father for lunch. They ate at La Toque Blanche. "You're looking well," his father said.

"You too, Dad. Very well."

"You've lost a lot of weight."

"I had whatever they call *la turista* in Greece. Except I'm fine now."

His father was drinking martinis. He had allowed his sideburns to grow, as well as the hair at his collar. He made a show of interest while Lawrence spoke about his time in France and Italy, the months in Rhodes. But it was clear he paid no real attention; he drummed his fingers on the tablecloth and looked around the restaurant at other diners, at the waiters, the walls. "I have something to say to you."

"Yes?"

"Something important."

"All right." Lawrence straightened.

"What I wanted to say is your brother and sister are not on my wavelength. Not people I can talk to anymore. I don't think your mother did it on purpose, but both of them are of the opinion that I'm somehow, oh I don't know, untrustworthy. The devil in a blue-striped suit. And I wanted to ask you to tell them I'm not." Rueful, his father smiled. "Tell them I love both of them, just the way I used to."

At the banquette in the corner a couple was laughing, uproarious. The girl was in a yellow dress, the man in a seersucker jacket, and they stroked each other's arms.

"All right."

"I *knew* you'd step up to the plate." His father made a swinging motion, wrists cocked, as though he held a baseball bat. "So have you decided?"

"Decided?"

"What comes next. What you're intending to do with your life."

"Is this a change of subject?"

"Correct."

"Remember what you said about 'the beaten track'? Well, it isn't exactly an outlaw profession—architecture. But you were right, Dad, I did need some time."

His father drank. "It's not like on Tuesday they answer the phone and on Wednesday refuse to; it's not like any single conversation or any particular thing goes wrong, it's just little by little until they're not home. Then your kids decide you're Antichrist—did I say that already? In a blue suit. The reason for marriage is to have children," he declared, maudlin, "and now I'm losing two of them. And you—you were away all year. Talk to them, Larry, okay?"

"I'll try."

"It's all we have," his father said. "Time. It's what we don't notice and let slip away and take advantage of and then one fine morning the alarm clock rings and you wake to it, wake *up* to it, and there's very little left of this commodity you think you've stockpiled and maybe even have too *much* of. Don't waste it, is what I'm trying to tell you, don't let it take you by surprise. Excuse me." His father stood up from the table and made for the men's room, weaving. The couple in the corner kissed. "And talk to your sister, okay?"

V

2004

SHE RECOGNIZED HIM INSTANTLY, AS SOON AS HE came up on deck. He was gray and thick and stooped, of course, but still completely Lawrence—not anyone else, or so Hermia thought, not someone she could ever fail to know. He stood the way he used to stand, both wanting to be part of the party and wanting to withdraw from it, holding out his life preserver as though it might protect him and be both shield and badge. He was wearing a windbreaker: black. His shirt was yellow, open-necked, and the tilt of his head was familiar; she *knew* that head, that neck.

Her stomach dropped; her heart leapt. Her breath caught in her throat. Those were inaccurate phrases, she knew; a stomach doesn't *drop*, a heart can't *leap*. But that was what it felt like, truly, standing ten feet apart from her old lover by lifeboat station 6, and it took her a minute to calm herself down and not rush to his side. She forced herself to wait; she *caught* her breath.

It was September 27, 2004. They had not seen each other since 1962. She had Googled him, of course, and found out where he worked and taught, the titles of his books—*Urbanism (Re)Considered; The Common Place*, the monograph series he edited—and the prizes won. She wrote down his office address. She considered a letter, or e-mail—*everyone* was doing it, *everyone* was hunting down lost friends. *Hi, Just thought I'd drop a line. Hello, here's a bolt from the blue. A blast from the past, baby, thinking of you.*

But none of it seemed possible, nothing made sense; she did not write him, or e-mail, or call. She thought about him often, as Lawrence had no doubt thought about her, but more than forty years had passed and the spilled milk was long since evaporated and water far under the bridge. There was nothing to say to him, nothing to ask, and no way to begin. *Hiya, remember me?*

It took her two full days. At first she wasn't sure she should, or wanted to, or what would happen if she did; how long would it take him, she wondered, to notice her instead? It was not so much the nerve she lacked as certainty; was this a good idea? *Should I, Will I, Won't I, Why not*, Hermia asked herself repeatedly, and could not decide . . .

She had started the cruise in Marseilles. The Mediterranean looked uninviting, the passengers were loud and dull and hell-for-leather-bent on having a wonderful time. She needed to be left alone; she did not want a wonderful time. Instead she spent the first days on the M.S. *Diana* avoiding importunate strangers, reading *The Leopard* and watching the water and wondering what to do next. In Nice she drank a glass of wine in the Negresco Hotel lobby bar; in Monaco she walked by the harbor and went to the casino just the way they urged her to, feeling both restless and bored. At Elba Hermia remained aboard and by the time they reached the port of Rome she more than half considered jumping ship. Therefore when he came on deck for Lifeboat Drill she could not quite believe it: the gods of coincidence dictating play and changing the rules of the game.

She remembered he had said that once, when they first met in Cambridge all those years ago. They had met three times that week, each time by accident, and Lawrence took this as an omen, as she herself had taken it; they saw each other at the Fogg, and then again at Elsie's, and then outside the Loeb. Those encounters, however, were not so surprising; they had shared a town and college and were walking the same streets. *This* felt different; this felt truly accidental: the gods of coincidence rattling the dice and inviting her to play . . .

She did not want to bet on things or, again, to play. Watching Lawrence where he stood on deck, she remembered how he'd hurt her, once, and asked herself if he retained that power still. This did not seem likely. She was thicker-skinned by now and had been hurt much more by others since 1962. He shuffled through the lifeboat drill or made conversation in the dining room or sat in his chair in the Elsinore Lounge, looking anything but dangerous, and cloaked in his pale solitude. *Will I, Should I, Why Not,* Hermia asked herself, and could not decide.

She watched him watching her. She waited a third day. But then, in the Luparium, he'd seemed so lost and lonely, so utterly forlorn, she approached him and reached out to touch his sleeve. When he stared at her—this grown man gone speechless—it was as though no time had passed, no distance was traversed. She caught her breath, her stomach dropped, her heart was in her throat. *Ridiculous,* thought Hermia, I'm sixty-three years old.

"WHAT ARE YOU DOING HERE?"

"What are *you* doing here?"

"The same as you." She tried to smile. "Admiring the view."

He colored. "Dirty pictures."

"Yes."

"The hell of a place to meet up with you, lady."

"Pompeii?"

He gestured. "Here."

"You mean, outside a whorehouse?"

"On a guided tour." Lawrence tried a joke. "With, as the man said, selling postcards, '*Feelthy* pictures stressing togetherness.' "

She did not laugh. "I mean, what brought you to the *Diana?*"

"My doctor. He said I should travel."

"Your doctor?"

"Wanted me to see the world . . ."

"You *used* to travel, didn't you? Or wanted to, at any rate."

"Yes. But that was then." His face was changing as she

watched—becoming youthful, softening. "And I've never been to Malta. Or Pompeii."

"Me either. Why a doctor?"

"Do you want lunch? A coffee, maybe?"

"It's good to see you," she ventured.

"And *you.* You look wonderful."

"No. No, I don't."

"You're here alone?"

"Alone," she said. "And you?"

"Not any longer. Not now."

THAT NIGHT THEY ATE TOGETHER at a table set for two. This way they could discourage company and begin, as she said, to catch up. There was so much to tell each other, wasn't there, said Lawrence, so much explaining to do. Well, not so much *explaining*, Hermia said, as filling in the blanks. She told him a little and kept back a lot, and he told her a little and kept back a lot, and they got through the soup and the salad and pasta remembering the things they'd done in Cambridge and Truro together.

This was easy to talk about: courses of study and houses and friends—what happened to Will and Silvana, for instance, the ones they stayed in touch with and the ones they'd both lost touch with—the graduate school he'd attended, the jobs she'd held and quit. He had read about her father's death and asked about her mother; was she still alive? She said, Mummy's living in England and a very old lady by now. She doesn't recognize me, or anyone, and hasn't for years. Hermia asked about his parents and he said they both were dead, they both had lasted till seventy-eight but his father had a heart attack and his mother a brain aneurysm later that same day. It was strange, said Lawrence, they hadn't spoken to each other except when it was absolutely necessary; they both had remarried and established other families, but in the end his parents died as though they shared a roof, a *fate*, and were inseparable; his mother had collapsed the night she heard the news.

Darko offered wine. She drank. They avoided the difficult subjects, the disappointment and trouble, the way things fell apart. Lawrence asked if she had children and she told him, Yes, a daughter, and he said he had a daughter too and two sons, by different wives. Are you married now, she asked him, and he answered, No, are you? She shook her head. There was, she said, so much to ask, and he said, Yes, so much to tell. And something in the way he said this seemed so familiar she wanted to cry; where has it gone, she asked him, where did it disappear to, and he asked her what she was talking about, and Hermia said, *You know.* He did know, he told her, he knew what she meant; then he advanced his hand and placed it on the tablecloth by the salt shaker and the spoon adjoining hers.

She left it there. It was too soon to take his hand. She remembered it had also been too soon the night of the cast party, although she'd let him kiss her then, and promised they would meet that Saturday or Sunday. Then when the weekend came at last and parietal hours permitted it he had invited her—so willingly, so trustful—to his wood-paneled bedroom in Claverly Hall: the second-floor room at the rear of the building, with the bark paintings he was proud of and that atrocious rug . . .

She remembered, she told Lawrence, everything. She remembered his bathroom, the pattern of cracks in the porcelain sink, the shirt he was wearing, the book by his bed. She had been blessed, she told him, with a retentive memory for details, cursed with it too; she had forgotten nothing and he said he also had forgotten nothing, or anyhow nothing important. What day was it, Hermia asked him, and he said March 21. That was opening night, she corrected him, but not the day we met; what was the name of the play?

I haven't forgotten, said Lawrence: *The Flies,* by Jean-Paul Sartre, and she'd been the stage manager. Who directed it, she asked, and Lawrence said, That's what I mean, I mean he was nothing important.

We were so innocent, she said, so hopeful then, and he said, Yes, there'd been no 9/11, no growing old or afraid. I have to ask you this, she asked, you're not, are you, Republican, and he said, Of course not, no, and she said, Well, *that's* a relief. They were—she tried to make a joke of it—in the same boat, weren't they, the two of them both passengers on a ship of fools . . .

"I'm very glad you're here," he said.

"I'll see you tomorrow?"

"Yes, of course."

"Ships passing in the night. *Colliding* in the night . . ."

"I'll see you tomorrow," he said.

THE M.S. *DIANA* WAS SCHEDULED TO ARRIVE at Naxos the next morning, via the Strait of Messina, and at two o'clock they passed the Isle of Stromboli. The volcano was—so the cruise director informed them on the intercom—a sight to see, worth staying awake or waking up for, and she watched it through her window because she could not sleep. Vesuvius, if not extinct, had been cloud-covered, unremarkable, but this one showed a cone of flame erect in the night sky.

They off-loaded at Giardini Naxos, which was where, their guide announced, the first Greeks in Sicily settled and prospered, but made the mistake of forming an alliance with their countrymen in the Peloponnesian War. It had been a fatal mistake. Dionysius, the tyrant of Siracusa, once he emerged victorious in battle, had razed the port and killed or sold off all the Greeks, and those few who escaped him dispersed to the hills and only centuries later did their descendants dare to return and again make the settlement home. Giardini Naxos was the port of Taormina now, but also a tourist resort. Here is your third volcano, said the guide, here behind you on the left is Mount Etna, where the Titans lie, and these days there is a lava flow to keep us, how do you say, honest. We have an expression in Sicily: stay mindful of—keep always in your mind the anger of—the gods.

She was sitting next to Lawrence, who made a show of nonchalance. He held out his hand to help her get into and out of the tender, then up the tour bus steps. Growlingly the bus ascended a series of steep switchbacks to the town of Taormina and disgorged them at the entrance gate; then they walked side by side past restaurants and curio shops. This time, however, the sun was out and the village, he said, seemed authentic; had she taken the tour of Capri?

Hermia shook her head. "I stayed aboard. I was having,

well, a migraine, and it didn't look like a whole lot of fun, but *this* is fun, isn't it, not too crowded, not yet overrun."

"The season's almost over. And there's the amphitheater entrance up ahead"—Lawrence pointed down the street.

"Have you been reading the guidebook," she asked, "or were you here before?"

"Years ago. When I was first in Italy."

"Oh? What year was that?"

He looked at her—his Borsalino tilted jauntily, sunglasses on—and said, "I can't remember." He was teasing her, she understood, reminding her about her claim to perfect memory . . .

"It doesn't matter?"

"No. And the director's name was Greg. The one who did *Les Mouches.*"

They reached the amphitheater. The night before there must have been a party, or some sort of concert, because teams of workers were cleaning off a raised wooden stage and dismantling loudspeakers and lights. The two of them climbed to the top rank of seats: stone benches cool in the sun. From this vantage they could see the sea, the pillars and brickwork and cypress trees in the distance and the slope of Mount Etna beyond.

Hermia took photographs. They sat. Lawrence pointed to the open space in the high wall opposite and said that was the place the Turks began to breach the structure, knock it down, but thank heaven for the nineteenth century, its devotion to picturesque ruins, or maybe just a lack of funds, because otherwise some officious someone would have insisted they fill in the gaps and we'd have no such sight line. It's the evidenced *absence* of closure we like; the view *between* pillars intrigues. An incomplete circle compels our attention much more than the one that's complete.

Then he was drawing a distinction between the ancient Greeks and Romans; the Greeks, he said, used such a space for politics and theater, and one informed the other, so when the citizens of Athens or in this case Taormina gathered together to witness, say, the Oedipus plays, they were engaged in civic action and democratic governance as well as entertainment. The Romans, though, preferred blood sports, and for obvious reasons—you don't want to let the lions escape or, for that matter, gladiators, you have to dig a moat and increase the height of the walls that contain them—they engineered these amphitheaters differently. They were spectacular engineers, the Romans, but this never could have been an authentic coliseum; the real word, Lawrence continued, for coliseum is *circus,* Circus Maximus, the one in Rome is called the Theater of Vespasian, and it isn't all that clear if the sign for mercy would have been thumbs-up or down. Thumbs-up, he said, is understood to mean *Good news* and thumbs-down *Bad,* but it might just as well have been the reverse, signifying *Die,* not *Live,* because the emperor would have known the crowd was hoping for the chance to see violent death: a slaughter, not reprieve. And so, thumbs-down might well have been a way of saying, Sorry, folks, I pardon the life of this fighter, I don't give permission to kill.

He went on and on in this fashion, not exactly lecturing but not not-lecturing her either, as though silence between them had become fraught and required the safeguard of speech. She did not require it. She looked at the cords of his throat, the underside of his chin where that morning he'd shaved sloppily and the stubble came in white. She wanted to tell him not to be nervous, not to impress her with all that he knew, and remembered, of a sudden, their first shared coffee in the coffee shop; he'd talked about his hope to be an architect, or maybe urban designer, attempting to impress her also then, and Hermia invited him, that Thursday, to opening night of *The Flies*.

"It's strange," she said.

"What?"

"*The Flies*. I was thinking about it: Orestes."

"Yes, the *Oresteia*. Why?"

"They might have performed it right here way back when . . ."

"That's true," he said. "They probably would have. Not the play by Sartre, though."

"No. Was it the Blue Parrot or Casablanca?"

"Casablanca was the coffee shop. And the Blue Parrot was the bar, I think."

"You do remember, don't you?"

"Yes. You were taking a spot quiz on Rubens."

"I loved you very much," she said. "I don't think I really knew it then. Or understood it, really. But I loved you very much."

THIS SILENCED HIM. He took her hand. She let him hold it, squeeze it, and studied the liver spots and network of veins and his wrinkled knuckles, the fingernails trimmed roughly and the cuticles he bit. A mist was rising from the sea and the light changed register; the construction crew beneath them was sitting, drinking coffee, and somewhere a radio played. She hadn't meant to use the word, had not been thinking "Love, my love," but the past tense—"I loved you"—afforded a kind of protection, and she was not sorry to have called his chattering bluff. If nothing else, she told herself, it made conversation serious; she'd altered the rules of the game.

Lawrence looked at her. His pale blue eyes were watering and hair sprouted from his ears. "Say that again," he said.

"I don't think I really knew it. It was, well, puppy love maybe—not the first time, but the first *real* time. They say you don't ever get over it."

"No."

"No you don't get over it, or no you don't agree?"

"No, you don't get over it."

Her temper flared. "Well, *I* did. I got over and over and over it, friend. Don't flatter yourself."

He squeezed her hand. "I was agreeing with you, Hermia. We don't, we never do get over it."

"Bullshit. Or, as you romantics say"—she tried an English accent—"twaddle, poppycock. A *crock.*"

"Well"—Lawrence stood—"thanks for the memories."

"Welcome. You're welcome." She'd hurt him, she knew; she had managed after all to pierce his smug assurance. "And that girl of yours upstairs, Charette, I *told* you I remember . . ."

"Bill . . ."

Now Hermia wanted to cry. Where had it come from, this

storm of emotion, this idiot shifting from sorrow to rage? She felt adrift, not tethered; she was veering wildly back and forth between her pleasure in his presence and old anger at his absence, and she did not want or need a lecture on the history of amphitheaters and their reconstruction. Clouds scudded through the sky. She wanted to talk about what had gone wrong, not the architectural distinction between a circus and a coliseum, as if any of that mattered, as if all they were doing was dancing around what neither was willing to say.

"Say it," urged Hermia, "*say* it," and he asked her, "What?"

"Oh, Jesus, I don't know. Say something that *matters*."

"I thought I was dying."

So now it was she who fell silent. The radio bleated beneath them, then squawked. "When?"

"Not when I saw you," said Lawrence. "This summer. Last July."

"Of what?"

"Heart trouble. Turns out I was wrong. I'm fine, I'll be just fine, the doctors are pleased with themselves."

She rose from the bench to his side. In the middle distance gulls were circling, swooping, and the umbrella pines had somehow turned dull gray. She willed herself to breathe, to not faint or slap or embrace him or do anything other than stand there on the topmost stair while she fought for composure and found it: a middle-aged woman in Italy, not being stupid, not hysterical, not anything other than calm.

"A transplant? A heart bypass?"

"Not even that." He spread his hands, sheepish. "An angioplasty—you know, the balloon. The ream-it-out and send-him-home. I'm fine, I'll be just fine."

"Let's have some lunch," said Hermia. "A great big juicy piece of beefsteak, if they have one here in Sicily, and a hunk of cheese."

He smiled. He touched her arm. They made their way back into town.

THAT AFTERNOON SHE KEPT AWAY, saying her headache returned. They ate together once again, but this time at a table with others; she and Lawrence made conversation about Taormina and Etna and the places in America the others at the table lived and the chances of peace in Iraq. One couple at the table said, We're from Columbus, Ohio, our names are Dick and Jane. Oh, we know that's just a joke—you remember the movie, don't you, *Fun* with Dick and Jane—and our real names are Richard and Janet but, hey, nobody's perfect, correct? The point is *everybody* in Ohio has yellow ribbons on their trees and wants to bring our boys home. But only after victory, after we've made certain Saddam can't try another 9/11 or be able to hit us again.

Lawrence objected. Saddam Hussein had nothing to do with the World Trade Center, he said, or Al Qaeda or Osama bin Laden or WMDs. The whole thing was a put-up job, an act of aggression with blinders. I hope we can talk about this and not be angry with each other, he told Dick and Jane, and I know I won't change your opinion. But it's getting harder and harder to see a way out, and this has been—he spread his hands—a great mistake we've made.

Hermia drained her glass. Although she herself had been silent, with little to contribute during the meal, she wanted him to know that she was on his side. His face looked boyish, nearly, its lines erased by argument; she reached out and touched his sleeve.

The others noticed this also. You two tree huggers, said Dick, you're both so scared of progress, but don't be a pair of pessimists, it's not the American way. The American way is be hopeful, is *act,* it's fix a problem when you see it and there *was* a problem there. Whatever way you cut it, we're making the world better, a safe place for democracy; that's the bottom line. Our boy will win the election and it will turn out fine.

Lawrence was undeterred. You're right that I'm a pessimist but you're being optimistic, he told the table over apple crisp: Iraq has been a hornet's nest, a can of worms, a Pyrrhic victory at best and one we can't afford. This war has been a terrible mistake and the thing is to dare to admit it. The whole world was with us on 9/12, completely in America's camp, and now it's completely against . . .

Hermia went up on deck. The M.S. *Diana* left Naxos at nine, and the high slopes of Mount Etna glowed, a fulmination in the sky made roseate by smoke. She had been away for ten days. The ship's port of call would be Siracusa, where they would dock in the morning; the next destination was Porto Empedocle, and the day after that would be Malta. They would visit museums and temples and shops; she reminded herself not to return empty-handed but to buy earrings and scarves. She could envision the end of the trip, the flight from

Valetta to Boston, and did not want to play the fool or indulge in a shipboard romance.

That was, she knew, the term for it: *shipboard romance.* It was what the widows dreamed of, and the divorcées, and the otherwise unattached: a caricature fueled by yearning and, here on the Mediterranean, wine. Behind her in the Elsinore Lounge stood passengers drinking and laughing. They were playing Parcheesi, or Scrabble, or hearts, and asking Marco the bartender if he knew the words to "Melancholy Baby" or could play "Hail to the Victors" on his acoustic guitar. They were tapping their sandals and snapping their fingers and chorusing "One More for the Road."

She could not bear it, not abide it; she had been alone too long to yield her hard-earned privacy. From her safe vantage on the deck the lava flow looked beautiful; it would not look that way, she knew, if near at hand. She went to bed at nine o'clock and slept a dreamless sleep.

IN THE MORNING, however, the sun was warm and bright and the port of Siracusa—with its seawalls and churches and sailboats, the busy hum of commerce—made Hermia, though stalled in traffic, happy; once more she sat beside him on the bus. Once more they had a tour guide, a short plump man named Luigi, who spoke through a microphone about the history of ruins and apartment buildings and the rock quarries they passed. In heavily accented English he joked about the Jolly Hotel and the way it earned its name; he pointed to a church and said it resembled an orange; then he made jokes about the Mafia and bad Italian drivers and the *dolce far niente* of traffic police.

He looks just like Danny DeVito, said Lawrence, a dead ringer for Danny DeVito, and Hermia agreed. Then in the cave where, rumor had it, the ancient tyrant Dionysius could hear each whispered secret because the acoustics were perfect and the echoes carried, Luigi sang "Santa Lucia." He took off his hat and fanned himself with a white crumpled handkerchief and held the high notes tremblingly, then bowed. I am, he said, not Pavarotti, but *Povarotti;* the other one is big and rich and I am small and poor. But you see we both are fat.

They drove to the old part of town, then left the tour bus and walked. Luigi showed them the cathedral that had also been a temple, and how the Greek pillars supported the roof of the church; it first had been a temple, next a Byzantine church, next a Muslim mosque, then when it was a church again the motif was Baroque. In here I must not sing, said Luigi, in here I must be quiet, and we must be grateful everyone still worships, otherwise this building would be pillaged like the world.

"Did he say 'pillaged like the world'?" asked Hermia, and Lawrence took her hand. "It's not," he said, "so terrifying."

"What?"

"Beginning again. People do it, you know."

"Begin again?"

He nodded. "I mean, every time I turn around I hear a story about high school sweethearts who meet after many years—*decades*—at their high school reunion. Or at kindergarten on Grandparents' Day. Or they call each other up after two failed marriages. Or they're widowers or widowed and meet at the funeral home—you know."

"I don't," she said. "I don't know, no."

"They hunt each other on the Internet. They subscribe to the same dating service or use the same search engine; they meet each other once again at the retirement party of friends. Or somebody's birthday party. I hear about it all the time . . ."

"All right," she admitted. "I Googled you."

He smiled. "Is that a verb?"

"I did," she said. "I looked you up."

"And what did you find there?"

"Your picture. Your address. A faculty blurb from the School of Art and Architecture. A list of your prizes and books."

"I know what Google means," he said. "And I thought about tracking you also that way, and wanted to write you often."

"You're not a very good liar."

"What I'm trying to say," Lawrence said, "is there's nothing surprising about reconnecting. Connecting. It's a thing you don't get over—or at least *I* don't, I never did—having been together way back when."

Now without warning her anger returned. "*Been together,* what's that mean?"

He colored. "You know what I'm trying to say."

"No, Lawrence. *Say* it. I *know* you, remember. You mean to say you spend your nights remembering women you slept with . . ."

"Is that what it sounds like?"

"It is. It does." She mimicked him. "'. . . *having been together way back when.*' Well, lah-de-dah."

They were walking now back to the ship. "You're a difficult person to talk to," he said. "You're not, are you, making this easy."

"And exactly why should I?" she asked. "Connecting, re-connecting—Oh, give me a break, Lawrence."

"Fine."

The M.S. *Diana* came into view. She took photographs. There was a gangplank, a potted palm in front of it, a roped enclosure through which they both passed.

"So why *did* you Google me?"

"I told you," said Hermia. "Love."

THERE WAS, she knew, no way around it; the only way was through. It was a thicket, a dark wood they walked through; it was undiscovered country and she did not know the way. This courtship—if it was a courtship, if what they were doing was courting each other—had caught her completely off guard. She had spent so many years alone, and those she cared for had demanded so much caring that she herself was lost. She went to her cabin alone.

The night before, at dinner, when Lawrence had been saying what Hermia also thought, it was as if their solidarity had needed no explaining: he'd spoken for them both. Dick and Jane, she understood, had seen them as a couple if not man and wife and believed them to be partners and, at least in terms of politics, aligned. She knew little or nothing about him, as Lawrence knew little or nothing about her adult life. But she had known him before. And the intervening years seemed unimportant, somehow; she felt a deep familiarity with her long-lost companion, a knowingness about his way of being in the world. Of *course* he would think this, of *course* he would say it; of *course* he was—she smiled to herself—a Democrat and not Republican; the boy she used to sleep with was the man she recognized now.

In the Valley of the Temples they walked together next morning; Porto Empedocle where they landed and the town of Agrigento took her breath away. Again the day dawned brightly; again they disembarked and sat together on the bus and were herded by a tour guide through a field of ruins and temples and rock.

Once more Lawrence tried to impress her, pointing out the plinths and capitals, describing the tricks of perspective that Greek architects had utilized: the way the columns appear of a uniform width, for example, but bulk slightly in the middle—the word for it's *entasis*, he said—the way the columns lean but nonetheless look perpendicular.

She let him talk. To silence him, she took his hand. When he asked what she was thinking she said, Oh, how long ago the people came to worship here, how many centuries ago they stared at the same sea. And the water was much nearer then, said Lawrence, it's been withdrawing since time out of mind—the Mediterranean ebbing away from, what's that word . . . ?

"The shingle. I *am* glad to see you again."

"Yes. I thought about you often and I know it sounds romantic but I did think about it. Us."

"You kiss me at this point, I think. We're staging a scene and we kiss."

Now it was Lawrence who drew back. "You're joking, right?"

"I'm joking, right."

"Well, wait till I adjust my teeth. Or brush them, anyway."

"All right," she said. "We're not staging a scene."

"I didn't think so, no."

She kissed him then, but briefly, on the cheek. He smelled of—what was it?—Paco Rabanne and what he had eaten for breakfast and a compound of toothpaste and sweat. He smelled of caution and age. With her lips she brushed his other cheek and trailed her fingertips across the rough white stubble and, stepping back, smiled. "Oh, but you do feel familiar."

THAT NIGHT the captain gave his end-of-cruise farewell banquet; Hermia had eaten it before. The meal repeated, course for course, what she had been served the night they docked in Rome, when passengers were disembarking at Civitavecchia. The waiters dressed in native costumes and sang drinking songs. They wore skirts and brightly colored caps and played what sounded to her like the ukulele; they said these melodies come from the Carpathian Mountains and villages in Croatia, and the captain wished everyone a wonderful trip and said well the weather was fine. You everybody did your best, he said, to wish for perfect weather and I am perfectly happy tonight because the moon is shining so my heart is also full. They ate lobster bisque and caviar and fish and meat smothered in cream, and by this stage in the journey Darko knew his customers; he poured Lawrence glass after glass of red wine.

She herself was drinking white. "Between the two of us," he said, "we lick the platter clean."

"Between the two of us," she said, "between you and me and the lamppost—except for meeting you, of course—I more or less hated this cruise."

"No."

"Sì. Veramente."

"But think of all you've learned," he said, "about Greek and Roman architecture. The difference between Doric and Ionic and Corinthian . . ."

"Don't start. I'm being serious."

"Do you think we would have met again in some other context?" He raised his glass. "Or in any other way?"

"Does it matter?"

"Not really, no."

"I mean, why would it matter? The world is everything that is the case."

"Excuse me?"

"Wittgenstein," said Hermia. "Or maybe it's Hegel. Schopenhauer." She giggled. "Kant."

" 'Will you, won't you join the dance?' That's Lewis Carroll."

"I will," she said. "Let's dance."

So they took their places on the cleared floor of the Elsinore Lounge, where couples were doing the fox-trot; others remained at the bar. One of the waiters was playing guitar, and one of them sat at the keyboard, with fixed smiles on their faces and their feet tapping the beat. Lawrence bowed. He held out his arms; they embraced. At first they were clumsy together, then less clumsy, then assured. She gave herself over to music, the tinny percussive mechanical tune, and something in Hermia quickened, and she twitched her hips. It was, she knew, the moonlight, the wine, the pleasure of dancing and all the old rhythmic enticements: the way his hand felt on the small of her back, the way he focused, frowning, guiding her, one, *two*, and three, and *four*. Then Dick and Jane were next to them and smiling, sweating, thumping up and down, and then they were out on the deck.

"Do you remember," Lawrence asked, " 'As Time Goes By'?"

"Of course I do."

"Your cabin or mine?"

She stared at him: he was making a joke. He was, she saw, as frightened as she; he did not know what to do next. The M.S. *Diana* was making for Malta, its engines thrumming, its wake white, and she was having her shipboard romance and staring out to sea. For an instant, Hermia shut her eyes and leaned against him, hip-to-hip, and he put his arm around her waist. It was, she knew, the thing to do, it was what she'd expected since she'd first seen Lawrence days before when he stood across from her by lifeboat 6. She lifted her head for a kiss.

And then she saw Patricia. Her daughter danced along the waves; her daughter rode beside her skimming the bright spume. The girl was dressed in black, as if for a recital, and her hair was cropped yet billowing, arms outstretched as if to play. Her feet in patent-leather pumps kept pace effortlessly on the water—suspended there, mouth pursed in concentration. Her neck was bent. As though she were a seabird and the *Diana* a part of the flock, her daughter glided a hundred yards off—dipping, swooping, hovering—and would not go away.

She screamed; she could hear herself scream.

"What is it?" Lawrence asked. "What's wrong?"

"I've seen a ghost," Hermia said.

VI

1977

W HERE SHE WENT WAS DOWN THE STREET. HER
friends Ellen and Robert Oppenheim had known
about her trouble, and they were ready to help. The couple
made her welcome, with a room prepared for her and her
daughter; they offered Hermia Valium and waited by the bedside until she fell asleep. That night she dreamed of Truro, of
the time when she was young, and free, and there had been no
damage. When she awoke in the morning, with Patricia safely
next to her, thumb in her mouth, her black curls damp from
sleep sweat, she felt as though they had escaped from a loom-
ing danger, and her own cheeks were wet.

On Friday they drove to Vermont. Their house in Arlington
was Hermia's to use, the Oppenheims assured her, a place she
could be safe. Robert was a therapist, a specialist in family
counseling, and he repeated she'd done the right thing. A psy-

chotic break has long-term implications, and recovery takes time; although he would no doubt apologize and try to win her back, her husband had entered a fugue state; he was taking acid—wasn't he?—and had had a bad trip. Ellen agreed with this, nodding her head; they all had seen it coming, and Hermia had been at risk. She shouldn't blame herself or feel ashamed of using Mace; she needed to protect herself and, of course, her child. Right now the man was dangerous, said Ellen, and she should stay away.

And so her long exile began. After the first weekend, the Oppenheims left her alone with keys to the house and a Jeep they kept in the garage and, repeating that Hermia had no reason to worry, returned to their jobs in New York. There was, they insisted, no way Paul could track her down, and anyhow he had been neutralized and posed no present threat. This whole episode was bound to happen, said Robert, it's been in the cards for years and would have happened sooner or later and you mustn't blame yourself, we'll make certain he gets help.

She and Patsy stayed in their benefactors' farmhouse off the River Road. The building was white clapboard, with green shutters and four chimneys and a picket fence; its front door displayed the number: 1828. The antique furniture was good, the wide pine floors had been burnished with wax, and the cupboards and closets were full. Split-leaf maples flared above the roof, and the roof was slate. To Hermia it seemed as though she'd stepped into a canvas straight out of Grandma Moses or, maybe, Norman Rockwell. Those painters had painted this landscape, and it looked familiar: steep-pitched hills, the rock-rimmed pasture where the neighbors' horses grazed, the plumes of chimney smoke.

She did try not to worry. She drove to the Enchanted Dollhouse ten miles north in Manchester and bought her daughter a dollhouse and elaborate series of dolls. She bought a television so they could watch *Sesame Street* together, and *The Electric Company*, and *Mister Rogers' Neighborhood;* when Mr. Rogers declared how pleased he was to be their neighbor—taking off his shoes and putting on his slippers and buttoning his cardigan—Patsy sang along with him, in perfect pitch, and clapping her hands when he clapped. The child was a glad chatterbox, burbling to herself all day and busy with crayons or dolls. She peered at books intently and loved to turn their pages and knew *Goodnight, Moon* and *The Runaway Bunny* by heart.

Still, Hermia did worry. She wanted to forget the past; she could not believe Paul would leave them alone or just let her live. In the beginning she was frightened—afraid of the doorbell or sudden night noise, convinced that he had followed her; outside, she wore dark glasses and a hat. She saw him, she was certain, at the post office or gas station or the convenience store. When she closed her eyes at night she saw her husband staring at her, glaring, his paranoia rampant and white spittle at his lips. All that first autumn she feared he would find them, his knife outthrust and waving, his jealousy intact.

But the Oppenheims assured her Paul was getting help. He had been hospitalized. He was heavily sedated and on medication when released, and then she learned he had returned to England and resumed his employment at Reuters. In February, from London, he wrote to apologize. Paul sent the letter to her lawyer, not asking for forgiveness because—or so he wrote— what he'd done was unforgivable, but he had come to under- stand their marriage had been ill advised, and he proposed a divorce. He wasn't, he understood finally, the marrying kind or cut out to be a father, and he hoped she would forgive him and perhaps think kindly of him or at least a little better in the fu- ture. He wished her and Patricia well.

There was a legal injunction, a series of letters from doctors and lawyers and, in the end, a divorce. This procedure took two years. During that time she and her daughter did every- thing together and went everywhere together and slept in the same room. She told her stepfather and mother often, on the telephone, how she'd tried to make the marriage work, but in this had failed. By the time Paul moved to Tokyo and Hermia felt safe again there was a play group for Patricia and, the next September, a nursery school down the road.

TIME PASSED. Unwilling to relinquish it, she rented out the house in Truro but gave up her apartment in New York. Be- cause she could not stay at the Oppenheims' indefinitely, she rented and then purchased her own home. It was half a mile from her friends' house, across from riding stables, and Hermia began to think of Arlington less as a place of refuge than as a place to remain.

The village was quiet; fishermen fished there for trout. More farm machines and pickup trucks than cars drove past the house. The Batten Kill River was famous, and there was a covered bridge and sugaring house: scene after scene of country life untroubled and unchanged. What changed was the weather, the wind.

On a level patch of lawn behind the porch, she installed a ChildLife jungle gym. She pushed Patsy on the swing and raised her up and dropped her down on the wooden seesaw and watched her daughter clamber up the ladders and dangle from the balance bars and slide down the slide. The spokes were green, the platforms brown, and it felt as though they had established a shared playground by the rhubarb bed. When the leaves fell they raked and raked, and Patsy loved to jump into the maple leaf piles and be buried there. They were never apart, not for a single afternoon or evening; they took naps together, baths together, and Hermia told her daughter they were "best friends."

Men and women of the village were polite but not intrusive; they plowed her drive and fixed the furnace when the heat shut down. They smiled at her and waved from the front stoop when she went driving by or, if they passed her on a tractor, tipped their Agway caps. Mother and daughter bought strawberries and blueberries and fresh-picked corn from roadside stands; they bought doughnuts and apple cider from the cider mill. Hermia planted a garden and had the house painted and, as before in Truro, trained pink climbing roses along the picket fence.

She reveled in the silence. She had had enough of noise, the whir and bustle of machinery, the sirens and traffic sounds all through the night. She had had more than enough of Manhattan, the "players"—in her parents' word—the runners-up and also-rans and the getting and spending and sex. It was not so much their isolation as the privacy that suited her, a New England reticence she liked. She wanted to be with her daughter, only with her daughter, and though they talked and read and sang together it felt as though they shared a healing quiet; they could shuck peas or corn, not speaking, or watch the sunset or TV or wild geese together in a companionable absence of speech, a silence that made her feel calm.

People left her alone with her child. She and Patricia had a private language, a way of knowing without asking how the other one was feeling and what the other was thinking—a sigh or a smile meant "I'm hungry," a tilt of the head meant "I'm full." They had an unspoken system of signs: "Let's go for a walk. Let's go home." It was as though, thought Hermia, great Nature had been wasteful when She made two separate bodies, because the two of them felt the same way—cold, hot, needing to pee or to sneeze—at the same instant and with no need to discuss it. And even when they disagreed—if Pat-a-Cake wanted to watch cartoons but Hermia wanted to go to the pond or, the other way around, when she just felt like staying home but the girl preferred bike riding—the disagreement was minor, a momentary shift of balance until balance was restored.

From time to time she felt her daughter should have someone else to play with, or that she herself required adult company, and was growing old, and dull, but then a playmate of Patsy's would come to the house after nursery school and the visit would suffice. It was astonishing how long a conversation lasted at the butcher's, or at the post office counter; an exchange about the weather—about the heat or rain or need for rain, about the snow or lack of snow—could slake her desire for talk. Most weekends the Oppenheims arrived from New York, and Hermia would see them and their company for lunch or at a picnic, and the social interaction would last her the whole week.

"Are you still happy here?" asked Ellen.

She nodded.

"Are you getting enough stimulation?"

"Do you mean am I lonely?"

Ellen nodded.

"No."

"I'm not talking about, oh, the movies. Or Broadway or museums . . ."

"Then what *are* you talking about?" Lately she could hear in her own voice her mother's forthright bluntness, the old arrogant directness.

"Nothing special." Ellen spread her hands. "Just I know I myself would go crazy up here. Without, you know . . ."

"I don't, no, know. Without a man? A vibrator?"

Her friend looked shocked. Then Ellen collected herself: "Next weekend we're bringing up Harry. You remember him, Harrison Laughlin. He's just been divorced and is dreaming of the country in leaf season—they're all leaf-peekers in October, aren't they—and he owns two of your dad's paintings of the dunes and asked, specifically asked me, if maybe you would come to dinner."

"The two of us? Can I bring Patsy?"

"If you prefer . . ."

"I haven't found a babysitter yet."

"Oh?"

"Let me try to explain it," Hermia said. "This morning we were making pies—apple pies together, because Patsy likes to roll the dough, she's getting good at it, she has more patience than I do—and she looks up at me and says, this five-year-old, 'Mommy, I love doing this, because it starts out one thing and it ends up another thing, but both of them are tasty. They change but not really, they're really the same.' And I thought to myself, 'Hey, that's not bad, that's quite an observation,' and she said, 'But the *real* thing is I watched these apples since they were only blossoms, just part of a tree.' And I said, 'You're Golden Delicious, you're good enough to eat,' and we laughed and laughed together, and so, no, I don't need company and don't feel alone."

"Still . . . ," Ellen said.

"All right. You're kind to ask. We'll come."

HARRISON LAUGHLIN WAS FORTY, an associate professor of English at Columbia, and when she told him she had written her thesis, way back when, on *Coriolanus* and *Cymbeline*, he took out his pipe and filled it with a pinch of nonexistent tobacco and said, "Good for you." He was attempting, he told her, to stop smoking, and he had a new system and was certain it would work. His strategy was to go through the motions of cleaning out his pipe stem and filling his pipe bowl and tamping it down and lighting a match but only in mimicry, only as a way of enacting the procedure and calling up the memory without any tobacco involved. This provided, he told Hermia, the satisfaction of reenactment, and he felt he got a smoker's rush by going through the motions and inhaling air. So too with Shakespeare, Harrison said, there were ritual observances in the late plays and romances that were mostly gestural; think of the masque, for example, in *The Tempest*, or the pageantry of *Pericles* or *Henry VIII*, and you'll perhaps see what I mean.

She did not see. She told herself that this was why she had avoided company—the babble and prattle and *me me me me*. For Ellen's sake, and Robert's, she had taken some trouble with her appearance; she had used lipstick and eye shadow for the first time since August, and she wore the purple shot-silk scooped-neck blouse Ellen gave her for her birthday. She could see the impression she made on their guest, the masculine *quack-quack* and *me me me*, and wished she had not bothered, had decided not to come.

The dinner, however, was good. Ellen was a first-rate cook, and she produced *coquilles St.-Jacques* and then *truite amandine;* they drank two bottles of Pouilly-Fumé. As always, the Oppenheims talked about retirement, what it would mean to live full-time in Arlington, and as always they concluded that they loved the city and their work—Robert more so than Ellen, who could take her job or leave it—and were not ready to move.

"And you?" asked Laughlin. "Any regrets?"

She shook her head.

"Hiding your light," he said, "under—I believe it's the appropriate image—a bushel." He laughed.

Though she had trained herself to not think about her father, Hermia found herself thinking about him: her dinner partner flattered her because of her last name. He spoke about the oils he owned, the two renditions of the dunes her father made in 1957, and how much he admired them, how the impasto of the beach, the very *essence* of the beach, was something he consulted daily and could not imagine not seeing, that line of light bisecting the dunes, the thick white line perpendicular to green and yellow waves, and how he had fairly *bankrupted* himself acquiring them at André Emmerich. But it had been, of course, an excellent purchase, a spectacular investment, and if Hermia felt the need or desire to see them again he would be delighted to invite her for a viewing the next time she came to the city, it would be an honor and they could have lunch.

Patsy was sleeping in front of the fire, holding her blanket and sprawled on the Oppenheims' couch; they would be going home soon. She had fallen asleep with a great noiseless crash, turning the pages of her Dr. Seuss book and then suddenly no longer turning them but sprawled spread-eagle on the pillow, her blanket at the corner of her mouth.

Robert offered his dinner guests cognac and *poire;* Hermia drank *poire.* They talked about the traffic in leaf season; this afternoon, driving up from the city had taken them six hours, though on an average weekend they expected only four. But it was worth it, said Harrison Laughlin, every minute has been worth it and that last hour on Route 7 was, if he said so himself, spectacular; is the word for it leaf-peeper or leaf-peeker or leaf-peaker, *p-e-a?*

The Oppenheims retreated to the kitchen, insisting they would do the cleaning up together, they preferred to finish up like this, they had their own private system, and it had been a long day. I'll take Patricia home in a minute, said Hermia, but I do hate to wake her, and Ellen said, Just let her sleep.

In the fireplace logs crackled and a piece of birch bark flared. Good night, you two, said Robert, yawning, stretching ostentatiously, and Hermia said the trout was excellent, thanks for everything, everything, and I'll drive home soon, I promise. I don't know, Harrison Laughlin was saying, if you've ever seen the trees in France with bottles tied over the blossoms, a ship in a bottle, so to speak, except the masts are growing fruit, and it's beautiful, spectacular. An orchard full of glass. And then of course once the apple or pear is safely in the bottle they add what we're drinking, a brandy: *Santé*. He raised his snifter and drank.

It was, she knew, her decision; he would take no for an answer. She could gather up Patsy and leave. She would not bring this noisy stranger home or permit him in their private space, but it was tempting anyhow to let the flirtation continue. If she did continue—listening to Laughlin and encouraging his talk about the English Department, his prospect of tenure, his colleagues, his hopes for publication, his windfall from a bachelor uncle with which he'd bought her father's oils at Emmerich ten years ago, his Columbia-owned apartment on Claremont Avenue now suddenly too big for him as divorcé, then waiting for him to explain what had gone wrong with his marriage, how the ex-wife was not a subject he wanted to discuss, and then discussing it anyhow, her arrogance, her self-regard, how he himself refused to make aspersions or be negative and then making aspersions, being negative—she could foresee the result. There would, she knew, be a third glass of *poire;* there would be his hand on her knee. Hermia could predict it all: the fireplace embers, the closed door of the library, the furtive grappling and clothes on the floor, the way the Oppenheims next morning would studiously avoid the subject of her behavior and offer her coffee and toast. Her home was inviolate, half a mile off, and all she had to do, she knew, was lift her daughter from the couch and say good night and go.

Nonetheless she fucked him. It seemed the thing to do. There was a friction, an itch to be rubbed, and though he himself was unfamiliar the procedure felt familiar. It was over rapidly—a quick ejaculation, a small hot spurt along her legs—and then there were the sighs, the smiles, the protestations of devotion, while she collected her clothing and woke her child and left.

THAT WAS THE END OF IT, however; she had had enough. He did call in the morning, but Hermia claimed she had a headache, one of her migraine headaches, and spent the afternoon in Manchester, buying a sweater for Patsy, avoiding the prospect of company and, when they came back again, not answering the phone. The next day the two of them made a trip to Albany, watching *Snow White* and *Cinderella* and *Bambi* all in the same afternoon for a Disney children's special, an extravaganza, and having dinner afterward and not returning home to Arlington till night. By that time Laughlin and the Oppenheims had had to leave, and when Ellen returned the next weekend she said, You made quite an impression. He couldn't stop talking about you, and Hermia said apparently he likes to talk but please let's not discuss him, or what he wants or wanted, okay? and Ellen said okay.

It was 1981; she was thirty-nine years old. The more time she spent in Arlington the more she saw its bigotry, the limits to the tolerance of those who mowed her lawn. What first had seemed a picturesque backwater now seemed merely back- ward, and cruel. This place, she told the Oppenheims, has come to feel provincial, and she did not like to think that she herself was living in the provinces or Pat had no real friends at school. Therefore Hermia drove her daughter every morning to the village of North Bennington, fifteen minutes south, where education was progressive. The founders of the Prospect School encouraged free expression, and the water table and the turtles were as important as arithmetic; during "quiet time" the students wrote down stories in their journals or built things out of clay. The teachers at the Prospect School wore homemade clothes and headbands and encouraged empathy with inani- mate things; they would tell Pat the "hot water wants to be turned off" or, at the end of quiet time, that her cubbyhole "wants to be cleaned."

One of the teachers, Anne Martineau, lived in a commune in Pownal. She had long blond hair and sturdy legs and a Ger- man shepherd called Max who went with her everywhere; she said Pat had a special gift for music and had her mother no- ticed how she never missed a note or forgot a tune she heard? Anne had been teaching for seventeen years and she was cer- tain, she told Hermia, this particular child had a gift.

Pat began to study the piano, and Betsy Harrington, her piano teacher, also was impressed. The girl could memorize music, not taking any trouble over it; the notes stayed, she said, in her head. She played with concentration for hour after hour: first improvising freely and then practicing her lesson book or the Czerny exercises, long arpeggios and plangent chords and, by her second year of study, Mozart. Hermia loved to listen and, just as important, to watch: her straight-backed child enraptured on the piano stool, arms out, so nimble-fingered. It was as though their silence had transposed itself to harmony, and Brahms or Grieg were visiting this child in thrall to song . . .

Betsy Harrington arranged a concert. There was a converted carriage barn across the street from the Prospect School, and it contained a Steinway grand; five piano students performed. The Carruthers twins played a four-hand thumping polka, the Cohen boy played a thick-fingered nocturne by Chopin, and teenaged Katharine Spencer played the sonata by Liszt. A composer from Bennington College arrived and joined the audience; he was Katharine Spencer's uncle and made a show of settling in—smiling, shaking hands. Anne Martineau and Max were also there, the great dog lying at his mistress's feet. It was a fine September afternoon, rain-rinsed and with a hint of chill, but Hermia was sweating; there were wooden folding chairs and a head-high vase of sunflowers and a table with cookies and punch.

Patricia came out and sat down. She wore a pearl necklace, a spray of roses in her hair, black pumps and a white wide-skirted dress that buttoned in the front. She did not carry sheet music; stiff-backed, she stared at the keyboard, then adjusted the height of the stool. For her part in the recital, she had selected Robert Schumann's *Kinderscenen,* and she played with emphatic restraint. "Scenes from childhood" filled the hall—the sweet simplicities, the lilting tunes and somber hints of sorrow yet to come. Swaying lightly to her own engendered rhythms, eyes halfway closed, head nodding, her daughter seemed to Hermia a creature from another world, a better world, a place where melody was everywhere and there could be no discord; when Patricia stood and curtsied there was prolonged applause.

Afterward, they praised her. "So poised," said the composer from the college, "so self-aware and yet so young."

"It's not assurance," said his partner. "To me it's the reverse."

The two men faced each other—one white-haired and flamboyant, the other with a close-cropped head and wearing a black suit. "What are you saying, George? Don't be so utterly *runic*."

"It's total immersion, correct? It's an absolute *lack* of self-awareness." George appealed to Hermia. "That's what's so charming, correct?"

Vladimir Horowitz, the piano teacher said, called *Kinderscenen* the hardest piece of all to play—not because of technical complexities, but because of its emotional demands. "Your daughter was splendid," said Betsy Harrington.

"Yes," said the men from the college. "She *must* continue her studies. She *must* be properly trained."

THE FOLLOWING SUMMER, therefore, Hermia sent her daughter off to camp. She did so with a heavy heart, a fear she both could name and not name that Patricia would be lost. She tried to hide this from the child and be enthusiastic, because the piano teacher said music camp would be just the thing. The National Music Camp was on a lake in Michigan, and Betsy Harrington had sent young people there before; she, Hermia, should think of this as a great opportunity and could be pleased and proud.

She did feel pleased and proud. She had produced this gifted girl, had done so by herself, and sooner or later it was bound to happen that her daughter would take wing. But it felt too soon, too rushed, and all spring Hermia was terrified, as she had been when first they moved and she feared her husband would find them. They had lived alone so long together in the house she could not bear to think about the prospect of true isolation when Patricia went to camp. She looked at maps of Michigan, at a place called Traverse City near enough to Interlochen so she could pay a visit, not just on parents' weekend but every other day. She imagined what it would be like to sit outside the practice rooms, or in the hall where students played, or by the lake just listening to and watching over the piano, not being in the way . . .

This would not, she knew, be possible. Their sanctuary had been breached, the place of their shared privacy was no longer private, or shared. As the date for departure approached, she felt her heart would crack. Having stitched her daughter's name into her shorts and towels and shirts and even on her bathing suit, for fear it would be lost, she packed Patricia's bags meticulously. She folded and refolded skirts and sweatshirts and a knitted cap for the cold nights, and Patricia's music books and the book about pioneer women and, for reassurance, her "blankety" with its frayed silk strip and wool worn thin from washing. She prepared a stack of post-cards and envelopes with stamps, all pre-addressed, and put them in a folder and the folder in the suitcase, with an "I Love You" sticker and her stuffed embroidered heart with the yellow *P.*

For breakfast on their final day she fixed everything her daughter liked—French toast and bacon, orange juice, hot chocolate—but neither of them ate a thing and, after twenty minutes, Hermia stopped pretending that they could. They walked across the meadow to the pond to say good-bye to the Muscovy ducks, and there were wildflowers everywhere and a groundhog and the blue sky she used to take for granted but could not now take for granted. On the drive to Albany it com-menced to rain and they arrived at the airport two hours early, in a thunderstorm, but the plane remained on schedule and there was no reprieve.

For the first leg of the journey, Patricia flew alone. The girl was traveling to Detroit Metro Airport, where she would meet a dozen other campers and a counselor and they would intro-duce themselves and proceed to Traverse City. A flight atten-dant met them at the U.S. Air counter and, because Patricia was flying as an unaccompanied minor, tied a red ID tag and ribbon to her wrist.

"Don't worry, Mom," she said—voice quavering—"I'll be okay."

"Of course you will."

"I will."

"I worry anyhow," said Hermia. "I have to keep the airplane up."

"You're joking, right?" the flight attendant asked.

"I'm joking, right."

"I love you, Mom."

"Oh, I *adore* you, darling. Have a wonderful, wonderful time out there."

"I'll write."

"And I'll write *you*, I promise. Every day."

They embraced. It was, she knew, the end of the beginning, but it felt like the beginning of the end. She watched her daughter—so small, so young, so determined—walk to the door of the plane, then wave and disappear. Hermia waited while the airplane taxied to the runway and watched till it was airborne and made her way back to the parking lot slowly, bereft.

Until she stopped sobbing, she sat in the car, resting her head on the wheel. Then, avoiding Route 7 and traffic, she drove the long way back to Arlington—leaving the Northway and winding through Mechanicville and Buskirk and Cambridge and along the Batten Kill on Route 313. The skies had cleared, the river gleamed, but it made no difference; the passenger seat was empty where at noon it had been full.

At four o'clock she reached her house and walked through the rooms with a bottle of wine, arranging, rearranging things, keeping the airplane in the air and landing it safely on time. She called to make certain the plane was on time. For no reason she could understand she pictured herself a beginner again, a girl studying in Cambridge all those years ago. The tune in her head was a tune she'd forgotten—plump Will with his head thrown back, eyes shut, warbling, picking out the minor chords on his guitar in Irving Street. There had been a party; there was beer and marijuana and their host was singing mournfully:

Black girl, black girl,
Don't you lie to me,
Tell me where did you spend last night?

In the pines, in the pines,
Where the sun never shines,
And I shivered the whole night through.

Anne Martineau called. She asked for a meeting with Hermia, and over tea confided there was trouble in the commune and she might need to move. There were these power players—well, Anne said, attempting to make light of it and not succeeding, attempting to smile, that's *my* side of the story, you might hear something different if you asked somebody else—and they made a grab for power, but our whole idea, our *charter,* is that that's just not acceptable, it's inadmissible, because if you stack a cord of wood it doesn't mean you keep it for your own use only, and if you're working as a bookkeeper at the tanning factory in Pownal you don't cook the books. She went on and on about the bad behavior of the man who owned the orchard, Mel, and how they used to live together but he'd become impossible, a kind of petty tyrant, a macrobiotic proto-fascist, and the point was, *is,* she admitted, that they had

had the kind of set-to that required cooling down, she and Max were persona non grata, well, Max isn't a person of course. They would probably want to keep Max. The long and the short of it—Anne rubbed her left wrist—was, *is,* she wondered if, just for a day or two, just while she was getting her feet on the ground and looking for a place to rent, or move to, she could borrow the spare room and crash in Arlington, out of harm's way for a while. The dog, she promised, would be no trouble and she had her own station wagon and cooking utensils and it was no emergency but she'd rather not sleep in the Ford.

Hermia said yes. She remembered how she too had needed sanctuary once, how the Oppenheims assisted her when she fled New York. Now it seemed her turn to help. Anne Martineau was grateful and arrived that evening, her station wagon stuffed with clothes, and pots and pans, and she and Max moved into the house and were a welcome diversion. The day or two became a week; the week became a month.

Anne cooked. She made elaborate stews of vegetables, lentils, rice, and discoursed on each ingredient and their healthful properties and how the juice and spices interacted. She said, "You don't mind, do you?" and lit joss sticks in the living room and positioned her tin Buddha in the hall. When the mail was delivered, and there was news from Patricia—after Hermia had read the letter to herself twice, silently—the women discussed it together and remembered being young, and how much they'd missed their own mothers when they themselves had first left home; if no postcard or letter arrived they spoke about the heedlessness of youth.

As time wore on they talked about their pasts. Anne was forthright, unabashed; she talked about the boys and, later on, the girls she'd had affairs with, the choices she'd made, and mistakes. Mel, for example, had been a mistake, with an ego that needed massaging nonstop, and this delusional sense of himself as a leader, a savior, this series of edicts he issued in Pownal—here she mimicked him, dropping her voice—"Don't worship Mammon or shave your legs or eat shellfish or *traife* and do everything just as I say . . ."

The Martineau family came from East Lansing, and Anne herself had attended the National Music Camp, which is why she'd known that Patricia belonged there, and agreed with Betsy Harrington, it was a dynamite place. The north of Michigan is worth a visit, and you'll be glad to go; the little finger, they call it—Anne spread her hand out and pointed—and Interlochen's right here. You'll *love* it, she told Hermia, just the way Patricia does, a place where everyone believes their art's the only thing that matters, really, and wants to be an instrumentalist or a composer; I myself was into singing way back when. It's strange, mused Hermia, my father was a painter and my daughter's a musician, but I'm just a go-between, a necessary interval between the generation that produced me and the one I produced . . .

They sat together at the kitchen table or on the west-facing porch, drinking tea and eating apples while the long days waned. Anne spoke about the pines and lake at Interlochen, how the winters there are difficult and how much fun Hermia would have when she went to see her daughter. Two nights before parents' weekend, however, she came down with a bad case of flu and was so violently sick to her stomach she could not leave her bed. Her fever climbed to 102; she sweated and shivered and was unable to fly to Michigan and had to cancel the trip. Uncontrollably she wept.

But Anne stayed by her bedside, nursing and consoling her, assuring her Patricia would be fine, just fine, and explaining to the counselors why Hermia had to stay home. When her daughter did return at last, at August's end—full of stories about water fights and bunkmates and new best friends from Chicago—she listened with amusement; this prodigy was still a girl, this performer still a child. And when the Prospect School began again on Tuesday after Labor Day, Anne and Patricia and Max the German shepherd drove there together every morning and back again each afternoon while Hermia remained at home contentedly, preparing dinner for the three of them, for only those hours alone.

VII

1964

LAWRENCE APPLIED TO ARCHITECTURE SCHOOLS
and was accepted by three of them and, after some un-
certainty, accepted the offer from Harvard; he had not
planned to live again in Cambridge, but the terms of the offer
were generous and the curriculum good. He found an apartment on Linnaean Street, behind the Radcliffe campus, and
walked every morning to Robinson Hall, the Graduate
School of Design. Making his way past Cambridge Common, he cut through Harvard Square and then Harvard
Yard. On those mornings he had time to spare, he took the
route through Radcliffe and looked up at what had been Hermia's window and asked himself idly where she might have
gone and what she might be doing now and if he should try
to find out . . .

The walk took eighteen minutes. A reek of tradition filled

Robinson Hall: the names of great designers incised above the portals, the gooseneck lamps bent low above scarred wooden desks. Portraits of retired deans stared out at the corridors sightlessly; blueprints of gardens and buildings hung framed and preserved on the walls. In glass-fronted freestanding cases he examined the school's history: the drawings and scale models of what had gone before. When he had time, between classes, he walked across the street and visited the Fogg.

Lawrence lived alone. White-haired professors, girls with their book bags, Cambridge matrons with leashed dogs and plastic rain hats: all hurried by him in the morning and again at night. They seemed both self-absorbed and affable, both conscious and unconscious of the presence of the past. At times he saw Hermia coming toward him, or pedaling a bicycle, or lying down sunning herself by the Charles—but it was never truly Hermia, her long-legged, dark-haired actual self, and he walked away.

In the preclassical period, he came to admire the Incas, the Egyptians, the Etruscans, and their methods of construction: their palaces and pyramids and tombs. Having learned the history of ancient Greece in terms of the terms of its buildings, he absorbed the role of roof beams and the lintels and entablature. From his glossary he learned the definitions of such sequences as *naos, narthex, nave, needle spire, newel, niche* or *triforium, triglyph* and *triumphal arch.*

But Lawrence focused much more closely on examples of modernist architecture; the studies at the GSD were future-facing ones. He took pleasure in technical drawings, the making of models and diazo prints; he studied the details of wiring and heat. In his class on urban design he was compelled by the charged interaction between the three professions of architecture, landscape architecture, and urban planning itself. Le Corbusier had completed the Carpenter Arts Center, his only realized building in America, and it loomed like a reproach and promise down the street: *Abandon all your ancient ways, ye who enter here.*

Those were the years at Harvard when the cutting edge that sliced through Cambridge seemed, in Dean Sert's curriculum, keen. Names like Gropius and Gabo and Hideo Sasaki each retained their currency, and the ideals and practice of the Architects Collaborative and Team 10 felt germane. Lawrence worked hard. He spent most of his time in studio, considering space *between* structures and learning to configure floor plans and rapidly develop a *parti.* The fruitful interaction between the shared professions—landscape architecture, architecture, city and regional planning—argued a kind of pluralist agenda; painting and systems analysis might share a common roof.

One of his professors, Serge Chermayeff, had a house in Wellfleet, on a secluded pond. In April he invited a handful of students to look at the modernist cottages of Breuer, Saltonstall and Morton—their attention to siting and landscape, their methods of construction. The group drove to the Cape in three cars.

Chermayeff himself was an angular presence: lean and aquiline, an associate of Gropius who spoke with a strong accent, the sort of émigré who would—or so it seemed to his students—have been at ease in the tsar's court. His *Community and Privacy: Toward a New Architecture of Humanism*—written with Christopher Alexander—examined those configurations that distinguished the public from the private realm; he discoursed on the Bauhaus while they walked along the beach.

The day was bright and cold. One of the other students, in answer to a question by Chermayeff, spoke of the flotsam that defines society, the accident of arrival and the intersection of climate and topography of which settlements are made. A trading post, for instance, will become a city so long as the commodity it trades in proves of value, or so long as the supply continues. And fails to meet demand, said Lawrence; it has to be—or give the *impression* of being—scarce. Explain your point, Chermayeff said, and he found himself discussing diamonds, the way that the De Beers cartel, if he understood it correctly, had convinced the world that diamonds were rare, not plentiful, and therefore should be prized. In *fact* a diamond is no more precious than, say, a garnet or turquoise, but if you manage the market correctly you can persuade the public it's a gem to treasure, a commodity to horde. It's not so much the eye of the beholder as the bank account that counts. What does all this have to do with architecture, asked the professor, impatient, and Lawrence admitted: not much.

Gulls scattered then settled behind him; a great blue heron flew past. He was, he knew, near Truro, and he thought about his time with Hermia, the weekends they had spent here in 1962. He would continue his studies and, in time, complete them; he would become an architect and, in time, successful.

But often, in the years to come, Lawrence remembered this landscape, the tide spawn and the clustered weed, the students walking on ahead and cold wind in his hair. Pretending to study the shape of the wood, he stared at his hand sightlessly, clenching and unclenching it; there was driftwood on the beach.

HE MET ANNIE GUNDERSON at dinner at the Sieverses'; she was blond and pert and committed, she informed the table, to social engineering—not B. F. Skinner or Karl Marx or any of those patriarch-determinist-authority types, but *voluntary* innovation, *voluntary* reconfiguration of the social contract. All social behavior is rooted, said Annie, in biological need.

"I'm not so sure," said Warren Anderson. "My own opinion is the reverse."

"Example?" asked Rick Herrick.

"Our society is organized to *counter* biological need. *That's* the social contract; it's what we agreed to when we came to this party in clothes."

"Speak for yourself," Annie said.

"If everyone followed their instinct"—Warren appealed to the table—"we'd be having food fights, we'd be jumping each other and humping each other and wiping ourselves with the tablecloth and stealing the silver, *n'est-ce pas?*"

"I *told* you we shouldn't invite him," said John Sievers. "I *told* you he couldn't behave."

They laughed. These people were accustomed, or so it seemed to Lawrence, to debate. Over pasta and then spareribs they had argued politics, the sincerity of Lyndon Johnson and the "single gunman" theory offered up by the Warren Commission and the management and prospects of war in Vietnam. He had been invited by the Sieverses; he knew no one else at the party and they knew each other well.

"Dystopia," Warren was saying. "It's not—by any stretch of the imagination—utopia. The social contract, I mean."

"But the female of the species"—Annie nodded at her hostess's dress—"may require multiple partners to ensure fertility. A stranger: a new male arrival, let's say, who doesn't belong to the pack. So the point of all our plumage is to cast it off."

" 'Off, off, you lendings,' " said Brittany Sievers. "That's *Lear.*"

"The heath scene, isn't it?" asked Rick.

" 'Pray you, undo this button . . . ,' " Julie Herrick said.

"Did we finish the Chablis?"

"Don't get me wrong," continued Annie, smiling down the table at Brittany in her black dress. "I do, I just adore chiffon—the way the sleeves billow, the collar. All your decorative finery, the things we wear tonight. But it has more to do with Darwin: *un*natural selection . . ."

When Lawrence asked her what she meant by that, she smiled at him: "You'll see."

"Are we imagining the Great Society?" asked John Sievers, serving apple pie.

"No thank you," Annie said.

"Sex," announced Brittany Sievers. "That's what she's been discussing. The politics of mating—games people play, am I right?"

Lawrence accepted a slice.

"What else is new?" asked Warren Anderson. "It's what she's *always* discussing." He passed his plate.

"The social utility of attraction." Annie smiled again. "Attractiveness." Her teeth were white, her lipstick a bright pink. "It's preening and planning and making the male of the species provide us with successors. So we can guarantee the next generation of women . . ."

"Bingo," agreed Julie Herrick. "You hit the nail on the head."

"How many takers for coffee?" asked John. "It's Blue Mountain coffee, the best of Jamaica . . ."

Everybody at the table drank, and they spent some minutes praising the blend, the taste of it, the cups the coffee came in, the region of Jamaica in which Blue Mountain coffee was grown. Rick and Julie Herrick talked about their time in Kingston, the year they spent together there after they'd been married, how it changed the way they looked at things, and not only because of the ganja, but because of how the music permeated everything, the way reggae lent its rhythm to their daily work, the *brilliance* of the island light . . .

"Can I be your willing subject?" Lawrence asked, half joking, and Annie studied him: "Fine."

She lived off Central Square, in a second-floor apartment. There were kilim pillows on the floor and photographs of elephants and warriors in war paint hanging on the walls. There were photographs of Annie in what she told him was Denmark, on a hillside surrounded by sheep. There was a photo also of her face enlarged, so the pores of her nose looked like craters and her cheeks a snowfield down which—when he focused on it—he saw minuscule skiers traversing the slope. These had been added to the blown-up image with a fine-tipped pen, and there were dates beneath the skis: 7/12/66, 8/17/66, 9/5/66 . . . beginning at her eyelashes and approaching the top of her lip.

It was December 12, and cold; the radiators clanked. "You should bleed them," Lawrence said.

"Bleed?"

"At your service, ma'am." With his pocketknife he turned a setscrew, and the steam valve of the radiator hissed.

"That's very impressive," she said. She had moved to Cambridge from Chicago, where her family owned real estate, and was working for a partner of her father's. She was twenty-five, high-breasted, and described the work as boring, though it helped to pass the time; it's what we're after, said Annie, a way to fill the week.

She offered him hash brownies, and he swallowed two. She was on the pill, she told him, and asked if he minded that she had had herpes; she was, she was sure of it, cured. The son of a bitch who had given her herpes worked in her real estate office, and she'd made certain that he got the axe. "Not literally." She smiled. "Not, I mean, on the offending body part. But Daddy fired him after I asked."

"You're serious?"

"I'm serious." And then she laughed and laughed.

They drank. Annie asked what are you doing here, what are *we* doing here, not I mean in this apartment, but walking up and down upon the earth. Lawrence talked about design, his dream of building something that might make a difference, *would* make a difference, to how people lived, our human impact on the planet and the way to contain urban sprawl. He talked about his teachers, the *busyness* of architecture, how we must learn to mediate between the actual and ideal.

The drugs were having their effect; he heard himself breathing as though underwater, and what he said seemed profound. Imagine for a moment you were living in a round house and not a square or rectangular space, Lawrence said; imagine what that does to physical orientation, the *shape* of social behavior: interaction, intercourse . . .

"Interaction, is that what you call it?" Sitting beside him on the couch, she leaned down and kicked off her shoes. "It's maybe the hash talking," Annie said, "but I believe we've got something going, I thought so the minute I saw you, I saw the ring around your head, the light I mean, the *halo*, really."

"Not really a halo," said Lawrence, and she said, "That's good, that's a relief, I like the way you wear those pants, why don't you take them off."

"With all these ski bums watching?"

"You noticed, didn't you, you're a noticing person, I like that." She leaned toward him and stuck out her tongue and wetly licked his ear. "It's my own private record, it's a way of keeping score. But I'll add you in the morning if you want . . ."

IN THE MORNING, however, she seemed subdued, and when he asked her if she felt all right she shook her head

"What's wrong?" he asked, and she told him, "It feels automatic, doesn't it, it all seems so predictable."

"What?"

"The way we got together. What we're going to do together."

"How do you mean?"

"Get married. Have a child."

"Excuse me?"

"Were you listening to me last night? *Weren't* you?"

He nodded.

"I saw it," she said. "I saw it the minute you came in the room. And when you sat down at the table, their table, that terrible table, just listen to me"—she counted it out on her fingers—"six *t*'s in a row at the start of a word, no, *seven,* that *terrible* table, I felt, hey, whoa, wait just a minute, girl, hold on to your horses, he's *mine*. It's what I meant when I talked about halo, it's what I saw when you walked in the room. Our marriage, the result of it, I mean, a baby girl . . ."

He wondered was she joking and saw that she was serious and wondered was she sane? Annie stared at her fingernails, tears in her eyes. "Blue Mountain coffee?" she inquired, mimicking John Sievers. "Or would you prefer Purple Hill? Myself, I serve Sanka, okay?"

She was the youngest child of three, and by the time that she was born, said Annie, her parents had a warring truce, a household arrangement as to who would be responsible for what. Both her parents had agreed she needed some other someone's attention, so she had a succession of nannies—that's what Mommy called them, she told Lawrence, *nannies, ninnies, nincompoops*—and then a crew of gardeners who worked around the house. One afternoon when she was fourteen a handyman called Brian—he came from Dublin, she remembered, and had a thick Irish accent, a *brogue*—raped her; she'd come home from school. Don't look so shocked, said Annie, it happens all the time. Then she asked him if *brogue* and *brogans* mean the same thing; aren't *brogans* the shoes Irish immigrants wear, like Paddy in the *paddy* wagon when they get hauled away?

It had been, she said, predictable: a kind of fondling—a kiss in the pantry, a hand on her ass, a flirtation she'd been proud of and been flattered by and had in its way invited until suddenly it wasn't flirting, wasn't friendly harmless petting anymore. That afternoon when she got home from school there was nobody else in the garden or house and she let him kiss her like she liked him to, then said, Okay, stop, okay? you're hurting me. But Brian had not taken no for an answer and knocked her down to the floor. The *greenhouse* floor, she remembered the tile, because they had had a greenhouse full of orchids on the south side of the living room. You're asking for it, Brian said, you've been asking for it, haven't you, well here it is, my girl.

Were you hurt badly? Lawrence asked, and she shook her head. What did your parents do, he asked, whatever happened to *him*? Brian too, she said, he got the axe, only this time the literal version—again she laughed—what you'd call a dickless Mick. But anyhow and since that afternoon I've never been able to appreciate orchids; Mommy kept orchids, she said.

He wondered if he should believe her. He wondered how much of what Annie told him—lying naked on the bed, her thigh across his knees—was true. She was self-assured, shored up by wealth, and at the edge of coherence. With her finger-nails she raked his chest, speaking in a monotone, saying he was, wasn't he, a Virgo, she could tell it from the way he walked, the way he matched his tie and shirt: a search for per-fection in others and precision in the self. It's why you'll be an architect, you *are* a Virgo, aren't you, she said, a kind of inno-cent with building blocks who dreams of building things. The risk is—she walked her fingers down his stomach—well, rigid-ity, but that's a risk we'll take. Let's take it again right now, okay? before you have to leave . . .

In years to come he wondered, and was unable to decide, what in fact had happened. He never knew how much she lied or if she believed what she said. He never knew, for in-stance, if there had been a carpenter called Brian or some sort of flirtation or rape. When she described her time at Smith it did seem pure invention, or at least exaggeration: the affair she had had with her history teacher, the way the old museum guard had caught them—Annie laughed, the phrase the dean used was—in flagrante delicto after museum hours on an eighteenth-century sofa in the upstairs gallery. They had been trying out positions on the furniture, and the whole thing was recorded on surveillance tape. She herself had been suspended but her professor was promoted and be-came—again she laughed—dean of the Office of Student *Affairs* . . .

She lied about her pregnancy, the pill she was on but had

not been taking, the diamond earrings she'd examined on a shopping trip and found for some reason one night in her purse. She lied about the Red Sox jacket in the hallway closet and what her brothers had done with the company shares, since they owned controlling interest. She'd not told the truth about Denmark, she confessed to Lawrence later; the photo of the hillside was Wisconsin and the place where her uncle farmed sheep. Her uncle had gone bankrupt and fallen in love with his sheep. When seven months after the wedding their daughter, Catherine, was born and her postpartum depression was at its worst she lied about the drugs she took, their quantity, their origin, the way her body changed and how it was *his* fault.

The marriage was brief, a mismatch from the start, and if she hadn't been pregnant she wouldn't have considered it. But she *did* want the child. What you were, Annie told him, was a necessary evil, I couldn't have done it without you, *we* couldn't have done it without you, but thanks a lot and no hard feelings and good luck. Katy and I are going home to Chicago and you can kiss her good-bye.

At first he had been angry, then unhappy, then relieved. There was a phalanx of lawyers, a series of discussions and agreements. By the time he moved to San Francisco and his job at Skidmore, Owings & Merrill—a job in part arranged for him by Annie's family—he found himself disposed of; he was twenty-seven years old with an ex-wife and daughter and visiting rights in the summer, as well as one weekend per month. Warren Anderson, it turned out, had been Annie's lover; the two of them resumed their old affair and moved together to

Winnetka. Do you remember, asked Warren, the night we met, that dinner at the Sieverses'? It was when she decided she wanted a baby, but *I* didn't want one or want to adopt, and you were the stand-in, he said.

Lawrence did his best to stay in touch. For the first years he did visit, playing badminton and checkers with his daughter; they went to the mall and the Field Museum together. His best, however—or so Annie told him—wasn't anything like good enough, and thank you very much. We're all entitled to mistakes and I was your mistake. She married Warren and divorced him and married again, in rapid succession, and by the time that she turned thirty and divorced a third time she was a Buddhist; the truth of life is suffering, she wrote Lawrence from an ashram in Colorado, and all of existence a wheel.

FOR THE THREE YEARS of apprenticeship, he worked at Skidmore, Owings & Merrill in their San Francisco office, moving from position to position and being supervised. He liked the city and the job, the feel of being entrusted with tasks both "hands-on" and conceptual while watching skyscrapers rise. Nat Owings himself would sometimes appear, and Chuck Bassett, the head designer, took the idea of apprenticeship seriously, preparing new arrivals for licensing exams and assigning each of them a partner to whom they should report. Lawrence wrote a paper on C. A. Doxiadis and the theory of ekistics, then a paper on Buckminster Fuller and the Dymaxion House. These were outtakes from the work undertaken at Harvard, but they seemed suited to the time and place—San

Francisco burgeoning, a city conscious of its past and enlarging future or, as his supervisor, Ted Hutchins, put it, "Westward ho-ho-ho!"

There was nowhere, of course, to expand to due west, and the fault lines from the earthquake seemed a stark reminder of the limits of expansion; the idea of urban renewal had gained widespread currency. Lawrence lived in a garden apartment on the east-facing slope of Nob Hill. He taught himself to cook. On weekends he would drive past Tiburon and Belvedere, the still-racy Sausalito and slopes of Mount Tamalpais and the flats of Stinson Beach. He admired the town of Bolinas, its ramshackle buildings, the planned haphazardness of plate glass and redwood and boxy shingled structures on the mesa, their concrete stilts. He told Ted Hutchins he was drawing up a master plan for Inverness: a small-scale version of Sun City or Reston for the rural working class. In *Ekistics* Doxiadis had written: "Following the ideas of Buckminster Fuller, we can also use the measurement of weight of construction per unit of space in an attempt to understand some of the real issues related to construction and to the necessity of a revolutionary approach to problems of mass construction for the great numbers of people who suffer from a lack of proper settlements."

Once every month his brother called. "Hey, brother, where've you been?"

"Here," said Lawrence, "at my desk."

"Right. Well, how the hell *are* you?"

"Fine, I'm fine. Where are you calling from?"

"Portland. Your time zone. We *share* it, remember, my man."

Then Tim would launch into his speech, his praise of the

commune he'd joined, how it had become his family, his own elected family and not the blood-is-thicker-than-water variety with its fascist assumptions of what people owe; it's not, he said, that difficult to understand why Kissinger and his jackbooted business thugs are goose-stepping all over Asia, because they're all pumped up—*ka-ching, ka-ching*—with oil and opium and keeping markets open for the Mafia men in D.C. How bright a good deed shines, Tim said, in a dark and dirty world; it's my mantra every morning, it's something I repeat to myself when I wash and meditate and it's the reason I'm calling and thing I need to talk about. Because *you* need to understand, brother, this poison in our system, the strychnine we were forced to swallow in grade school and high school and college and even, yes, at home. What Mom and Dad fed us each morning was propaganda pablum; they didn't *know* it, maybe, they weren't to *blame* exactly, but what we inhaled with our orange juice and Cheerios was America as apple pie and what they failed to mention were the corporate jackbooted thugs. Or this crazy, crazy war. Just look *around* you, Larry, and take the blinders off and tell me what you see . . .

He was looking at the spec sheets for a marina in South San Francisco. Tim talked on about apocalypse, the big wind blowing east to west, the *universal* dust storm brewing up like tea around America, and tea leaves settling everywhere, the murk of it, the reek of corruption, and faded in and out until finally Lawrence hung up.

His mother called. She and Robert had a proposition for him, she said, or not so much a proposition as *proposal*. She was sad about how far away she felt from her two boys, how little they saw of each other, but she and Robert had just now completed the purchase of five acres of farmland on the shores of Lake Champlain. They were hoping for a summer house, as well as a place to escape to in winter, and they wondered if Lawrence would like to design it; this had been Robert's idea. That's the sort of man he is, she said, and money's no object, or not an *objection,* and we think of it as a retirement home. We aren't ready for retirement, we're not talking ramps and wheelchairs, but it's such *beautiful* property, we can't wait for you to see it: please say yes.

He did. He had no license to practice, but one of his classmates from Harvard was licensed as an architect in Vermont and could sign off on the plans. Lawrence flew to Burlington, and met his mother and stepfather there, and they drove him to and walked him through the site. It was, indeed, well chosen: a meadow sloping gently down, a rise with wide views west and south, the great blue lake beneath.

"We think of this," said Robert, "as a new chapter for us both—you see what I'm saying, no *baggage,* no *history,* nothing except what the two of us bring to it, your mother and me, and you too are starting out, so let's do this together, okay? As I see it, it's win-win."

He designed a multilevel house. The living quarters were at entry level, so they did not need to climb, and the upstairs was a steep-roofed sitting room with views in the four directions and a sleeping balcony for guests. The master-bedroom suite and balcony faced west, and the second floor could be sealed off when not in use. His "clients" wanted the feel of a farmhouse, a contemporary structure with rough-hewn wooden beams that nonetheless might seem as though it had been standing in the field for generations. Lawrence convinced his mother and Robert to clad the whole in Cor-ten steel. It was expensive to install, but there would be no maintenance, and the rusting siding would look, from a distance, like wood. The roof was corrugated tin.

This juxtaposition of modern and old was the organizing principle for what became his first commission and completed house. "What we can do with steel these days," he remembered a teacher declaring, "makes the imagination of even Piranesi look a little hidebound. If it's *doable*, do it, why not?"

He added a silo for storage. This cylindrical structure too was sided in corrugated tin, and the local workmen—taciturn but skillful—treated him as though he were a well-heeled madman, warily. The house was sixteen hundred square feet, but the twelve-foot ceilings made it feel more spacious, and both the middle-distance views and those of Lake Champlain seemed somehow a part of interior space. In private, though he did not tell his mother this, he felt the whole to be derivative of—or, to put it generously, an act of sculptural homage to—Le Corbusier. On a whim he sent a set of plans and photographs to the National AIA Honor Awards Program and heard nothing for six months; then he received a letter of congratulations and an official citation.

This pleased them in the office, but he designed a second house—this time for his father, on Long Island—and his supervisor warned him not to spend so much energy on private commissions. "We're glad to see you working hard," said Ted Hutchins, "but remember you work *here,* at SOM, and at *least* forty hours each week."

Ted Hutchins was affable, plump. He wore a goatee and suspenders and had crescent sweat stains in the armpits of his shirt. He was proud of his young protégé, he wanted Lawrence to be clear this wasn't a reproach but statement of fact: sooner or later, not yet but someday, there might be a conflict of interest, and we'd like to keep you here or send you to the office in Chicago. You're doing fine now, you're part of the team, and let's keep it that way, okay? Having completed his apprenticeship at Skidmore, Owings & Merrill, Lawrence took the three-part exam and did receive board certification as an architect in California; licensed, he entered the profession and asked himself what would come next.

What came next was the Mason house in Inverness—this one solar-heated and facing out on a fenced pasture with Black Angus cows. Here the material was redwood and old railroad ties, and the second-story windows were a set of salvaged portholes from a Port Townsend tug. That motif—his client owned a mail-order "Nautical Supply Shoppe"—was reinforced by outsize anchors framing the entry drive, and a series of hurricane lamps. There was a three-page pictorial spread in *California Living,* and the house photographed well. It too was carefully sited, and it too received an award.

Henry Mason, however, was not a relative, and although his wife, Denise, seemed pleased, he himself proved querulous. Mason complained about the expense of the construction and the shadow of the overhang and problem with the fireplace draw, once the mason had laid in the smoke shelf. "It's *my* nickel," he was fond of saying, "*I'm* the one who earned it and it's me who decides what to spend . . ."

"Well, sort of," Lawrence said.

"They told me—everybody told me—that you double the cost estimate; you should plan on twice as long and twice as much as the contractor says. But I never expected, not ever, to multiply by three!"

"I'm sorry."

"Bullshit you are."

"It was *you* who kept adding things, Henry. The deck. The hot tub. The wine cellar just last week . . ."

"It's *my* nickel," Mason repeated. "And it was Denise who wanted the hot tub, not me."

There was a threatened lawsuit, and although it never went to court the specter of a lawsuit troubled Lawrence greatly; his client belonged to a different world. The state of California had real estate developers and conservationists in almost equal measure, and if the car you drove or clothes you wore made a political statement, then certainly the house you lived in also staked out a position: *By their dwellings ye shall know them,* as Ted Hutchins liked to say. To oppose the war in Vietnam seemed somehow connected to low-income housing, and solar energy would reduce dependence on oil. "Bullshit," said Henry Mason, "we're talking cost overruns here."

His client's wife was seductive; she poured Lawrence wine while they studied the drawings together. Denise threw back her head and, laughing throatily, let her fingers graze his thigh.

She complained about her husband, his lack of taste and—let's be honest about it—imagination. But Lawrence felt uneasy, unable to reconcile what he had hoped might prove to be a visionary modular system with the need to turn a profit: high-end custom structures, although a challenge to design, were not now the point.

WHAT *WAS* THE POINT, he asked himself, and bought a white Volvo P1800 with red leather seats. He liked the car, its handling, its solidity and the fact—although he had not known this when he purchased it—that the Volvo once was featured on a television series called *The Saint*. Strangers would point at him, smiling, and sometimes they asked for his autograph; he assured them he was not a star, not a TV celebrity, but nonetheless liked the attention. On weekends he took trips.

Lawrence drove south to Big Sur. The woman he was seeing, Marissa, joined him for dinner at Nepenthe and they spent the night together at the Big Sur Lodge. Marissa herself had a home in Carmel, and she had driven to meet him; they drank wine and watched the sunset and made love with enthusiasm and, over coffee and croissants and homemade jam in the morning, discussed the future: if he was free to join her next weekend and make a commitment or not.

"Do we have to decide?"

"It's not," she said, "irrevocable. I don't mean *that* kind of commitment."

"No?"

"I'm not your jailer, Larry. It isn't a *prison*, commitment."

"I thought we were discussing what to do next weekend. San Diego, San Simeon, whatever . . ."

Marissa was a child psychologist, and when they argued—which was often—she said his was a case of arrested development: he was a perfect example of an American boy-man, the type who refused to grow up. It isn't refusal exactly, she said, it's more an inability or what we call a deficit, it's being fixated on actualization but not *self*-actualization, and he should read Abraham Maslow and try, just a little, to act like an adult, all right?

"Does that mean making choices?" he asked. "And abiding by them?"

She nodded; she patted his cheek.

"Can I choose to get out of here?"

Marissa paled. "If it's what you need to do, yes."

Lawrence pulled on his sweater and left.

HE MOVED TO A LARGER APARTMENT that was half a house on Filbert Street and remained at SOM, working on regional projects, writing articles and playing tennis each Tuesday after work. His brother ceased calling and dropped out of touch, although every so often a postcard arrived with incoherent messages: *Oink-Oink!* or *Little Brother Is Watching You!* or *Kropotkin had it right!* His sister came to visit. Allie had earned an MBA and was being recruited by a firm in San Francisco, but there were competing offers and she was planning to accept instead the one from Philadelphia. "I'm an East Coast gal," she said.

They went out to dinner at Ernie's, and the headwaiter treated them as though they were a couple, romantically involved, and not brother and sister. This amused her, and she said so, and they spent the evening discussing their childhoods, the new families their parents had acquired and the houses he had built. Allie was wearing pearls, a tailored suit, and in the years of business school had acquired a hard-edged authority; her fingernails and lips were crimson and her gestures brusque.

"What I don't understand," she said, "is how we all got through it."

"What?"

"The years and *years* of bickering. The endless arguments."

"What I mostly remember," said Lawrence, "is silence."

"You mostly weren't home by then, brother."

He smiled at her. "That's true."

"Can I ask you," Allie asked, "what it felt like to repeat it? Divorce."

"Excuse me?"

"Did you ever believe you were copying them, repeating a failed marriage? Or being *influenced* by them—our parents?"

"No."

"No?"

He heard himself saying that what he had gone through was mostly denial, mostly a way of ignoring the past: who I miss is my daughter, not wife. When she asked about divorce, Lawrence admitted, he'd not made the connection to their shared family history; I do believe in marriage, except not the one I had . . .

She was blushing, he noticed, and biting her lip. He drank. Then his sister said something that shocked him: you fall in love once only, or anyhow that's what I think, and all the rest is playacting, a way to pass the time. And I've done it, said Allie, I've gone and *done* it, goddammit, except it's a kind of addiction and I've been trying to quit. The best reason, she confessed, to come to California was to put a continent between herself and Mr. Wrong, since her own love affair wasn't working and was, it turned out, hopeless, the oldest cliché in the marital book. The man she was seeing was married and had two children of his own and wasn't planning to leave them, not ever; there was only so often she'd answer the phone and be disappointed or come running at his say-so, only so many hotels and motels, because he was fifteen years older, a kind of daddy substitute, a sorry excuse for their own absent father, or that's what her doctor suggested, and maybe her doctor was right. For the longest time—for three *years* now—she had refused to believe it, had not taken no for an answer but convinced herself, or tried to, that maybe tomorrow or next week or month they'd turn a corner together and he'd wake up and see the light and the two of them would live together happily forever and ever amen.

She continued in this fashion, looking down at her plate, describing her trouble in detail, her new resolution to end the affair and not pretend there'd be a happy ending, no wedding band or bed of roses or full moon in June. The waiter, hovering, inquired, "Another bottle, sir?" and he looked at his sister questioningly. She shook her head, eyes misting, and Lawrence asked for the check. Allie scraped back her chair and, standing, linked her arm with his, saying, "It's excellent to see you, brother, and have someone to complain to. Someone who knew me way back when . . ."

But he had become inattentive, adrift, remembering what she had said, *You fall in love once only, or anyhow that's what I think,* repeating the one word in silence: *Hermia,* his name for what was lost.

VIII

2004

THE HARBOR OF VALETTA, THEIR TOUR GUIDE SAID, "is impregnable. These seawalls has never been breached. The Knights of Malta from earliest times are warriors and healers; they have always been Crusaders and ministered the sick. They has, you see, two duties: they are soldiers and Hospitallers both. When the Knights were driven out of Rhodes because of Arab siege," the tour guide continued, her voice high-pitched, "they settle here in Malta to make of the island a stronghold—and which it is remaining until the present day. These battlements and forts are similar to those of Rhodes, although the stone is different; maybe you visited that other island, yes? The stone of Rhodes is red, of course, but here the walls is white."

They walked beneath an arch. The town of Valetta, their guide explained, was founded in the sixteenth century by the grand master of the Knights, Jean Parisot de La Valette. "He make a stronghold for his peoples commanding in position. Is a military community," she told the passengers from the *Diana*, "according to the Roman model."

"What's that?" asked the man from El Paso.

"Streets slope from down the heights for soldiers to keep watch from, see? And also the architects bring us fresh water. This one is not a town by accident, not just something that arrange itself—how do you say?—by circumstance but *planned.*"

A bell chimed eleven o'clock. In contrast to the negligent clutter of Sicily, the streets of Valetta, though crowded, were clean; the traffic too was orderly, and there were traffic police. This town seemed less a tourist destination than a place where people lived and worked; young men with leather briefcases and women swinging handbags bustled past.

"There's an overlay of Englishness," said Hermia. "It feels English, doesn't it?"

Lawrence agreed. "Retirement heaven, a tax haven . . ."

"Here is a very ancient place, a very ancient peoples and civilization," continued their guide. "You will see in the museum the goddess of fertility, and the peoples from the Stone Age are excellent workers with stone. In our entire history only the little Napoleon succeeded to conquer the island and only when the soldiers decided not to fight. This was because the Knights of Malta elected from France refuse to battle with their emperor, and the grand master of the Knights say, well, in that case, *Seigneurs,* we make him welcome; if we do not lift our arms together we lay them together all down."

The tour guide was petite, and trim, and wearing a yellow beret. She walked with an umbrella and used it to extend her arm, pointing at buildings and sites. The sky was bright.

"Are you all right?"

"Not really, no," Hermia said.

"What's wrong?"

She shook her head. For what in fact was there to say; how could she ever explain? Last night she'd clung to Lawrence, but it had not helped. "I've seen a ghost," she said to him, and when he asked her what that meant she shut her eyes.

"What's wrong?" he repeated.

Her daughter rode ten feet away, suspended on the wave spume by the railing where they stood. The dress was diaphanous, body just bones. The face, however, was unchanged: near and dear and beautiful, mouth pursed in concentration . . .

"What sort of ghost?"

She could not confess why she stiffened, or how Patricia haunted her and danced beyond the rail. "Take no for an answer," her daughter had said, the final time they argued, and slammed the kitchen door . . .

Behind them in the Elsinore Lounge someone was playing a polka. Hermia trailed her fingers down Lawrence's cheek and, shivering, left him on deck.

So now it was bright day again, the last day of their trip. "My name is Amelie," their guide announced, "and I pass my whole entire life on the islands of Gozo and Malta, except for two years in Scotland, are any of you Scottish? No? In that case I confess to you because of Edinburgh I very much esteem the weather here, the lack of soot. We have, in the dry season, dust."

Her English was inaccurate, her accent strong, and yet she managed to suggest they had been strolling down Bond Street or through Piccadilly Circus in the rain. The sun was hot.

"Except just now we were discussing the little Napoleon," said Amelie, "that is how we call him in these parts, the Corsican Buonaparte, who was presented the keys to the city, and he assure the Knights they would no one be harmed. Indeed, he keep his word. But after three days he collected the plate—all the silver and gold from the church, the auberges and the palaces—and melted it to bullion to pay for the campaign in Egypt with ill-gotten gains that had been the Knights' treasure. This was the one time Valetta was taken and only because we do not choose to fight."

Lawrence and Hermia smiled. They did so at the same moment, and Amelie noticed. "It took your great Admiral Nelson," she said, "to be blockading the harbor and force away the French, because by that time the Corsican he understands this is not a hospitable place. Since then we have been English or belonging to the Commonwealth, and King George in the Second War was grateful to us all. The Maltese people refuse to be beaten by Germans no matter how harsh the bombardment or how relentless the bombs. And afterwards he honor every person on the island fortress for their suffering and steadfast ways: you see here the George cross."

They were standing in a courtyard, by statues of Crusaders.

Jane from Columbus asked about the agriculture on the island, and what the people grew. Their tour guide answered questions; she discussed the crops of Malta, the density of population, the balance of payment problems and retirement communities and desalinization plants and the question of the European Union and the Maltese debt. She was enthusiastic, voluble, and the passengers from the *Diana* made a small circle as she spoke. The language here is half-Sicilian and half-Arabic, she explained; not many people speak Maltese but it is a beautiful language, you must listen when you walk. And visit the elegant shops.

Next she described the Knights of Malta—their chastity, their vows and power and crusading zeal. "One hand the sword, one hand the bandage, see? There are three categories," said Amelie, "and every member of the knighthood is a candidate from one of these—the nobility, the wealthy and the serving men.

"By serving men I do not mean," she continued, "a servant; I mean only they has some particular skill and use it for the profit of the Order. The painter Caravaggio, for example, take refuge here and became a Knight of Malta but could not offer money because at the time he has none. Caravaggio could claim of course no previous nobility; instead he offer what he promise is his largest and would be most important painting— the only one he sign. In the Cathedral of St. John you will see it when you go."

Outside once more, she pointed her umbrella at the sea. "Notice the sight lines past the fort," said Amelie, "the esplanade, the way the townspeople has ample warning always if an enemy approach. The harbor is on all three sides protected and the fort is—how you say?—impregnable to breach. Imagine for a moment what it feels to climb these ramparts while the soldiers up above you drop down rocks or cannonballs or heat their boiling oil!"

Brandishing her umbrella, she continued down the street. There were many people shopping, people striding purposefully, but Lawrence and Hermia lagged behind. The gaily decorated shops and old stone houses made a maze they wandered in; he took her hand.

"Let's let them go, all right?"

"All right."

"We've elected the privacy option."

"You don't want to see the Knights' armor?" she asked. "Or, in the museum, the goddess of fertility?"

He shook his head. They descended an alley with clothing boutiques, a bank, a travel agency and, at the corner, a café; he ordered them both cappuccino and they sat to drink it at a table with an umbrella and two chairs. The chairs were green, with red wooden slats, and the tablecloth had brightly colored variations of the eight-pointed Maltese cross. She remarked upon this, and he asked her, "Do you want pastry, a croissant?"

"Coffee's fine," said Hermia. She pressed her lips together; her single dimple showed. "They stuff us, don't they, on the ship."

"Agreed."

"I'm still digesting dinner. And must have gained five pounds since Rome . . ."

"Not so I've noticed."

"Well, three . . ."

"You're fishing for compliments, lady."

"Yes. But I don't want a pastry."

"I want to know," said Lawrence, "if you're angry at me." He drank. "And if you're angry, which you are, I think, what I can do about it, why . . ."

"This isn't about you. Not really."

"Oh?"

"Except you've been so eager. You were always so, so *eager*—that's the word for it—so puppy-dog ready to please."

"Is that what it looks like? Is that how I seem?"

Now it was she who raised her cup. There was froth at the rim of it; Hermia drank. "You're right," she said. "I'm being dismissive. But not unfair, exactly. You've been thrusting your-self at me all through the trip—or, anyhow, since Pompeii. And I'm not a college girl and things are not the way they were and we can't pretend we're children, we've *got* children, we had chil-dren, and it isn't just a matter now of, what did we call it, wham bam, thank you ma'am, I'm sixty-three years old."

"I know that, remember, I'm sixty-four."

"Old enough to know better," she said.

So the mood between them lightened and the tension less-ened. They finished their coffees; he paid. She took photo-graphs. They made their way through little squares and thoroughfares into a public garden, then found a bench and sat together in the sunlight watching children playing, watching the elderly walking their dogs, watching the light in the trees.

"Do you want lunch?" Lawrence inquired, and she shook her head. "Your cabin or mine?" he asked again, and this time Hermia laughed. They found the road down to the harbor and walked together past the Customs House, smiling at the men in uniform who sat smoking by the seawall, and through the roped enclosure of the M.S. *Diana* and past the potted palms.

The ship had numbered brass medallions for the passengers, a system by which the cruise director kept track. A board hung by the gangway with a list of names beside it; when disembarking, those who went ashore would lift off and pocket their numbers and, when returning, replace them. That way, the cruise director explained, we know who's here and who's not.

He returned his number, 63, and hers, 71, to the registry board. Most of the medallions were missing, since the excursion to Valetta was the last one of the cruise, and only a few passengers elected to stay on the ship. Sailors were polishing brightwork; sailors were mopping the deck.

By the purser's desk she told him, "I'm in the owner's cabin."

"Oh?"

"They rent it out if he's away; it's on the upper deck and does have views." She smiled. "Etchings. Would you like to come on up and see them?"

Lawrence nodded yes. His own quarters down below were cramped and unforgiving, with exercise clothes on a hook. So he followed her upstairs and waited in the hallway while she fumbled in her handbag for a key. At length she found and used it, and they stepped inside.

Spring and Fall

. . .

THERE WERE WRAPAROUND WINDOWS that gave on the harbor, a seating area, a chaise longue. The curtains were of watered silk, and Oriental carpets festooned the hardwood floor. This gave him pause. It altered the equation, somehow; it made him feel foolish, a little, as though he'd been pursuing her the way a passenger in steerage might chase some great bejeweled lady in first class. The captain's bridge was just above; she had a private balcony and, during their absence that morning, the bed had been made up. Silk pillows with the name *Diana* lay plumped along the headboard, and the bedspread was embroidered with a clipper ship, sails furled.

There had been a movie, a soap opera he'd seen years before of a street-brawling boy and rich girl who sailed on the *Titanic*. They fell, of course, in love. She had been carrying Picassos and Cézannes and was supposed to marry an arrogant aristocrat but in her heart of hearts adored the boy instead. There was, of course, a storm at sea; there was an iceberg and a rending crash and great catastrophe; there was an orchestra playing "Nearer, My God, to Thee." Nature's nobleman had saved his darling's life but drowned . . .

"I'd forgotten," Lawrence said. "Well, not forgotten, really . . ."

"What?"

"You're an heiress, aren't you? You always take the penthouse suite."

"Don't be unkind," she said.

"I mean it as a compliment. I'm being respectful, madam."

"Bullshit. All it is, is money."

"Yes."

She moved to him, half teasing. "Would you like to close the curtains?"

He did.

"That's better. Thank you, Jeeves," she said.

They were enveloped, of a sudden, in the protective dark. Hermia kicked off her shoes and therefore was less tall than he; he straightened his shoulders and held out his arms. A bouquet of white lilies had been arranged on the bureau. Their odor was pungent, suffusing the room.

"Well?"

"Well."

"Wouldn't you, would you like to kiss me?"

She moved against him yieldingly and pressed her lips to his. At last the moment had arrived—in this romantic setting, this owner's stateroom on the topmost deck—but Lawrence felt constrained. They stood by the armchair together. While he was touching her and holding her he told himself he could continue or not; he could proceed with these maneuvers or stop staging them, stop kissing her; it did remain a choice. He coughed. She stepped away. Hermia found herself remembering, long years before, the choice she'd made in Arlington, that time she'd slept with the Oppenheims' friend—what was his name, the one who owned her father's paintings and taught English at Columbia?—and how she had asked herself then also if the game was worth the candle; *will you, won't you join the dance?*

Again he cleared his throat. They leaned toward each other, pressed against each other, and she wondered what her breasts would feel like if he kissed them as he used to, and what would happen next. She saw them in the mirror, two bent gray heads adjacent in the ornate gilt-framed glass, saw them touching lips and cheeks as though performing for the camera in some sort of time-lapse photography, a present overlay upon the distant past. The stubble at his chin was white. The folds of his neck were—what was the word for it?—*wattles,* and they were going through the motions of seduction but clumsily, anxiously, feeling their way past the layers of clothing and flesh. It was as though the camera became a movie camera, and she was her own director, holding the viewfinder, watching. *Take one,* she told herself, *take two, all right, people, try that again* . . .

They sat at the bed's edge, his arm at her waist and her head on his shoulder, and the muted light through the curtains illumined the wall opposite: the bureau, the mirror, a painting of a shepherd with his flock and sheepdog and flute. Briefly Lawrence shut his eyes. Briefly she closed her eyes also. In the ensuing silence she could hear machinery: the hum of idling engines, the system for heating and cooling, the tick of the clock.

"Do I," Hermia began to ask, then stopped.

"Look beautiful?" He smiled at her, gallant. "The answer is yes."

She blushed. "That's not what I wanted to ask you."

"Well, what?"

"Do you feel up to, up for this? Oh, this is so embarrassing. I don't mean *up,* I mean ready."

"We don't require Viagra," said Lawrence. "If that's what you've been asking . . ."

"No."

"But it does feel *important*. It doesn't feel like something we can take for granted . . ."

"No." And now she did feel safe with him and took his hand and pressed his fingers one by one and traced the deep lines of his palm. Haltingly at first, and then with a sense of rising relief, she spoke about Patricia. She told him what they'd fought about and how they had argued and flailed at each other till the girl walked out in anger and did not return. She'd slammed the kitchen door so hard the calendar had fallen—Hermia could *see* it, *hear* it crumple—to the floor.

The kitchen door had slammed before, the disappearing act was one with which she'd grown familiar. It had been the early spring of 1992. It had been April 15. That was, she remembered, the day she paid taxes, and there were tax forms awaiting her signature and checks to write and envelopes to send them in; her accountant had filled out the forms. She could remember her anger, her grief, and every single thing the two of them had fought about all winter. She could recall each hurtful word and what was in the oven and where, above the radiator in the sunlight by the south-facing window, bread dough rose . . .

For there had been another kitchen, another fight and rapid flight when she escaped New York. She could not bear to think the wheel had come full circle and could not be reversed. It was too obvious, too neat by half to think that Patsy—Pat-a-Cake, Patricia—did what she herself had done, that all of this was preordained, some sort of blood taint or DNA for retribution implanted by her husband. There had been, said Hermia, a can of Mace, Paul's paranoia, and then the years of hiding in Vermont. For the first days she waited, for the first weeks had been hopeful and then fearful and then terrified and at last had understood—with a deep blank certainty, an icy recognition—that the girl had left for good and would not return.

L AWRENCE DISEMBARKED AT THREE O'CLOCK, too restless to remain aboard and needing open air. The scene in her cabin accompanied him; her cheek on his shoulder, her tears. He walked by himself into town. Leaving Hermia, he'd offered, "If you want me to, I'll stay," and she forced a smile and said, "I'll be all right, I promise, I'll see you later on."

He took the road they'd walked before, and in the center of Valetta found the Cathedral of St. John. There he made his way through heavy doors and, entering, was shocked; the austere façade of the building had not prepared him for the pomp within, the splendor of the windows and ceilings and multicolored floors. Beneath his feet the Knights were buried, square by inlaid square. Triumphal death was signaled everywhere: the skulls that grinned at him, the portraits of grand masters and bones crisscrossed on marble crypts were Baroque in their exuberance. *Step lightly*, they seemed to be saying, *we too were fleet of foot.*

After some time he located and sat in front of *The Beheading of St. John.* It moved him very much. The red of the saint's cape, the red of the blood pooling under his neck, the doorway's arch, the window, the elderly couple recoiling: all these signaled mastery. A muscular killer leaned down with a knife while a maiden at the painting's left leaned forward with a basin; was she a servant come to fetch the head or perhaps the princess, insatiable Salome? In any case the artist knew what he was doing, whom to please . . .

Lawrence was sweating; with his sleeve he wiped his face. Every afternoon of the journey except for this one he had used the treadmill on the M.S. *Diana,* and fleetingly he wondered if the twinge in his chest was a warning. He had not made love since June. He had not wanted to. But Hermia was changing that, had challenged his long solitude by offering her story, and he asked himself and did not know if he could start again . . .

"The Beheading of St. John," a tour guide near at hand was saying, "is Michelangelo Merisi's gift to this cathedral and his masterpiece. A large composition—the largest he painted, the only one we know he signed, and here he use his pen name: Caravaggio. What he was doing in Malta, eh?"—the museum guide inquired of a listening group—"because he flee from Rome to Naples and then from here to Sicily and then again he quarreled, this man was always quarreling, he was a very great painter but difficult person, I think.

"Consider the men in the window; they are watching this terrible scene? Do you think they like to see the blood or fear because their turn come next; are they excited by the spectacle or also prisoners perhaps? Caravaggio of course is famous for how he paint light, the Einstein of the period, the one who first invented what we call *chiaroscuro,* eh, and though the saint himself is brightly, how you say, illuminated, the painting here is dark. It is in honor of the patron saint for whom we name this building; St. John had a shipwreck on Gozo, the island next to

Malta, and pray for safe deliverance, which he discover in this place. Caravaggio is telling everybodies, I believe—the Knights, the grand master of the Knights of Malta to whom he offer this picture—we live in darkness and die in the light. We must be prepared, the artist say, for the girl with a basin and blood on the floor, the one who studies sacrifice, and she is standing waiting for both our beginning and end."

"How was your walk?"

"I missed you," Lawrence said.

"I'm sorry I didn't come. Come with you, I mean. Oh, Jesus"—she spread her hands, sheepish—"why does *everything* have to sound . . ."

"Suggestive?"

"Idiotic. I feel like I'm a kid again."

He sat. "That's one of the things I've been thinking about. Somehow—since we met again, the day you found me in Pompeii—I've been behaving like an adolescent. Or pretending to be grown-up, the way I did at Harvard. But it isn't all that bad, I think, it makes me feel so *hopeful*."

"Really?"

"Hopeful, I mean, that the future is bright. What's that expression, 'The world is my oyster'?"

Her hands were trembling. "Is it?"

"No. But why's the world an oyster—does that mean we swallow it?"

"Or 'happy as a clam'?" she asked. "Why should a clam be happy?"

"I think because it's smiling. And you should *see* the Caravaggio. But the whole cathedral, Hermia, the way the Knights filled it to bursting: how ornate the carvings are, the skeletons and all those skulls and bones."

"Cheery little business."

"What I'm trying to say," said Lawrence, "is I'm back to being optimistic. To thinking things are *possible*, not over . . ."

"Not over, no. Except we've waited forty years."

"Who's counting?—forty-two. Two out of every three years of your life."

"Oh, I've given up arithmetic." She leaned across and kissed his cheek. "That too."

AT DINNER LAWRENCE AND HERMIA joined an elderly couple from Boston and a pair of newlyweds. The gentleman from Boston was distinguished in appearance, with a mop of white unruly hair and a carefully tied bow tie; he patted his lips with his napkin each time he started to speak. He had worked as a geologist, and he regaled the company with stories of eruptions throughout the Mediterranean, the recent behavior of Stromboli and Etna as well as the more famous eruption of Vesuvius and the kinds of volcanic activity one might hereafter expect.

"I've always wanted," Hermia said, "to look down at lava."

"You never do get used to it. It's something special, lava bubbling."

"It is," his wife said, "laughable. We dearly love to laugh."

That this was inappropriate seemed somehow not to matter; she picked at her chicken and played with her carrots as though herself a child. She was, she confessed to the table, a little hard of hearing; they lived on Beacon Hill. Lawrence knew the street, he said, and as an architecture student did a set of elevations of the rooflines of Newbury Street. The chimneys in particular, he said, I do remember the chimneys. "You *must* come and see us," said the geologist, "you and your wife will be welcome," and Hermia began to correct him and declare they were not married. Then she decided not to; it would have been no kindness to tell these old people the truth. Lawrence smiled at her and said, "We'd love to. Next time we're in Boston we promise we will."

The younger couple worked in advertising. Bruce and Judy lived in Connecticut; did Hermia know Westport? They lived in the center of town but had met each other, Judy explained over salad, at a copywriters' convention in North Carolina this spring. All blessings—she fashioned a cross in the air—upon the Grove Park Inn. She had lost her husband six months before in a car crash on an icy road, and though she did feel guilty, *terrible* about it, the truth was their marriage had been going nowhere and was heading for divorce court that same week. Bruce himself had been divorced, and when they met in Asheville they knew they were made for each other, had been incredibly lucky, if you can call it fortunate when there's divorce and death. So this was their honeymoon voyage, their chance to get it *right* for once, and to adjust for what went wrong, and she was bound and determined now to get it right. Had Hermia been to Asheville and did she know the Biltmore House and how romantic the gardens could be? Judy proposed a toast to everyone's good fortune and, gesturing at Darko, held her glass out for more wine.

So they were one of a group of three couples, and talked about the trip. The best parts, they could all agree, were Malta and Agrigento, the worst was the Isle of Capri. "It has to do with weather," said the elderly geologist; Hermia tried to re- member his name. It was too late in the evening for her to ask his name again; his wife said, "Yes, but there is inner weather also, inner temperature. Isn't that so?" She was wearing bracelets with large turquoise stones embedded in the silver; her husband patted her arm.

"Indeed," he said. "We're ninety-eight point six . . ."

After dinner Lawrence and Hermia stood at the railing, and the moon was high. She steeled herself to look over the bowsprit, but there were no ghosts. Flags fluttered in the breeze. The fort of the Crusaders and the high stone battle- ments loomed floodlit and imposing.

"Did you enjoy yourself?" he asked.

"When?"

"At dinner?"

"I've been having a wonderful time."

" 'Wish you were here.' "

"And what about you, Lawrence, have you been having a wonderful time?"

He gestured at the seawall. "Hard men, the Knights."

She was feeling happy now, alone with him, loose-tongued a little because of the wine. "Hard?"

"Yes, unyielding. Famous for their discipline . . ."

"Then what a shame," said Hermia, "they took those vows of chastity."

He smiled. "I don't imagine they kept them . . ."

"And you," she asked, "are you still being courtly?"

"Chaste, you mean?"

"Since the afternoon . . ."

"I do repent me," he said.

So they went up again to her cabin and this time the curtains were drawn; a pink lamp glowed softly by the bed, and the bed linen had been turned back. They kissed, and this time meant it, and she felt Lawrence stiffen against her. In silence they took off their clothes. She stepped out of her dress and unfastened her bra; he had trouble with the laces of his shoes. She kept on her slip, he his shirt. He switched off the light by the bedside and they stood together there; the darkness aided her, and alcohol, but even so she was afraid.

"Are you all right," he asked, "with this?"

Speechless, Hermia nodded. They sat. It had been so long, she wanted to say, so long since she'd been naked with another naked creature, so long since she'd been touched, had touched, she did not know how to begin. He began. He kissed her mouth, her arms, her breasts; she fingered the back of his neck. She focused on his tongue. "Doesn't this feel strange to you; does it feel familiar?"

"Mm-mn."

"I'm out of practice, a little. A lot."

"Are you all right?" he asked again.

A tenderness rose in her: "Yes."

And now in the annealing dark they touched each other, probing, uncertain, tentative, until it was as though the love they'd made when young returned as body memory; this was, he thought, the way she felt and used to feel, the way she'd looked and smelled and touched and sounded all those years ago. He leaned above her, hesitant, then dropped his head and sucked her breasts and she pressed his head to her nipples and reached for, found his penis and held and stroked it, throbbing. Her breath was sweet. She could hear herself breathe. Raising her slip up over her knees, he worked his way down past her stomach; she was dry at first and unresponsive and then slowly felt herself loosen and moisten and spread her legs to him, arching.

Somewhere deep in his throat, Lawrence sighed. She kissed him, kissed his cheek. In her mind's eye she was a girl once more and they were in each other's arms and there had been no interval, no severance or sundering; this stateroom in Valetta and the student room upstairs in Claverly had fused, were one, and when at last he entered her it felt as though they both were beginners together. Time stopped.

THE MORNING'S DEPARTURE was scheduled for six. In separate cabins they packed their suitcases and set them out in hallways for off-loading. Then, having collected their passports from the ship's purser, they left tips for the personnel and took a taxi to the airport; there they stood on numbered lines—he for the plane to Amsterdam and she for Rome. He would fly from Schiphol Airport to Detroit Metro Airport and she from

Fiumicino to Logan in Boston; he would return to Ann Arbor and she to the house on Cape Cod. Once their tickets had been processed and their luggage checked, they went through the procedures of security together.

The officials were polite. Nonetheless he divested himself of his jacket; she smiled at him as though again in her cabin, undressing, but this time on public display. Courtly, Lawrence carried her carry-on bag and offered his arm to balance her while Hermia stepped out of her shoes. She took off her coat, he his belt. They passed through the metal detector; she raised her arms, he his. Once they had dressed and collected their coats they walked into the waiting room and found an unoccupied corner beneath a plate-glass window and sat down.

The chairs were plastic, molded, and a fine mist cloaked the runway; the day promised to be fair. Do you want a coffee? he asked. She shook her head. He had asked the same thing yesterday, but somehow this morning the question seemed changed. It was the identical question, but everything had changed. She wondered if she could say this out loud, and if he would agree. The banality of travel, Lawrence was saying: a thousand years ago this would have been astonishing, a hundred years ago worth noting; now we travel for a day and cross continents or oceans and the airport is a modern common denominator for what feels like symbolic transport and no actual journey at all. There's no categorical difference, he declared, between this airport in Valetta and the one in, say, Cedar Rapids, or the airport in Kabul.

"Have you ever been to Kabul?"

He shook his head.

"Then how can you be sure of it? Sure, I mean, what the airport looks like . . ."

"I've seen photographs. We don't compare a horse and tree but might a horse and cow. So there are differences in airports and we *notice* them, but the essence of the contemporary experience of travel is the same."

"Do we have to keep talking like this?"

"No, we don't have to, I'd much rather talk about *us*."

"That's good," she said, "that's better."

"Will I see you again?" Lawrence asked.

"I've changed my mind, I could use a coffee. Do we have time?"

"Will I see you again?"

"With milk, please. And no sugar."

"In the ancient stories they ask this question three times. Thrice. Will I see you again?"

She smiled at him. "Just Google me."

"In Truro? Should I come to Truro?"

"Do you want to?"

"Yes."

IX

WHEN PAT BECAME PATRICIA, TEN, SHE WENT TO
the Pine Cobble School, and then high school in
Manchester. She attended Burr and Burton for four years. Her
friends were the children of lawyers and doctors; her grades
were good. Yet something secretive arose in her, something hidden and guarded and inward, and Hermia felt she was raising
a stranger—well, not a *stranger* exactly, she said to Anne in the
kitchen, but someone she couldn't predict. There was a time
she had known without asking the things her daughter wanted,
the things her daughter felt . . .

"It's called adolescence," said Anne, "and nothing to worry
about."

"No?"

They were stacking plates and cups.

"Or what I mean to say is *everyone* goes through it, and
though you're right to notice, there's nothing to be done."

"Of *course* there is," said Hermia, "or anyhow there ought to be; do you think she's doing drugs?"

Anne laughed. "I don't, no."

"Are you sure?"

"I'd recognize the smell of pot. And so would you."

"I didn't mean she's smoking in the house . . ."

"No, of course not. She's just restless."

"Restless?"

"The music," Anne said. "Have you noticed what she's playing?"

"Bach? Busoni?"

"The Bangles. I don't mean what she's practicing, I mean the stuff she listens to."

"Oh, *that*," said Hermia.

" 'Why don't we do it in the road?' "

They laughed. They reminded each other what it had felt like—the miserable nights when young, the nameless yearning to escape, the posters of Brando and Newman and Dean: all those hormones raging, those training bras and braces and waiting by the telephone for calls that never came. Hermia scraped the table leavings into the pail of compost and rinsed out the bottle of wine. They were relieved, they both agreed, to have put adolescence behind them and to become middle-aged.

But it was a slope that grew steeper, not flat; it grew worse and not better with time. It wasn't opposition, really, not out-and-out rebellion, but a kind of staged departure while mother and daughter drifted apart. She rarely said the word aloud but what Patricia said each time she spoke was *No. No way, not now, not ever. What you want from me is not what I want, and whatever you're asking the answer is no.* In Interlochen, Hermia knew, something had happened to her child and was happening again in school; when Patricia turned fifteen she brought home friends called Rain and Perdita and Ocean and announced, We'll be a band. You'll like our name, proclaimed the girl, we're the Radical G-String Quartet.

Max the dog turned fifteen too; he hobbled, and one eye went blind. If Hermia encouraged him to join her on a morning walk he pulled himself to his feet with difficulty, wheezing, spittle hanging from his muzzle, and after a few hundred yards would look at her with what she felt as reproach and lie down in the shade. Rain and Perdita and Ocean said, *He smells, he stinks!* Squealing together throatily, they wrinkled up their noses like the girls they pretended no longer to be; they sang "Manic Monday" and "Eternal Flame." They wore beads and bandanas and miniskirts with fringes and flea-market secondhand vests with patches saying *LOVE.*

"She has a head on her shoulders," said Anne. "I know it doesn't look like it, but the girl does have a brain . . ."

"Yes, where?"

"Don't be so hard on her."

"I'm not. I'm *not* being hard. I adore her, you know that, I'm just disappointed."

"Well, don't be. Or, at any rate, don't let her know you are."

Hermia began to say, and stopped herself, that Anne who had no children couldn't understand the way it felt to be going through this: the flesh of her flesh growing up and away, growing separate, *scornful,* aloof. If she reached out for a touch or hug, it was as though she were contagious, and Patricia shrank away. She remembered the time at the Albany Airport when she'd consigned her child to a uniformed attendant and watched them while they walked together down the jetway, disappearing: the jaunty resolution, the brave face the girl put on. She had been proud of her behavior then—how her daughter turned back and was waving—but had known already the loss was irretrievable. Once, the two of them shared everything, and now they shared nothing at all.

For *this* face was a blank. It wore purple lipstick, then black. The Bangles gave way to new models and were declared passé; the Radical G-String Quartet, next summer, patterned themselves on bands with names like Pussy-Posse and T-N-T and Slot. They wired the milk shed for sound. After breakfast every afternoon the girls clumped out of the kitchen and beat a path up through burdock and thistle, carrying their instruments and saying, "Whoa, it's *hot!*" Soon an eardrum-threatening cacophony would thump across the pasture: a bass, a drum, a saxophone, with Patricia playing keyboard, pounding away in a frenzy of elbows and tossing her dark hair down over her eyes like a creature in pain or possessed. Max followed them, then fled. "I got to get *out* of here, got to get *out*" was the refrain they caterwauled, and the only lyric Hermia could understand: all the rest was *wa wa wawaaa . . .*

THAT FALL RYAN JOFFREY ARRIVED. He did so on a motorcycle, roaring up the River Road, wearing goggles and a ponytail and reeking of patchouli and Old Spice. He played the acoustic guitar. She and Anne were horrified, but the girl admired him, and they sat together on the porch or drove the roads of Arlington or practiced in the milk house and talked about Bob Marley and Jimi Hendrix and Jim Croce and Otis Redding, the great dead. "What about Janis Joplin?" Hermia inquired, and Ryan said, "What about her?" and she said, "I was only asking," and he turned away.

His earring was a cross. He braided his ponytail thickly and had pimples all over his chin. She could not bear to picture him pawing at her daughter, her lovely corruptible child. When she did the laundry and found blood on Patricia's underwear, she said, "Honey, do you want to—don't you want to—talk to me?"

The girl shook her head.

"We need to talk," said Hermia.

"There's nothing to talk about, Mom."

"That can't be true."

Patricia turned back to her book; it was, Hermia saw, *Black Rage*.

"Okay. Except I have a question. Do you miss your father?"

"Whoa. Where'd *that* come from?"

"Nowhere. Left field."

"I don't," she said. "I don't even *know* him."

"Me either," Hermia said. "I'm not sure I would recognize the man, in an airport, I mean, or know where he's living now. And the two of us got along fine, I think, or thought, or used to, you and me, not your f-father and me"—she could hear herself stuttering, making no sense—"before all this, oh, what would you call it, *disruption*. But sometimes I wonder if there should be—should have been someone—a man in the house. Somebody adult to stand at the door."

"What are you *talking* about?"

"Ryan. Protection. I don't want you pregnant . . ."

The look she got was withering; Patricia stalked out of the room. As if on cue and by way of an answer she heard the staccato bleat of the machine in the driveway, scattering gravel and clearing its steel throat. There was a pause, an idling, and then they roared away. Ryan called his motorcycle "Hardly" and polished and buffed it to gleaming; he lived with his parents south of Rutland, which he called the sticks. "It's a downshift town," he said, "second gear and a stop sign; it's like that song the G-Strings do, 'Got to get *out* of here, gotta get *out* . . .'"

Max died. One morning Anne discovered him, in the kitchen, on his pillow bed, motionless and stiff already, with his sightless eye unblinking and pink tongue hanging down. She screamed. Hermia came running; she had been brushing her teeth. The friends clung to each other, crying, trying to comfort each other and failing until finally they knelt and stroked the shepherd's lifeless fur and placed a biscuit near his mouth as a propitiatory offering and covered him with a sheet.

They buried him that afternoon, in a trench Ryan dug by the pond. He worked uncomplainingly, and for this the women were grateful; he dug deep. The four of them stood by the grave for some minutes, burying the dog's leash and collar and a box of biscuits, taking turns with the shovel and the clumps of clay and topsoil. Then Ryan finished the job.

. . .

AFTER THIS THE HOUSE on River Road seemed less and less a haven. If Patricia did come home alone, she stayed in her room or on the phone; the piano gathered dust, unplayed, and when Hermia asked if she wanted it tuned, her daughter only shrugged. The Radical G-String Quartet ceased performing; Perdita and Rain and Ocean went their separate ways. Patricia herself seemed not to care; she said, "We weren't that good, *they* weren't that good, and it was going nowhere, *we* were going nowhere and Rain thought she was, like, God's gift to performance but it was like this ego trip and had *zip* to do with the music, okay?" When it was time to talk about college, which ones to apply to and which ones to visit, she said, "That's *your* scene, Mom."

"Whoa. Everyone . . ."

"Not *everyone* . . ."

"Well, what else would you be doing?"

"Lots of stuff."

"Like?"

"Lots of stuff."

"Is that an answer?"

"It didn't sound like a question. You weren't, like, *asking* me anything, you were just making assumptions. Me and Ryan . . ."

"Ryan?"

Patricia nodded.

"What's *he* got to do with it?"

"You asked me, right? You were asking a question."

"What I wanted to know about is what *you're* thinking. If we should be planning, oh, campus visits; you've got a counselor, don't you, an adviser with suggestions?"

"Radcliffe. Your precious Radcliffe. The place you went and expect me to go . . ."

Hermia stiffened. "I never said that."

"You didn't have to, Mom . . ."

"Never *thought* about Radcliffe," she lied. "I couldn't care less where you go."

"Then let's just forget it. Cool."

"Well, this is fun."

"What?"

"Trying to talk to you. Trying to talk *with* you. Having any sort of conversation."

"Right."

"It *used* to be so easy."

"Right."

"Oh, what's the use. Have it your way. Let Ryan be the expert here . . ."

But Ryan too stopped visiting, and soon there was someone called Danny who went to Keene Valley Community College, then someone called Pete, then Jimbo, great hulking boys with Mohawks who thumped up the stairs of the porch. She tried to tell them apart. She wanted to ask what had happened to Ryan and to have a conversation with her daughter, or just to be easy with silence. But it felt impossible; the silence was not easy, and she couldn't bring herself to ask about Danny or Pete or Jimbo, their interchangeable bodies, their faces like boxes, their lives in the workaday world.

That autumn Anne moved out. She rented the top floor of

a two-family home in North Bennington, down the street from Prospect School. She was bone-weary, she told Hermia, of driving back and forth to work—especially in winter, especially alone. "I can't handle it," said Anne, "not being with him in the house, not having him here—Max, I mean. It's just too sad, too much a reminder, I need not to be here, okay?"

"Okay."

"Try to understand," said Anne, and explained herself at length. She didn't want to be the uninvited guest, the one who came to dinner who moved in all those years ago, and needed to move on. It was 1991. She had planned to stay maybe a weekend, a week; *now* look at us, she said. Those car trips with Patricia, when she was at the Prospect School, well, it wasn't exactly *commuting*, but it did feel like company, and *this* was, wasn't it, a kind of empty-nest syndrome, an empty front seat twice each day, and she needed to move into town. She would leave her rocker in the living room because they had bought it together, that time up in Hartland Four Corners, and keep her brown rice and wok in the kitchen, since she was planning to use them whenever she drove back to visit, not planning to leave in a *serious* way, just making some space for herself. She was forty-nine years old and needed her own private space.

Hermia too felt ready for a change. And though the women stayed in touch they were no longer intimate; the things that had united them—a dog to walk, a child to raise—no longer could be shared. It was, she told herself, a period of transition, a period to get through, and sooner or later—the sooner the better—Patricia would come to her senses and return to her old ways. It was, she thought, a long wakeful nightmare, a dream she would have to endure.

BUT THIS WAS A DREAM she couldn't stop dreaming, a nightmare she failed to escape. One afternoon in the kitchen, when Hermia was baking bread—the loaves in their pans rising—her seventeen-year-old brushed past, wearing boots with so much mud in the treads that everywhere she stepped turned brown, and there were pebbles and straw on the rug.

"You could, couldn't you, take off your shoes? Would it be too much trouble?"

"Yeah."

"Yeah, what?"

"I could."

"Well, all right, take them off."

"Except I'm heading out again."

"Oh, where?"

"Out."

"Don't overdo it, darling, don't be *too* much a caricature. You sound like you've been practicing."

"For what?"

"For the part of the insolent child. The one with no manners . . ."

"Fuck manners."

"Excuse me?"

"You *heard* me. Fuck manners."

She could hear herself breathing. "And why?"

"Because I *live* here," said the girl. "It has nothing to do with good manners."

Spring and Fall

"The mud . . ."

"If housekeeping's *your* thing, why don't you clean it up?"

She gripped the tabletop. "You're doing this on purpose, right?"

"Not *purpose*, Mom. I walked into the kitchen, that's all."

"And can walk right out again."

"You mean it?"

"Yes."

"You hear what you're saying?"

"Yes."

"You won't try to stop me? Take no for an answer?"

She shook her head.

"Okay."

AND THAT WAS THE END OF IT. It had been Wednesday the fifteenth of April 1992. Patricia grabbed her hat and parka from the hanger in the pantry—the straw hat with the turkey feather and green parka stitched with *PEACE*—and slammed the door and clattered away down the steps. There was the now-familiar noise of an engine starting, a door that opened, slammed again, a spray of gravel in the driveway and music thumping, blaring, and the loud acceleration of the car that bore her off. Hermia barely saw it disappear—big, dented, maybe ten years old—and did not go outside but stayed in the kitchen and watched through the window where there were muslin curtains and bread loaves rising in their pans and a pot of geraniums blooming; she'd been so furious she wouldn't, *couldn't* trust her memory for details, but was certain the car had been brown.

When policemen asked her, later, if she happened to notice the make of the car, or the license plate number, or state, she shook her head. She hadn't been paying attention, or paying *that* kind of attention; she had been dealing with anger and cleaning the mud off the floor. She could describe Patricia. She did this with precision, and also the hat and the parka and the stone-washed jeans and boots. The parka was dark green, from L. L. Bean. The letters *PEACE* were yellow, maybe six inches tall, and had been stitched across her daughter's chest, with *PE* on one side of the zipper and *ACE* on the other; her daughter stood five foot ten. Her daughter had black hair.

But Hermia waited to file a report, thinking the girl would return. The first night felt no different from other nights of waiting, of staying awake and falling asleep exhausted and waking up at two or three or four a.m. when a car rumbled into the drive. The first day had been no different—a list of griev-ances, a mounting rage—and she in fact expected Patricia to come back. All Thursday she pursued the argument—those tracks on the floor, the heedless self-absorption, that "Fuck manners, Mom"—and came up with right things to say, the way to deal with accusation and make her answer clear.

It was then she most missed Max, and Anne, their shared companionship. Always before, she'd had company, waiting, and someone to complain to or sit up with through the night. Anne would have distracted her; they would have talked and shared herb tea and built a fire in the winter, if the living room felt cold. Max had been a watchdog, and he would hear a car on River Road a long time before its arrival. His tail would wag or he would bark in welcome or in warning, and all his life—

even near the end of it, even fat and blind—make his loud way to the door. Now Hermia sat by herself, by the window and the telephone, while her daughter refused to come back.

The second night *was* different, and she had trouble sleeping, sitting in the rocking chair and waiting for a car, or call, or any sort of sign, and hearing the house silence envelop her like noise. Then it became Friday evening, but often before on a weekend Patricia had what she said was a sleepover date, with friends at whose houses she slept. Her child was not a missing person, Hermia assured herself, not yet. She thought about the way that she herself escaped a house—their old apartment in New York—and how the wheel had come full circle and would continue to turn.

The police were dutiful. They answered her questions and came to the door and took her deposition at their headquarters out on Route 7 and distributed flyers in Bennington and Manchester. But it was clear this had happened before: a runaway girl is no sort of story, and there are teenagers all over the county who leave home, then show up again. Odds are—they tried to comfort her—your daughter is just fine. They would look, of course, and keep on looking, but she should try not to worry; there was no evidence of kidnapping or violence. They would, they promised, stay on the case and update, on a weekly basis, the Missing Persons Report.

Night after night she waited; day after day she drove the streets of Manchester and parked at the entrance to Burr and Burton, or went inside and interviewed Patricia's teachers and her friends and college guidance counselor. None of them had anything useful to report, or any information. She drove to

Williamstown and Rutland, and managed to find Ryan there and ask what he'd heard; his blank stare was convincing, however, and he could offer no help. He always had been a know-nothing, and now he knew nothing at all.

Some nights she slept in Patsy's room, hoping the girl's restless spirit would declare itself, her breath rise from the pillow as it once had done routinely, her body's leavings—hair, a fingernail, foot scrapings—emerge from the clothes closet or the carpet or the dresser shelves. Some mornings she wore Patsy's clothes. If she waited very quietly, and closed her eyes and held her breath, she felt a second presence breathing in the room; if she could only *locate* it, she told herself, her daughter could be found. Fingernail parings and old clothes and scent all seemed to her a proof of life: her daughter was alive. And some deep part of her stayed calm; she would have known, she told herself, if her child was in danger or—worst-case scenario—harmed. Worst-case scenario of all, of course, was more than mere danger or physical harm, but this she refused to believe.

On Memorial Day the telephone rang. Hermia was gardening, dealing with the first spring peas, which needed to be thinned and staked; then when she came inside there was a message from Patricia, saying, *Mom, it's me, don't worry, I'm okay, I'm just fine.* The red message light on the machine was blinking; the call had been made seven minutes before, but there was no telephone number. She pressed star 69, because she had been told star 69 would reconnect to a previous number and return a call. But there was only a buzzing, a blankness, and then a mechanical voice announcing, *If you'd like to make a call . . .*

Next week another message came: *Hello again, it's me, don't worry, I miss you, I'm okay.* The week after that: *Mom, I'm fine.* It was uncanny, nearly, the way the girl would telephone the few times Hermia left the house, or hang up if she answered—just a pause, a breath, a click. The relief was enormous, of course. The relief was the important thing, and she tried to tell herself her daughter would return. She recorded a new message of her own—*Patricia, please tell me the best way to reach you*—but decided not to offer money or to ask for a telephone number or to plead *Come home!*

There were five calls by September, and then a postcard with a postmark out of Santa Fe, and by the time the card arrived Hermia was angry. What had she done to deserve this, she wondered; why hadn't her daughter just come out and said it: *Mom, you're making it too hard to stay here, I don't* want *to be a musician, I'm not good enough for Radcliffe*—or however she'd explain herself; *Mom, time to set out on my own.* Why couldn't the girl be straightforward, she wondered; what was this need for secrecy? *I* need *my space*, Patricia wrote, *I* need *to not be anybody's family for a little while. I'm well, I'm learning a lot, I hope you're okay too.*

In October she hired a private detective with an office down in Bennington, but he was incompetent, a waste of time and money. She did not begrudge the money or time yet hated the way he made his report: the ignorance, the lewd suggestiveness and back-alley speculation there had been drug dealers involved. The trail is cold, declared the detective—and used that expression, *The trail has gone cold*—but he could warm it up again, he promised, if she wanted to keep trying and was willing to keep paying. Hermia said no.

The autumn leaves were dull, and fell, and winter came early and stayed. The snow was unremitting. When her horoscope read, "A person very dear to you will come into your life again," she cut this out of the paper and pasted it on the refrigerator door. "All is not lost," she read next week. "What you believed you'd lost you'll find." This too she cut out and kept.

Then as the months and months rolled by she stopped awaiting news with the same urgency; the police said the same thing always: they had no tips, no leads, and there was nothing new. She posted a reward. She took out a post office box for the purpose, but it was stuffed with misery: requests for help, long rambling letters from strangers blaming Jews or godlessness or crack cocaine, advice that she *Trust in the Lord*. From time to time a person called, but what they wanted was money, and their clues were worthless; they told their own sad stories, and in March she withdrew the reward.

SHE HAD TO LEAVE VERMONT. When a year had gone completely past and it was April 15 once more, Hermia knew she could no longer wait in the creaking, wheezing house alone. Vermont had seemed a refuge once, a place of safety and escape, but now it offered no refuge. She did not sell the house, because her daughter might return to it, but could not bear to live alone through spring and summer, fall and winter in this place again. The year she'd waited felt like ten, the seasons were interminable, and she knew she could not last it out through 1993. Instead she thought about the house in Truro, empty all this time except for summer rentals, and where she had been happy once when young.

Anne called. "You're leaving?"

"Yes."

"How long?"

"I don't really know yet . . ."

"I don't really blame you."

"Blame?"

"You know what I mean, Herm, it's like when Max died. *I* couldn't hack it."

"She's not dead."

"I'm sorry, of course not. That's not what I was saying."

The receiver crackled; there was static on the line.

"Would you rent the place out, maybe?"

"No."

"Take care of yourself, okay?"

"Okay. Thanks for calling, I'll try."

It surprised her how easy it was just to leave, how little she needed to do. She arranged for the mail to be forwarded and changed the telephone message to say *I'm on the Cape.* She took more than a parka and rain hat, of course, but what she packed for Truro barely filled the Volvo, and Robin, the caretaker, promised to check on the furnace. He drained the pipes and lowered the heat and fastened the shutters upstairs. Robin stopped by once a week to check the lights and windows; he mowed the lawn when the grass grew and raked the leaves in autumn and kept the driveway plowed. The house on River Road had lasted, Hermia told herself, two hundred years without her, and it could last a few more.

She called her mother in England to explain about the move. Her mother was a widow now, and inattentive, fading, saying, "That's nice, dear," routinely. She was growing deaf as well and complained about the phone. She kept saying, "What? Speak up, don't *mumble*," and it was hard to know for certain what she understood or failed to. Hermia did not discuss Patricia, nor did her mother ask; "Give my best to the Baileys," she said. The Baileys—Frank and Annabelle—had been their neighbors in Truro in 1959 and were long since divorced. Frank Bailey had remarried, and Annabelle Bailey was dead.

After the first shock of it—on arrival, Hermia thought, *How small, how dark*—the house in Truro too proved simple to arrange. She unpacked and stocked the pantry shelves with what she'd brought from Arlington. Fortunately, the previous winter, she had had the interior painted, and the walls were freshly white and the wood floors of the living room and parlor and the staircase gleamed. Her father's presence filled the place—his paintings on the walls, the portrait he had done of her when six years old, with Tigger, the Ekoi mask above the fireplace and even an unopened case of bottles of Jack Daniel's on his studio closet floor. These totems of her youth were, if not comforting, familiar; there was a great deal to cherish, and she felt her spirits lift. She remembered dinner parties, dancing parties, the ruckus of celebration when her father was finished with work.

The ghost of Lawrence welcomed her also, waiting on the couch. The braided rug, the trundle bed, the bathtub, each re-

vealed him; as before, he raised his arms. She remembered
making love with him that first time he had seen the place, in
her childhood bedroom, standing up. Hermia remembered
walking together down to the beach, and how he offered his
peacoat in the offshore wind. Now she was fifty-one. It all had
happened years ago but still felt like yesterday: the key on the
nail by the woodpile, the way they'd warmed each other, the
slap of flesh on flesh . . .

She had had no other lovers on the Cape. In Vermont
there'd been some months of pleasure with a lawyer up in
Manchester who met her at the Equinox Hotel and whose
marriage, he assured her, was a marriage in name only. For a
while she had been hopeful, had felt the first stirrings of yearning, but then his wife gave him an ultimatum: either divorce or
fidelity, and he had had to choose. He had chosen the latter, of
course.

The chimney needed pointing, and a mason came and
dealt with it; his cousin pruned the apple trees and left a stack
of applewood to season for the winter. She trimmed the climbing roses and had someone from Consider the Lilies clear the
flower beds. The house began to breathe again, to feel lived in
and welcoming, and she always kept a lamp lit in the living
room and played music while she cooked.

She joined a reading group. She volunteered for meals-on-
wheels, and the Safe House Auxiliary Service, and she mar-
veled at how rapidly the weeks and years went by. People
offered her five hundred thousand dollars for the house. Then
they offered her a million dollars, then two million dollars; then

the real estate agents said just name your price. You don't understand, said Hermia, I *live* here, I don't plan to sell. When the days and weeks felt empty, it was easy enough to fill them, and she was astonished, a little, the year that she turned sixty, by how easily she'd settled in and down.

At JAMS and the post office Hermia met old friends. Time had bent and altered them, but not beyond recognition, and she felt at home on the Cape. There were sculptors and poets and retired airplane pilots and State Department officials from the Kennedy administration; there were, it seemed, psychiatrists and psychoanalysts in every house on Bound Brook Island or on the rise of Corn Hill. One man, Arturo Tucci, had been a painter-friend of her father's, and he said, "My dear, I'd like to paint you. If you're able to sit still, that is, I'm a creature of habit and cannot be rushed."

Arturo was seventy-six. After years of realistic landscapes, his seascapes grew abstract and he became a colorist; now, he said, he was doing portraits because only faces continued to be interesting; did Hermia agree? He had done a series of portraits—line drawings, charcoal sketches, watercolors, oils—of his wife, Irene, and when she died three years ago he'd been, he said, unable to keep working. He couldn't paint for months. He hated his easel, his studio, *everything;* he couldn't hold a brush. He turned the collection of portraits of his wife's face to the wall.

Then he decided what he had to do before he died was travel; they had always hoped to see the Hermitage in St. Petersburg, and he procured a visa and took a bus from Wellfleet to Hyannis and then to Logan Airport and flew from

Boston to Frankfurt and from Frankfurt on to St. Petersburg as a present to himself for his seventy-fifth birthday. As a way of doing by himself what he and Irene had planned to do together, he visited the Hermitage, that astonishing collection of impressionists—Bonnard, Utrillo, and the greatest of them all, Matisse!—until he started dreaming in color and decided to come home.

Since then, Arturo said, the only important thing was faces, and he wanted to paint hers. She took this as a compliment and drove to his studio daily; he greeted her with a piece of short-bread and a cup of tea and sat her down in Irene's chair and told her, "No more talking now." Then he commenced to draw. In the chair, in the north-facing light and the embrasure of the window, with this elderly painter observing her, his hand moving over the canvas as though disembodied, Hermia felt young again, and wished she had a dog to pet, a blanket on her knees. He squinted, frowned; he shut first one eye then the other; he peered at her intensely. But he was dissatisfied, he told her; there was something missing in the face, some expression he couldn't get right. Often, she would return for a sitting to find the canvas painted over or a new one waiting, blank.

His hair was white, his eyebrows too, and when he finished the day's labor he would shake himself free as though from a dream, and say, "Another cup of tea?" and she would make it for him, at ease in his old kitchen. Then they would talk. Arturo knew many people on the outer Cape, and he regaled her with gossip: who was well or ill or sleeping with whom or who had gone bankrupt or mad.

. . .

THE OPEN WOUND OF HER DAUGHTER'S DISAPPEARANCE closed over, a little, with time. It did not truly heal, of course, but when she thought about it now she thought of Patricia as someone in childhood, not as a woman turning twenty and then twenty-five. To think of her lost darling was like fingering scar tissue or pressing on a bruise. She rented out then sold the house on River Road. Hermia entered into the community of Truro—its close-knit full-time residents, its summer cele-brants—as she had never, quite, in Arlington; her parents had been famous here, and she'd learned to ride a bike and drive a car along the side roads by the beach. And when the letters came each year—on her birthday or at Christmas—she read the nothing they told her as if the lines came from a stranger (*I'm fine, I like it here, I've been working as a temp and sometimes I bor-row a piano; I know you're on the Cape, I hope you're okay, I'll be in touch again soon*), and folded and preserved the letters in a leather folder on her writing desk. There was never a return address or way to answer back; it was a one-way conversation and there was nothing to say . . .

Her neighbors Bill and Helen Watts returned from a cruise of the Mediterranean, and had had a wonderful time. They in-vited her to dinner, along with the Wilsons and Banners and Arturo, and bored everyone all evening with the details of their itinerary, the cities and sites they had visited; they returned with a bottle of grappa purchased duty-free in Fiumicino, and they poured everyone grappa and set up a screen in the living room and showed an assortment of slides. "*This* is Vesuvius," said Bill, "and *this* is the town of Pompeii; *this* is where we had that guide—what was his name, Helen?—who kept announcing, remember, 'We are making refreshments out of antiquity.' Each time we visited a temple or stopped at an excavation our guide said, 'We are making *refreshments* out of antiquity,' and he wasn't joking. Remember how much fun we had in Naples, how perfect the weather was for us every single day?"

Arturo had fallen asleep. The Wilsons and the Banners too sat stuporous in armchairs, nodding, and so Bill and Helen turned to Hermia, insisting that she take the trip. They talked about Sardinia and Sicily; they believed a trip like theirs would be just the ticket, exactly what Hermia needed, and they went on and on about the excitement of sightseeing, the value of a change of scene. Are you auditioning for the job of cruise director, she wanted to ask, do you get a commission?

But Bill and Helen were unstoppable, laughing together and reminding each other about what they'd eaten and done. The two of them meant well, of course, and poured out the last of the grappa and continued to show slides of blue-green water and white temples and each other smiling in front of each *"bella vista."* Bill translated the phrase repeatedly, saying it meant "pretty view," and they'd had a spectacular time.

At evening's end, to silence them, she promised to look into it, and the next day a travel agent in Orleans called her, saying, "Your friends the Watts suggested I should get in touch and send you some details, okay?"

"Okay," said Hermia, and two days later a brochure arrived. To her own surprise she found herself reading it with interest: the cruise would last two weeks. Except for visits to her mother in England—who no longer recognized her and to whom it made no difference, seemingly, if she were in the room—she'd not left the country at all. It would be a change of pace, a change of landscape mostly, and Hermia reserved a cabin for the trip.

X

1973

W HEN HE TOOK THE JOB IN ANN ARBOR HE RENTED
an apartment near the farmers' market. Lawrence
liked the town, its coffee shops and jazz bars and, everywhere,
its low-key midwestern affability. As half-time adjunct assistant
professor in the architecture program he made friends on the
faculty and with those who worked downtown—designers and
lawyers and real estate developers who asked him to join them
at lunch. There were concerts and basketball games to attend;
there were parties to go to and give. On his thirty-third birthday he joined a health club and started to work out four mornings a week; he enjoyed the anonymity, the nodding
acquaintance with men on adjacent machines.

Again he wrote steadily, liking his classes and liking the students, preparing his lectures with care. They would, he believed, make a book. His course Public and Private Space was

popular, and his editorial "Urbanism and the Public Realm" was published in *Architectural Record;* this pleased him very much. Lawrence divided his time between the Art and Architecture Building and the local firm of Spence & Mills Design Group, spending Monday, Wednesday, and Friday afternoons on North Campus and the rest of the workweek downtown. At times—consulting on a shopping mall or the condominium complex adjacent to the golf course—he wondered what had happened to ambition. Early on he'd hoped to change the shape of things, to be a kind of Frank Lloyd Wright or Buckminster Fuller of his own generation; now here he was producing drawings for a downtown four-story parking garage . . .

Still, he felt at home in Ann Arbor; the city paid attention to its common space and parks. There were walkways by the river and playing fields and bridges where the students clustered, a pond out on North Campus where he sat and smoked. On fair days he would walk or jog through Gallup Park along the Huron River, and sometimes he drove out to Baseline Lake or Whitmore Lake and rented a canoe. He met his second wife in the Arboretum, drawing a willow tree with its roots exposed on the bank of the river. Janet was sitting on a blanket, and he stopped and praised the way she rendered sprigs of willow leaves.

Silent, she smiled and returned to her work. She was wearing a tie-dyed wraparound skirt and a T-shirt with a toxin sign.

"Do you do this for a living?" Lawrence asked. He introduced himself.

Squinting, she looked up at him; he was standing in the sun. She had a clipboard and a sketch pad and set of drawing pencils.

"I'm sorry, I don't want to interrupt . . ."

"But you're interrupting anyway," she said, and offered her hand. "Janet. Janet Atwan."

"I mean, you're very good at this."

"You're standing in my light."

"Oh, sorry. Is that a suggestion?"

"It is." Again she bent back to her work.

IN YEARS TO COME he remembered the line, the way she instructed him to step aside. It was, Janet told him, a quote. Alexander the Great once made a pilgrimage to the beggar Cynic Diogenes, asking the seated man what he desired; you have only to ask for a favor, said the reverential emperor, and it will be conferred. The philosopher had answered—or so the story went—with the phrase she repeated to Lawrence: *Get out of my light, Lord, I'm cold.*

All through their marriage it felt the same way: he standing, smiling, praising her, and she beneath him, elsewhere-focused, saying what bitter Diogenes said: *You're casting a shadow. Move on.*

Janet had her own career and proved successful at it, working as a bookkeeper for an insurance firm, and then as a certified public accountant, and then preparing taxes for well-heeled individuals and corporations in town. There were years she earned as much as him, and years when she earned more. But always she seemed to be nursing a grievance, always reminding him how much things cost—not in financial so much as emotional terms—and what she gave up to have sons.

They produced two of them—Andrew, then John—and in

1977 purchased a one-story home on a two-acre lot in Ann Arbor Hills. As the children grew, so did the house; Lawrence remodeled it, building a wing to the rear. He designed a series of glass-enclosed bedrooms facing the woodlot, gesturing at Philip Johnson's Glass House but from a respectful distance— as Johnson had gestured at Mies. There were skylights and freestanding chimneys and a wraparound Florida porch.

At Janet's urging, when Andrew turned three, they acquired a golden retriever the family named Daisy, and then a cat named Peek-a-Boo and hamsters and a parakeet and, until it grew too large to keep, an alligator called Rex. When the boys were old enough for school, and if the weather was pleasant, he and Daisy walked them there, through tree-shaded winding streets. The neighborhood children cried "Daisy" and ran to pet her fearlessly; she wagged her tail and rolled on the ground and let them scratch her belly and pull at her soft ears.

Lawrence liked being a "dad." He had many happy memories—games of Frisbee on the lawn, the barbecue he built himself, springtime dinners at the picnic table where white azalea bushes and rhododendron bloomed. When he collected his children from school, they were always glad to see him and, hurtling out the door, would rush into his arms. He liked helping with their homework: the spelling and arithmetic and the building projects with cardboard and construction paper; he fashioned, in the basement, a platform for Lionel trains. It was bilevel, with tunnels and hills, and they spent hours together downstairs establishing freight yards and passenger stations and ramps. Fixing lunch for his sons was a pleasing routine: the peanut butter sandwiches and potato chips and chocolate chip cookies and boxes of fruit juice he packed into brown bags. They drove to the Toledo Zoo and Greenfield Village and the Henry Ford Museum when Catherine came to visit, on those rare occasions Annie sent her east. He tried very hard to be faithful and to make his marriage a success.

But there were women everywhere: the lighting designer from Cleveland, the client from Grosse Pointe Shores in the throes of a divorce, the secretary in the office of the dean of engineering who wore tight skirts to work. Over time, it seemed to him, Janet grew more and more distant—preferring her Monday Quilting Club or Saturday morning Live Model Class to staying home with him at night or staying, on weekends, in bed. He told himself he needed sex more often than she, more urgently, and if he lived in France or Argentina there would have been no stigma in acquiring a mistress; it would have been *expected,* and not an issue at home.

The woman from Grosse Pointe Shores owned a building site in Petoskey and asked him to design a lakefront house on the property. She had been referred to him because of his experience with solar panels and the Breuer house in Wellfleet, of which he'd made a model and on which he'd lectured in class. She came to his office in North Campus, saying, "Money's not an issue, not *at* issue anyhow, the main thing is getting it right. Don't you agree?"

He agreed. He asked her what she wanted, and she told him what she did and did not want—how she thought of the new structure as a getaway, a hideaway, a place to be alone. "I *vont* to be alone," she said, imitating Greta Garbo, and then she laughed and said, "Not really, that isn't at all *vat I vont.*"

They made a site visit together, driving north, and that night she came to his hotel room with a bottle of white wine and said, "I'm lonely, aren't you lonely?" and undid her blouse. Her name was Marianne, and her husband turned out to prefer—to have a marked preference for—men. It undermined her self-esteem to be so obviously not the partner he wanted; did Lawrence find her attractive and would he object if she took off the rest of her clothes?

He did find her attractive and did not object. She was passionate beneath him, scratching at his neck and back, and he felt young again and somehow deserving, as though all of those days making breakfast for the children and all of those nights doing homework had earned him this session with reckless Marianne in bed. In the morning he visited her room instead, and they took a shower together, and she turned around and soaped herself and fitted him inside her, saying, "This is what Nathaniel likes."

"Nathaniel?"

"Nat. Mr. Soon-to-Be Ex."

When he returned to Ann Arbor Janet appeared not to notice the welts on his neck, and he settled back to his routine with a briefly slaked desire; he was solicitous with the boys and did the grocery shopping when tax time approached and his wife worked overtime. Lawrence remodeled the home of the man who owned the Porsche and Volkswagen dealership and then the loft of a couple who owned Main Street Music; he too spent long hours at work. But often he pictured Marianne beneath him, her brazen nakedness, and although she decided not to pursue the beach-house project, he did try to see her again.

She refused. When he called from the office, she said, "It's a bad idea, it would be too damn confusing, and anyhow we've gotten back together. Me and Nat, I mean, we're going to give it the old college try." To solace himself he slept with Dana, the lighting designer, after her presentation on North Campus, in the motel she was staying in off Plymouth Road. She too was ardent, unrestrained, and when she left for Cleveland she said that she'd had a good time. "I'll see you next fall," Dana said. "Or you could visit me in Cleveland, if you want . . ."

Again for a month he felt happy at home, and that spring he planted a vegetable garden on the flat lawn up above the barbecue. He did not fence it, however, and rabbits and groundhogs ravaged the lettuce and beans. Daisy ran after them fruitlessly, too fat and slow to catch her prey but enthusiastic nevertheless at the prospect of the chase. While John and Andrew watched TV he sat out at the picnic table, sketching a plan for a sauna; Janet joined him with a gin and tonic and a plate of cheese.

"This isn't working, is it?"

"What?"

"Marriage," she said. "Our marriage."

"Excuse me?"

"You know what I'm saying. You heard me."

"No."

"No you didn't hear me, or no it isn't working?"

"No, I'm not certain I know what you mean."

"Come off it, Lawrence."

"No, really . . ."

She offered him cheese. There was Stilton on crackers, a wedge of Emmenthaler and sliced Brie. "Dana called."

"Who?"

"Dana. She seemed surprised you had a wife. She tried to pretend the number was wrong, but I told her she was right. Correct, I mean, to think you won't be married soon."

"What are you *talking* about?" He looked at his sketch.

Janet took his pencil from the picnic table and reached across and x'd out the drawing thickly, twice.

"You don't want a sauna?"

"Denial. You've been into denial for *years*. Just because we don't discuss it doesn't mean I haven't noticed."

"What?"

"How unhappy you are, Lawrence. And how unhappy you make me."

"I do?"

"How we don't belong together, never did . . ."

Janet drained her glass, then emptied it out on the grass. She seemed matter-of-fact and bemused by his shock, explaining herself to him as to a child; she had known about his escapades, his little adventures, his—the word for it was—*flings*. Ann Arbor was too small a town for him to keep behavior hidden and she didn't love him, hadn't ever loved him maybe, didn't think she could forgive him and wanted a divorce. They had done what they could to pretend marriage worked and they belonged together, but in fact and all along they should have stayed apart. They had made a mistake getting married, and for a while, for the sake of the children, she'd tried very hard to ignore her unhappiness and to hope things would improve. But it wasn't working, wouldn't work, it was no favor to the children and they'd all get over it; she wanted him out of the house. This is, she said, the end of it; I need to get on with my life.

HIS OWN, he decided, had gone wrong. The schedules that his children kept no longer seemed to require him, the noise that once seemed a distraction now was a fuss he missed. Lawrence drank. He mourned the clattering ruckus of domesticity, the busy jumble of the house. In his furnished apartment on Ann Street, he tried to focus on his work, writing an essay on postmodernism in which he praised Moore, Graves, and Tigerman, also acknowledging Venturi in "this rejection of the Modern Movement." Watching his sons play baseball or soccer, he kept his distance in the stands; he slept again with Dana, but the edge of desire had dulled. He was forty-eight years old, a bachelor, assailed by a sense of the passage of time and how it was passing him by; he consulted a therapist, twice.

The sessions were not a success. He positioned himself on a brown leather couch while the therapist—Alan McDiarmid, who had been recommended by a colleague—sat in a BarcaLounger. McDiarmid had a close-shaved head but thick black eyebrows and a mustache and attentive, purse-lipped expression; during the second visit he interrupted Lawrence, saying, "Let's get to the point."

"I'm not sure I know what you mean . . ."

"Meaning?"

"*Point.* Does there *have* to be something I'm after? Some problem I'm supposed to solve?"

"Well, why else are you here? Why did you make an appointment?"

"I thought maybe . . ."

The therapist seemed impatient. "Yes?"

"Maybe what I'm going through is, you know, representative? A predictable pattern in middle-aged men? A rite of passage, somehow . . ."

The wall clock audibly ticked. There were leather-bound books and a gaslit fireplace and above it a framed painting of a stag bending down at the edge of a lake; outside, there was traffic on Liberty Street. Lawrence coughed; he had been trying to decide, he said, if he wanted a permanent teaching position, if he should go up for tenure or be mainly a practitioner. He was at a turning point, he told McDiarmid, some sort of— what would you call it?—fork in the road, and could use help with directions.

"Oh?"

"What I'm trying to describe," he said, "is everything feels out of sync—like one of those movies with bad splicing. Bad *editing* maybe. I open my mouth and language comes out, except the audio is poorly dubbed, and there's a difference—a split-second difference—between what the character says and how his mouth moves. It just isn't right . . ."

"You called yourself a character." The man seemed unconvinced.

"Did I?"

"Why?" McDiarmid made a note. "Why would you do that, I wonder."

"Do what?"

"Why do you *think* you use the third person? Or talk about bad editing? You mean you're not able to say what you mean?"

He shook his head. "It's just I feel so far away from what I dreamed of early on, from who I thought I'd be, or be with."

"And this feels like a problem?"

"Almost everything feels like a problem, but none of it touches me really. I'm not really here, if you know what I mean."

"No . . ."

McDiarmid's therapeutic style, he recognized at last, was confrontational. "No *what?*" Lawrence asked.

"Who did you think you'd be with?"

"Does it matter?"

"If you think it does."

"This conversation makes no sense. All I do these days is work, and even the work isn't working . . ."

"Oh?"

Now he repeated what Janet had said: "We don't belong together, never did."

STILL, HIS TIME WITH THE THERAPIST clarified things; he decided to stay in Ann Arbor. On the basis of two P/A Awards and *Ekistics and the Common Space*, the College of Architecture and Urban Planning proposed him for tenure; in 1991 he became a full professor. This promotion gratified him to a degree he found surprising, and he told the dean how thankful he was for the vote of confidence. "It's a slam dunk," said the dean. "We didn't break a sweat . . ."

While the boys remained in town he tried to be an active father, attending practice sessions and tournaments and concerts and carpooling with the other parents and paying the Greenhills tuition. With Janet's grudging permission he took them out on rafting trips and, for Tigers games, to Detroit. They liked the Detroit Lions also, and he bought a set of tickets, but the games were cold, and long, and the Lions rarely won. Lawrence solaced himself with the notion that all children sooner or later leave home, but in the case of *his* children the process had been reversed.

While his daughter was in college they saw each other often; Catherine enrolled in Oberlin, a three-hour drive away. She and her friends spent weekends in Ann Arbor, and if he himself went out of town he left her the key to the place. "Daddy-cool," her roommates called him, and this pleased him mightily, though he could not escape the suspicion that the nickname was intended as a joke. By junior year she began to display her mother's pampered recklessness; he worried for her safety and—when she argued with him—what he thought of as poor judgment. "Please be careful," he would say, watching irritation play across his daughter's face. Still, he urged Catherine not to drink and drive or trust in "the kindness of strangers"—Annie's phrase for casual sex—and, though he dared not be specific or too stern a moralist, could not keep from warning her about the risks she ran.

"Don't think I'm being . . ."

"Being what?"

"Oh, I don't know. Censorious?"

"A censor?"

"Someone you have to keep secrets from. Or someone you need to *behave* for."

"Why would I think that?" Catherine shook her golden mane at him and shrugged and turned away.

Then the boys too left for college and ceased being in regular contact. How did it happen, Lawrence asked himself, that the person in the mirror was sprouting liver spots and wrinkles and hair in his nostrils and ears? How did it happen that his wives and children found him an irrelevance, a stranger to be tolerated and, when possible, avoided? His waistline had thickened, his neck too, and he found himself comparing the price of real estate and cars and clothes with prices he remembered from a quarter of a century before. Increasingly he worried that the world of pleasure that once seemed so available was closed to him, foreclosed.

He went to his thirtieth Harvard reunion and reported to the tent where his classmates gathered, putting on badges and hats. They seemed old and fat or wizened and bald; at first he believed he had made a mistake and gone to the wrong tent. The class representatives had no difficulty recognizing him, however, and handed him his "welcome" folder and slapped him on the back.

There were panels and speeches and parties; on Friday night there was a dance. Turn by turn he danced with classmates' wives and trophy wives and classmates, trying to enjoy himself, full of self-pity and Scotch. Next morning, nursing a headache, he sat on a panel on urban revitalization, comparing Newark and Birmingham and Atlanta and dealing with the three cities in terms of city planning and the shift in profile of their population base. Lawrence took the position that the cutting edge of architecture was a serrated blade, or ought to be, and that what Dean Sert accomplished in the 1960s had been a conscious agenda: the Harvard Square they all dimly remembered was a kind of shadow footprint in the traffic pattern today. When it came his turn to talk he reached for the microphone and, remembering the couplet from Samuel Beckett, recited it: *Spend the years of learning squandering courage for the years of wandering . . .*

"That girl of yours," someone asked him at lunch. "Whatever happened to her?"

"Who?"

"What *was* she called, I can't remember. The one with all that hair, what, Harriet? Henrietta?"

"Hermia?"

"*Hermia.* Right."

"I don't know," Lawrence admitted. "We've dropped out of touch."

"Me, I've got grandchildren," said the man. "Five of them. Amazing, isn't it—remember that old Latin saying, *Tempus, fugit.*" He laughed. "Bottoms up. It's what I tell my grandsons, bottoms up."

"Where are you living, Larry?" asked Tim Bell. Tim Bell wore a blazer and wide crimson tie.

"Ann Arbor."

"Oh. Retired yet?"

"Not yet."

"We've just done it," said Tim Bell. "The missus and me and *Betty* makes three." He smiled. Then he explained that

Betty was a forty-foot sloop, a rig he had brought up to Camden and was planning to sail back to Tortola before hurricane season, then winter over in the Virgins, and he told the others at the table there was nothing like it, nothing like a sailboat with a favoring breeze and the British Virgin Islands—Tortola, Virgin Gorda and the rest—for pleasure-cruising, push come to shove; the Drake Channel made everything worth it, those *years* at the office spent sucking it up.

"I never would have figured you for the retiring type," said Sammy Lax, and everybody laughed.

"Did you say *Virgin* Gorda?" asked a man whose name he did not recognize. "Is that the one where the resort is Little Dix? No *wonder* it's still virgin—get it?—the Rock Resort is only Little *Dix*?"

Lawrence tried to join in the general merriment, but could not. The men were wearing crimson caps, the women crimson scarves. He looked around him at the dining tent—this herd of well-dressed, well-fed citizens—and asked himself how he arrived at this place and how youth had drifted away . . .

FOR THREE YEARS he served as chair of the Architecture Program, dealing with issues of recruitment and curricular reform and retention of lecturers and the President's Planning Advisory Commission for the allocation of campus space. He wrote and taught. There was a kind of comfort in imperatives of detail work, the sense that something was expected of him hourly, daily, weekly, and the printout of individual appointments and committee meetings his secretary compiled. He was

sitting at lunch in the Michigan League, working on arrangements for a joint exhibition with the Faculty of Art and Design
at the new ArtSpace, feeling tired, feeling restless and, although
he tried to hide it, bored. Once the discussion was over,
Lawrence paid and left. But his progress was impeded; a crowd
of young people appeared. Great clusters of them filled the
hall. Exuberant, wearing dreadlocks and caps and denim jackets, they cascaded through the lobby doors and blocked the exit
stairs.

He could not move. He tried; there was nowhere to go.
Streams then a river of children poured past: laughing, shouting. One aspect of increasing age, he told the associate dean at
his side, is how hard it is to guess the ages of young people;
these are high school students, aren't they, not college level yet?
Remember how, when we were young, we couldn't tell about
old people—if they were forty or sixty or eighty; well, now it's
become the reverse. Who are they; why are they here?

Why they were there, it developed, was for a poetry slam.
This was, Lawrence discovered, the midwestern regionals and
there were high school students from the area as well as teams
from Ohio, Indiana, Illinois, and the Upper Peninsula of
Michigan. They wore insignias and headbands and T-shirts
emblazoned with logos and jostled each other happily; they
wore earrings and nose rings and metal in their eyebrows and
patterning their cheeks. They were high-fiving each other and
adjusting their Walkmans and drinking water from small plastic bottles and jostling for position in the hall.

He checked his watch. He had, he realized, an hour until
his next appointment—too little time to return to his office, too

long to loiter and wait. So he found a chair at the edge of the room, just inside the paneled door, and listened to the poetry slam until the crowd would thin. It did not thin. It packed the room and aisles and hallway, and there was an insistent beat, a jubilation everywhere. A platform stage had been erected, with a podium and set of microphones; groups of young people were twirling their arms and punching the air in near unison, shouting. The beat of the music was loud. The microphones hummed, thrummed.

A series of poets came out on the stage, reciting their verses and watching the clock, taking turns. They did dance steps or shuffled and shrugged. What he heard or thought he heard, because the speech was hard to follow, shocked him: *Mother-fucker, sucker, motherfucker, sucker, it's another word for used-to-be Chic-A-Go; when you tell me clean the place and clear some space I hear my daddy doing time, my mammy saying ain't no crime, like T&A, like whatyousay, like all that shit is IT!*

A boy with a cherubic face and rolls of baby fat declaimed, *Hey you you bitch, come scratch this itch, I got a song to play ain't got all day it's pitch and catch, you twitch your snatch and let's get it ON ON ON. Because what I say is what's the point let's blow this joint, our gov-uh-ment is up-for-rent and everythin' is sinkin', stinking in this land of Ford and Lincoln.* Then his friends joined in the chorus, saying it to-gether: *The game of fame is pitch and catch, you twitch your snatch and let's us get it ON!*

A girl walked out onstage. She was tall and thin and black-haired, in a tank top and black jeans. She was older than the others, Lawrence saw, and moved with the coordination of a dancer, rangily, snaking the microphone wire behind her, tap-

ping her heels and the hand on her hip. He was too far away
to see her well, but she possessed authority and the seated audience knew it; they shouted out approval while she stood and
stared. If this had been a show she would have stolen it; if this
had been a chorus line she would have been the star. Speaking
softly at first and as if to herself, stamping her foot to the beat
of the rhyme, and meditative somehow in the middle of this
public space, she spoke to those who listened as though to each
alone: *You say you'll wait another day—eternity for me, you say—and
that you're near though far away. But when I left I was bereft and what I
do is take you too, your heart comes with me on this ride, the seat belt
cinched across my side, each breath I breathe is You!* The rhyme pattern
was predictable but nonetheless compelling (how she had fled
her home to roam, how she ranged from coast to coast from
east to west but yearned for rest), and then it was blank verse
and words he could not follow, only halfway heard, long skeins
of language raveling while around him the audience roared.

She held out her hand and went silent; the timekeeper
waved her away. Fierce, she moved to the side of the room.

Lawrence left. He had twenty minutes now to make his
meeting at OVPR, and he started walking. The figure of that
black-haired girl remained with him, however: on State Street
and in the Fleming Building while they wrangled over space,
and cost, and the proposed center on North Campus for Information Technology; all during the afternoon seminar he led on
posturbanism and re-urbanism—an unlikely pairing, admit-
tedly, but conjoined in its repudiation yet guarded embrace of
"everyday urbanism"—and a reception for the lecturer that
evening, a "green" architect visiting the program from Seattle

who was urging conservation and the use of recycled or salvaged material in skyscrapers, and dinner afterward, she stayed with him. Then when finally the day was done and he was back in Ann Street, kicking off his shoes and taking off his tie and finishing a Scotch and water as he sorted through the mail, he understood at last what memory had been aroused and why he sat there watching and what he had responded to: the image of Hermia, young.

CATHERINE ANNOUNCED SHE WOULD MARRY a lawyer; at the wedding he sat next to Annie and was shocked to see the change in his ex-wife: wan and thin and wearing strong perfume. The minister described the happy couple as selfless, devoted to each other, and spoke at length about who Catherine was, describing someone Lawrence failed to recognize: his daughter as *Samaritan,* so generous to those in need and unstinting as a volunteer and ready with a hand held out to anyone who asked for help. On the dance floor afterward, while he was piloting her back and forth, she said, "Oh, Daddy, I'm so lucky. So grateful for all that you've done."

What had he done, he asked himself, what could she be grateful for and who was this man she had married?—fairhaired Philip fresh from law school and earning six figures already. The wedding party was boisterous, lawyers and doctors and account managers, and of Catherine's college friends there were one or two he remembered. But Lawrence felt unsettled, and Annie in this incarnation was a stranger totally.

"Isn't it amazing," she asked him over wedding cake, "we produced this girl together? How did we *do* it, I wonder?"

"By interaction," he wanted to say. Once, this would have amused her, or occasioned a response, but the matron at his side was picking at her wedding cake and drinking sparkling water with a slice of lemon, then a cup of decaf coffee, and would not relish the reminder of her old abandon; she had become the very image of propriety, good breeding, and he held his tongue. "*We* didn't do it," he managed instead. "The credit's entirely yours."

Annie patted his hand. "That's sweet."

"Sweet?"

She nodded. "I *will* take the credit. She's sweet."

Then his sons too got engaged—Andrew to a friend from college and John to a high school history teacher who was half-Korean. The three weddings happened in rapid succession, as though his children were competing to establish separate families and see who could move away farther and faster; by 2001, when he turned sixty, Lawrence had grandchildren whose birthdays he registered dutifully and of whom he was fond. Andrew's wife, Vanessa, was an ebullient redhead, and John's wife, Irene, a solemn dark-eyed presence, and everyone seemed happy and got along well together. Andrew settled in Phoenix and John in Vail, and when Lawrence had business in the Southwest he made a point of visiting, and if they came to visit him he made a point of "treats." But year after year when the visits were done he had a sense of exhausted relief, and his children and their families felt very far removed.

Once more he shared meals with women and was their

companion at concerts, and once or twice he slept with them, attempting to enjoy himself as he had done when young. But it all seemed automatic—a bodily memory, like walking or breathing, that he performed from habit and without conscious application. Elise Aronoff, for example, was smart and fierce and, as he was, twice divorced; she had a brittle energy Lawrence found attractive. She owned and operated the Artists' Collaborative Space on South Main Street, a three-story brick building with studios and galleries and, in the lobby, a shop. He met her at the display case while buying earrings for Catherine, and he confessed that, after all these years, he couldn't quite remember if his daughter had pierced ears or not; she said it didn't matter, wasn't a problem, he had a fifty percent chance of getting it right, and they could adjust the clip-ons if he got it wrong. Therefore he purchased the earrings—amethysts in the shape of a teardrop, with a thin gold coil suspending a second, smaller stone beneath—and Elise commended his choice. She gift-wrapped the box carefully and added a black bow.

They had coffee together and, later that same week, a drink. She invited him for dinner and prepared a cassoulet, first having determined that he was not a vegetarian or allergic to the ingredients, and he admired the style of the meal and praised her for it lavishly. They drank a bottle of rosé and, for dessert, Muscat de Beaumes de Venise; Elise caressed his cheek and shoulders while they were sitting on the couch. They talked about their children, where they lived and worked and how rarely anyone *saw* anyone these days, how the geography of distance had grown commonplace for families. "It's much too fast," she warned him, "don't you think we're rushing things?" but, heavy-bellied with the cassoulet, he folded her into his arms.

The love affair lasted six months. It *was*, he told himself, a love affair, there had been something lovable about her passionate convictions—the way she hated Cheney, Bush and Rumsfeld, for example—and how meticulous she was about arranging the flowers when he brought her a bouquet, or how she insisted on shopping at the farmers' market on Saturday morning instead of at Whole Foods. Her body was firm-toned from yoga, and she enjoyed herself, or appeared to, in bed. She took a proprietary interest in his grooming, reminding him to have his hair cut or his shoes resoled, and twice she bought him shirts. The prospect of intimate companionship no longer felt welcome, however; he preferred his private space, he told her when she suggested a week together up north, and the idea of starting out anew with Elise Aronoff did not excite him. At the Artists' Collaborative party in June, he threw a pass at Susan Ward, one of the ceramists exhibiting pots, and made certain that Elise was watching, so later that night when she complained about his embarrassing behavior Lawrence told her he himself had been embarrassed only by Susan's refusal, because he was a free agent, just as she, Elise, was a free agent, and would remain that way.

She flung her white wine at him, missing. He said, "Some women are beautiful, angry, but it doesn't make you beautiful," and then she slapped him twice, and beat his chest, and he was coldly conscious that this was a pivotal moment; he could stay and sleep with her, aroused by her excitement, or break it off instead. "You bastard," she said, "why don't you just get out of here?" and he said, "Fine. Okay." He did this with a twinge of regret but mostly with conviction; he was sixty years old, no longer moved by romantic theatrics, and unwilling to accommodate another person's needs. Lawrence left.

IT WAS TIME ONCE AGAIN to take stock. He was a tenured professor of architecture, a published presence in the field now nearing the age of retirement; he consulted, often, on the size of his portfolio with TIAA/CREF. He had, he decided, thrown away—or perhaps in truth had never been presented with— the possibility of a career as an architect of consequence; what he nibbled on were table scraps from other men's achievement feast: Gehry and Pelli and Eisenman and Foster, the long list of those who did or were doing what he had hoped to do. He felt winded during tennis and tired after mealtimes and took catnaps when he could, but mostly he conducted business as usual and, more and more often, was bored. He was a father and grandfather, twice divorced, and more and more a solitary who read the *New York Times* with attention, then did the crossword puzzle. Lawrence signed a living will, directing his survivors not to take extraordinary measures to resuscitate or keep him alive if impaired.

XI

2004

IN DECEMBER HE DROVE TO CAPE COD. THEY HAD called each other often, e-mailed daily, written letters; her handwriting, he told her, was unchanged. She signed her letters *Love*. In the e-mails, they exchanged opinions rapidly: discussing the weather, the tasks of the day, the trivia of plumbing problems or the lack of progress in a local murder mystery, a woman killed the year before whom Hermia had known. The police were asking everyone—all the men of the area, anyhow—to provide them on a voluntary basis with samples of their DNA; this might or might not prove useful, she wrote, but it's a civil liberties issue, and everyone in Truro has an opinion one way or another; should the government be adding yet more evidence to what they have compiled already as a dossier on their citizens? The dead woman had several lovers, but they all had alibis, and what bothered her, wrote Hermia, was the

cloud of suspicion that hung over Truro, the pall that had settled in town . . .

Ann Arbor seemed, to Lawrence now, full of senior citizens.
On sunny days he passed them in the park. He saw them at the
farmers' market or doing tai chi at the gym. Anxious, still,
about his health, he was preparing for retirement; scheduled to
teach in the winter, he was feeling valedictory about the seminar next term. It was Urban Design and Urban Planning, with
a focus on the distinction between anticipated and preexistent
conditions—as in, for example, what General Oglethorpe designed for Savannah and Baron Haussmann for Paris; is it easier to start with a blank slate or work with the existing urban
fabric? What have the City Beautiful Movement and urban renewal done—or failed to do—with the American town-and-
cityscape? There would be case studies on Brasília and what
"Corbu" achieved in Chandigarh.

The prospect of Thanksgiving made him, as always, uneasy; he could not invite his children and did not invite himself
to visit them instead. His sons' wives had families also, and he
would have been welcome in Phoenix or Vail, but the idea of
travel that weekend was daunting and the fuss and ruckus of
collective celebration seemed, if not more than he could handle, more than he desired. He was fine, he told them when they
asked, just weary a little from the cruise and ready to stay
home.

Halfheartedly Catherine inquired, "Dad, what are you
doing?"

"When?"

"For Thanksgiving. Your dinner, where will you be eating it?"

"Spence & Mills," he lied, "has a party at the office and we're all invited to eat there if we stay around."

"Really? Who's cooking?"

"A Moveable Feast. It's the catering service; I'm fine."

"You're sure?"

"Fine," he repeated. "Unless *you'd* care to join me . . ."

"Come to Chicago," she said.

But Lawrence remained in Ann Arbor. On Thanksgiving Day he watched the Lions game on TV, then went by himself to a movie—a holiday screening of *Bringing Up Baby*—watching Cary Grant and Katharine Hepburn and Charlie Ruggles and the rest disport themselves enchantingly with leopards and puppies and cocktails and dinosaur bones. When hero and heroine kissed at film's end he joined in the applause. What he hoped for, he told Hermia on the phone, was to spend more time with her, and with her alone.

"You mean it?"

"Yes."

"You're not being polite?"

"No. Yes, I'm not being polite."

"Are we rushing this?" she wondered.

There was static on the line.

"You *asked* me, remember? In Malta."

"Of course I remember. And it's a straight shot from Boston. Or T. F. Green in Providence, and then you rent a car. Or you could fly to Provincetown and I'd collect you there."

"I'll drive," he said. "It's time for a visit. And I'm not bringing a moving van or planning to turn into fish."

"Fish?"

"It's an old expression: after three days all guests smell like fish. I promise to shower."

She laughed. "You're welcome whenever you want to . . ."

"What, shower?"

"No, visit. Do come."

They agreed he would do so in early December, before the real winter set in. He would drive from Ann Arbor to Truro, spending the night in the Finger Lakes maybe, or Buffalo or Albany or one of the towns in between. "I'll be driving my mother's Impala," he said. "You know, the gray convertible. The horse does know the way."

"You're joking . . ."

"Yes."

"I remember that car."

"I remember the backseat," he said.

On December 1 he began the journey east. That first night he traveled no farther than Cleveland, and the next day drove past Erie and then Buffalo to Seneca Falls, where Susan B. Anthony and Elizabeth Cady Stanton had composed the Women's Bill of Rights. Then Lawrence drove south to Geneva and spent the night by the lake. It rained. On Friday morning he set out early, driving in the rising mist, and following I-90 till the junction with Route 495; "Come ahead," she told him when he called. "I'm waiting, I can't wait."

Yet Hermia did worry, fearful she'd made a mistake. What did she really know, she asked herself, about this man, and how he would behave? She had trusted him in Malta, and years before in Cambridge, but more than forty years had passed, and who he was in 2004 was a person she no longer knew. A night on shipboard in a foreign country is a night on shipboard in a foreign country, nothing more. And *that* was not her life or world, but *this* was her real life and world, and inviting him to Truro felt very different to her. She hoped it was not a mistake.

Now everywhere, or so it seemed, she read or heard stories of courtship: old friends reconnecting, old high school classmates or graduates tracking each other down on the Internet, then meeting again after years. "If auld acquaintance be forgot" was the theme song of such stories, and they ended with a kiss and "Auld Lang Syne." Old friends were reunited, old friends would meet and marry and their love, long dormant, bloom.

But "Auld Lang Syne" seemed too good to be true. It was a fairy tale. She did not believe, she told herself, in "happily ever after"; it was not the way most stories ended, and all those tales of friendship and courtship left out the sad parts, she was certain—the parts about disappointment, the parts about failure and viciousness and fraud. Waiting, she thought about Lawrence, and she remembered the things that went wrong, the trouble he had been . . .

On Friday she made up the guest room. Airing it, then shaking out the blankets with their smell of camphor and disuse, she recognized how much time had gone by since she'd had guests, or entertained, or had what they used to call sleepover dates. For the Sunday of his visit she planned a dinner party, intending for Lawrence to meet her good friends—the Wilsons and the Banners and Arturo—and wondering how he'd fit in. She reminded herself—if he tracked in mud on the soles of his shoes, or if he left dishes unwashed in the sink—not to complain. Patricia had behaved that way, and sometimes appeared to have done so on purpose, testing her limits and patience and waiting till Hermia snapped.

She vacuumed; she tucked in the sheets. Then, patting the pillow, she froze. She understood that what she'd done was think about her daughter, preparing for his visit, and those closed wounds were opening and she was raising the stakes. This is *not* about, she told herself, abandonment; this is *not* about departure but arrival and he's coming for a weekend and it isn't a big deal. Old habits die hard, Hermia reminded herself, and solitude was a habit by now. The wallpaper was peeling and would have to be reglued. You're all grown up, she told herself, you're a big girl: behave.

WHEN HE CROSSED THE BOURNE BRIDGE it was raining; by the time he got to Truro there was sleet. His cell phone did not function and he called her from the phone booth by the post office, in the wet dark. She directed him toward the ocean, on the Pamet Road, and told him where to turn and look for the sign to her driveway: two rights and then a left.

He found it; it was five o'clock, and his headlights raked the house where Hermia was standing by the door. The trees were bare. Beneath the dripping overhang she raised her smiling face to his and offered him her hand. "Welcome," she said. "Welcome back."

"How *are* you?"

"Fine. I'm happy you're here."

"It beats Geneva," Lawrence said. "The Finger Lakes were

the middle of nowhere. But *this*"—he extended his arm, ex-
pansive, pointing to the pine trees and the dune beyond—"is
civilization."

Hermia studied him. "Why *did* you drive?"

"I'm not exactly sure. It felt like it would give me time. And
be a proper pilgrimage . . ."

"They landed just up the road, the Pilgrims, and stocked up
on water and fruit. I'll take you there tomorrow, maybe, if the
weather's better."

"It looks just the same. The house, I mean. I remember the
driveway, that fence there, the woodshed . . ."

"A century ago," she said. "Come in."

He collected his bag and a bottle of Pommard and followed
her through the door. The table had been set for two, and there
was a fire in the fireplace; the pictures had been painted by her
father. The bookshelves were as he remembered them also:
narrow, crammed full of leather-bound books, with oversize art
books piled high on the chairs and the floor.

Silent, he stopped for a moment in front of the portrait of
Hermia, young—now hanging in the dining room where once
the Edward Hopper hung—and holding the dog in her lap.

"Should I take off my shoes?"

"No. Not, I mean, unless you want to . . ."

"My coat? Where do I hang it?"

She showed him. "Your quarters, sir."

He looked at her questioningly. Hermia smiled: "Separate
cabins. Number 63."

"And you—you were 71."

"Welcome, world traveler. Fresh water, berries, a drink?"

"I clocked the distance, coming here—it's just about a thousand miles. Not as the crow flies, maybe, but I did take some detours."

"Remember that song?" She did not hum it. " 'If I go ten thousand miles . . . ' "

"I think it's time you kiss me," Lawrence said.

She did so, then drew back. He smelled of exhaustion, the long day's drive. "Do you want a shower?"

"I want us to not be so nervous. I want to relax, first, a little."

"Mi casa es su casa," she said.

HE DID RELAX; he used the toilet, then washed his hands and face. They drank Pommard and sat by the fire together. The Hopper and the Motherwells, she told him when he asked, were sold, and what he was hearing in the kitchen on the CD player were the nocturnes of John Field. "I thought it was Chopin," said Lawrence.

"The Irish version of him, yes."

"It's beautiful here."

"You like it?"

"It's a beautiful house. You know that."

She raised her glass, sipped from it. "Yes."

"I keep remembering," he said, "how long ago I came here, first . . ."

"In 1962."

"Most people on the planet weren't even *alive* then, Hermia."

She smiled. They talked about the weather and the coming winter, how isolated it could be, how inward-facing on the Cape—but that was what Hermia loved, she explained, the silence of the woods and beach and how different it felt from the summer and the constant roar of traffic on Route 6. It's a different town in August, she told him, hard to find a parking place for Ballston Beach, and sometimes it's so crowded people park at JAMS—the place by the post office you called from—and walk. He asked her if she felt afraid with that unsolved murder mystery, or not so much afraid as—what's the right way to put it?—suspicious. I've lived alone too long, she said, to have any personal fear here in Truro, and the horror of that killing is the killer seemed to know her, or anyhow that's what police assume. I'm sorry, Lawrence said, I didn't mean to worry you, and she said, I'm not worried, but let's change the subject, all right?

They did change the subject. They talked about the Finger Lakes, the museum he'd gone to in Seneca Falls, the sight lines in the Valley of the Temples at Agrigento and how the photographs she'd taken somehow failed to register the particular transparency of Mediterranean light; I have an album from the trip, said Hermia, but it's a disappointment—the album, I mean, not the trip. I'll show it to you later: you were always saying *formaggio*, remember, *Gorgonzola, Bel Paese,* never *cheese. Pecorino Romano,* he said. That's about the extent of the cheeses I know, the Italian ones anyhow, pardon my French, and they smiled at each other and drank.

Outside, the rain solidified, tapping at the windowpanes. It isn't, Hermia said, predicted to amount to much, the weather's supposed to improve. They spoke of the little fat tour guide who sang, who called himself Povarotti, and the way the captain of the M.S. *Diana* pronounced "Henglish" and the red cone of Etna at night. They tried to remember the names of the couple from Boston, the gracious white-haired gentleman and his deaf wife at the final shared supper, those people who lived on Newbury Street, not Dick and Jane—remember them?—and the waiter who played the banjo up in the Elsinore Lounge.

The windows were small-paned, six over six, and where the panes remained intact the old glass had rippled and bubbled. He admired the wide pine flooring and the hand-fashioned bricks. When was this house built? Lawrence asked, and she said 1790, or thereabouts. Thenabouts, I suppose is the word, and it's been added onto but the center section hasn't changed, this room's the original part. "My father loved it here," she said. "He died outside."

He touched her arm.

"Well, not outside the house, in fact, in fact it was down in Hyannis, but this is where he crashed the truck and for the longest time I couldn't see that stand of pine at the first curve past the driveway without being reminded, without being haunted, a little, by everything he'd left unfinished or just left behind—his paintings, my mother, the waste of . . ." Her voice trailed away. "I mean, when he died he was younger than *I* am. Than both of us."

Lawrence changed the subject. "Whatever happened to Vermont?"

"I sold *that* house. There was too much Batten Kill under the bridge . . ."

He looked at her. She was wearing a black cowl-neck sweater and cotton pants with flared cuffs. "For a big-city girl you seem to be spending your life in the country . . ."

She raised her glass.

"Have you noticed," he inquired, "how it's easier to talk about the things we did together than what we did apart?"

"I've noticed, yes." She drank.

"The way time flies and crawls," he said. "That's the thing I've been thinking about. I don't *feel* old, or as old as I look, and I'd guess that's true of everyone: these ancient wheezing hulks we are—not you, of course, you look terrific—still shocked by the face in the mirror and planning to play hooky or skip home from school."

"The school of second chances . . ."

"Right . . ."

An ember flared. They watched it. "There's dinner. I've made dinner."

"I'm not hungry yet."

They kissed. This time she moved her lips and tongue and this time he held her closely and she did respond, pressing herself against him, and while the Irish pianist John O'Conor played the music of the composer John Field, the two of them embraced. After some moments Hermia rose and led him wordlessly past the guest room she'd prepared, and past her own adult bedroom to the space of her childhood next to the porch where decades earlier they'd made love standing up. This time they used the bed. This time they were cautious, a little, and unhurried in the empty house, and he felt when he entered her fortunate, fortunate, and thought of how he'd thought himself, long years ago, first holding her in this same room, to be luck's shining child.

The music in the kitchen ceased; a shutter, somewhere, knocked against the siding. The bedsprings were loud. Sleet beat at the roof, tattooing the window; the furnace hummed. And she, beneath him spread-legged, straining on the mattress, told herself there was no damage, nothing broken or misplaced or lost, and shut her eyes to the surrounding dark and, yielding, lifting, as though she were young again, came.

NEXT MORNING THE WEATHER IMPROVED. At dawn there was a fine white glaze upon the branches of the trees, and everything looked crystalline, but by ten o'clock it melted and at noon the sky was clear. On Saturday they ate and drank and talked and slept together happily, driving to Eastham and Orleans and walking the beaches and, in Wellfleet, walking dirt roads between ponds. In the Stop & Shop they bought ingredients for the dinner party next evening, and she would not let him pay, so he purchased six bottles of wine. That night they ate in Provincetown, and he talked about the course he was preparing for the winter and how much he liked to teach. I'll bet you're a wonderful teacher, she said, and he said, I'll miss it, I do enjoy class. Please take this as a compliment, said Hermia, smiling in the candlelight across the restaurant table, with its red checkered tablecloth, but you were always a talker and it's easy to imagine you behind the podium. Point taken, Lawrence said.

On Sunday evening her dinner guests arrived. Formally she

introduced him to Arturo and the Banners and the Wilsons, and they had a fine time together, eating fish pie and complaining about the horrors of a second term and the Republican majority. The Banners in particular were horrified, and said they were thinking of leaving, or refusing to pay taxes, but there's nowhere to go to that feels any better or any country, really, that *wants* Americans nowadays. I was wrong, said Lawrence, utterly wrong; when we were in Italy in October I was certain George Bush would be thrown out of office, but there were all these other people on the cruise—remember, Hermia?—who said their boy would win. In a town like Ann Arbor you never quite notice, and maybe that's true here in Truro as well, you think America's *sane.*

We get what we deserve, declared Jon Wilson sadly, the ones who vote for God and country are the ones who get sent to Iraq. I pray to the God I don't really believe in we survive for four more years.

Arturo pointed to her father's art and said it shouldn't hang so near to the fireplace, darkening. It's a fine fireplace, excellent draw, but anyhow there's smoke. You may not know, he told them, how William Hogarth was angry that his own work fetched a lower price than customers were paying for old masters. And so he did a mezzotint, *Time Smoking a Picture,* showing the artist as graybeard, painting and making rips in the canvas with a scythe balanced over his shoulder and his pipe puffing out white clouds of smoke; that way the new composition would quickly look old and Hogarth could demand a higher price. I never understood, Arturo said, why I myself had so much trouble with your portrait, Hermia, that time we tried and tried, but tonight I understand, it's that painting on the mantelpiece, I just couldn't get it out of my mind. I didn't even *know* I was thinking about that portrait of you sitting here with the dog—but it's too damn good, it's brilliant, and it was in my mind's eye always: a reproach.

"And *Time Will Darken It*," Jon Wilson said, "wasn't that Bill Maxwell's book?"

"Its title, yes. But he must have been quoting. I *do* wonder whata he was quoting," said Gabriela Banner. Her intonation was Italian, strong, and although she had been living in America for fifty years she seemed wide-eyed and astonished by the customs of the country; her English was impeccable but made no concessions to accent. "I *missa* them, the Maxwells," she said. "Dear Bill. Dear beautifula Emily. Dead."

Hermia offered to look up the phrase; the book was, she was certain, sitting somewhere on a shelf. But Arturo said, "Don't bother, what we're talking about here is natural, *age*, and it's the addition of pigment, not underlayment, that counts. That's the difference, isn't it—not the only difference but an important one, I think—between the way we work on surfaces today and how they used to manage. If there's anything anywhere left . . ."

He was on the verge of tears, it seemed, then suddenly was weeping, and Joanna Wilson put her arm around the painter's shoulders and he said, "I miss her so much, I miss Irene so much, I think about how happy she'd have been to be here with us. Just sitting in this room."

"We miss her too," said Hermia. "Everybody does."

She looked around the table at her friends and felt a rush

of, if not pleasure, satisfaction: not, of course, at Irene's absence, but the presence of this company, those who had known and mourned her together and were telling stories about the scarecrow in her garden, the way she dressed it in Schiaparelli scarves and Thrift Shoppe Calvin Klein . . .

"It was the best-dressed scarecrow on the Cape," said Henry Banner, smiling, "and all the crows minded their manners. Rabbits too."

"I'm doing a show," said Arturo. "Next spring—just Irene's face. Sketches, lithographs, one terra-cotta head I tried. And twenty-seven oils."

Lawrence felt a tightness in his chest. These people knew each other well, and had long shared memories; Arturo's wife, of whom they spoke, was someone he had never met. For dessert they were eating a strawberry fool, and he picked at his food while the others discussed her—her dream of visiting the Hermitage, a dream that Arturo alone had fulfilled, her gift of mimicry and how much she loved to dance.

"Remember the square dances," asked Gabriela, "the ones downa by the dock? Remember how she'd *skip* to do-si-do?"

Jon Wilson raised his glass. They drank. Lawrence attempted not so much to join in the discussion as to join in the shared sorrow, but the memory of Hermia's father and Arturo's wife remained abstract, incorporeal, and he focused instead on the painting: the young black-haired girl with the dog on her lap, the yellow chair she sat in with its cushions shaped like hewn stone blocks, the patterned carpet underneath and window in the top right corner of the canvas, giving out on a garden beyond. She was smiling at the dog but somehow also straight ahead, and this was what seemed masterful: that doubled gaze, the upward angling of her eyes so that she seemed to shift, immobile in the seat.

After coffee and brandy the others departed. He helped her cleaning up. They stood side by side in the kitchen, a domestic couple—he rinsing off the plates, she stacking them according to her system in the dishwasher—and when the machine was full she said to him, "Leave it, okay? We'll do the rest tomorrow."

The tightness in his chest, however, did not go away. At midnight Lawrence excused himself, saying, "It was a terrific meal. But I need to get some rest, I'm tired, dead on my feet."

"Poor dear," said Hermia. "Plumb tuckered out . . ."

He joined in the joke of it: "Used me all up."

"Not *all,* I hope. There's always tomorrow."

"No. Yes."

"Did you like them?"

"I liked them very much. Admired them, really. You've got excellent friends here, I think."

"Yes."

"Old friends. That's one of the things we can no longer do."

"Excuse me?"

"Make old friends, I mean. We can make *new* friends, not old."

She smiled at him. "In my better moments, I think we're being both."

They kissed good night. Then, wearily, he took himself to bed.

• • •

THE PARTY HAD BEEN, Hermia told herself, fun: the meal was good, and Lawrence and her company did seem to get along. She was happy now, she told herself, happy, happy, and tomorrow she would ask him to extend his stay. She could not sleep. She listened to the furnace, listened to the wind outside, and thought of her mother in London, in the establishment in Golders Green, and what it would be like to bring her back to this house she would no longer recognize because, for years, her mother had recognized nothing at all. We wait and wait, thought Hermia, and sooner or later the thing we wait for does in fact appear: the statue moves, the painting comes down off the wall. She saw a statue move, a painting fall, and knew that in fact she had fallen asleep, was dreaming, and the image of her mother—immobile in the nursing home, washed and fed and put to bed but insensate and wholly unknowing—and the image of herself when young, and then Arturo's wife, Irene, in portrait after portrait fused, were one.

Lawrence lay wakeful in the windy dark, counting backward from two hundred and attempting sleep. He pictured the buildings of Moshe Safdie, of Rafael Moneo, of Mies van der Rohe; he thought about his children and grandchildren and the woman in the next room no doubt also awake. His knowledge of her habits was old but incomplete. The word *choleric* came to him, and he made a chorus of it, repeating "choleric, choleric," emptying the word of meaning, placing it next to *caloric* and hearing the two of them rhyme. Noiselessly he sang. He thought about "enfolded negativity" and a phrase the

Smithsons used, in London, describing the interior space of their buildings as a "charged void"; he repeated the phrase: *charged void*. Again he counted backward from two hundred and watched the clock register 1:11 and tried to make a pattern of it: time.

IN THE MORNING, when he woke, he knew he was at risk. The band of pain across his chest and taste of tin were what he'd felt in July. Over coffee he told Hermia—who came into the kitchen smiling, fresh-faced, wearing slippers and a beige terry-cloth robe—that if she didn't mind he'd drive himself down to Hyannis for an EKG and maybe a stress test, it was nothing to worry about, not serious angina, but better safe than sorry as they say. What are you *talking* about, she asked, and he said, It's Monday morning, the third day of my visit and I smell like fish. All right, she said, this isn't funny, will you be serious a minute and he said I probably shouldn't have driven, probably shouldn't be pushing myself and if you have a doctor here I think I'd better visit him or the simplest thing is just the emergency room.

She drove him to Hyannis. It was December 6. He said that, in Ann Arbor, he'd had to wait through the Fourth of July, and the timing was much better now, this time it was Pearl Harbor Day, or almost, Bombs Away. I know you're trying, Hermia said, to joke about it and keep me from worrying, keep *yourself* from worrying, and it's very impressive but not very funny; do you mind if we don't talk like this and talk instead about the way you feel? So Lawrence did describe it: the shortness of breath, the ache in his chest, but repeated that he wasn't worried; he was catching it, he hoped, in time and they'd warned him before it might happen again since the stent could be rejected, or, more likely, there's another problem in another artery and he shouldn't have eaten dessert. It's not as severe, not halfway as bad as July, he said, and I was joking of course about dinner, the strawberry fool was superb.

She gripped the steering wheel tightly. She was trying not to cry. In the stretch of single-lane traffic past the rotary they were caught behind a line of trucks, and she could not pass them, and wondered if they should have called an ambulance instead, or 911.

He touched her wrist. "It isn't an emergency."

"We're almost there."

"That's fine. I'm fine."

"*Was* it the fool? Something you ate?"

He shook his head. The day was gray.

"Or—oh God, I hate to ask this—what we did together?"

"When?"

"On Friday night. Saturday. Yesterday afternoon."

"Listen to me, Hermia. You mustn't—no—don't blame yourself."

"There *was* heavy cream in the fish pie. And butter, oh God, butter everywhere. I'll *never* cook that way again . . ."

"Please," he said, "I'm being careful. That's all it is, a precaution."

"Promise?"

"Love, I want to live."

In silence they drove the last mile. The outskirts of town

were blocked by construction, and a man with a *Drive Slow* sign he swiveled to read *Stop.* Traffic slowed to a crawl in Hyannis; she passed a row of buses, a cement truck, a stalled car. But it was as though all things had changed: he'd called her "love," and she who'd held herself aloof was desperate to help. His weakness enlisted her strength. At the emergency room entrance Lawrence waved and walked carefully in through the door while she watched, then went to park. It was ten o'clock. After some circling in the parking lot she found a spot and got out of the car to join him. Then, locking it, swinging her handbag up over her shoulder and starting to walk to the hospital, she felt the world go dark.

Hermia leaned against the window of the Volvo, breathing deeply, standing, seeing black spots dance across the curtain of her eyes. The air was cold. She was, she knew, going to faint. It was, she knew, a migraine, or the onset of a migraine, the announcement of its stalking her: a distant thing, then not so distant, near. What terrified her was recurrence: this hospital she had avoided—not needing more than an annual checkup with the family practice in Orleans and, routinely, a series of mammograms and Pap smears and once, when the test results were less than routine, the procedure up in Boston—for all the years and decades since her father's accident. It *could* not be, she told herself, that Lawrence came into her life to depart it on a stretcher; it *could* not be he'd joined her just to be taken away. Oh please, she heard herself saying, oh please please please it can't happen again, I can't lose this one also, not lose everybody. Please please just let him be all right.

And as though it was a prayer and her prayer had been answered he was lying in a hospital bed, smiling at her when they let her visit in cardiac care, attached to tubes of oxygen and an IV and wearing a white smock. "The second time around," he said. "I've been repeating myself . . ."

"Don't talk. Are you supposed to?"

"Where Louis Kahn collapsed was in the men's room in, I think, Grand Central Terminal. Or maybe Pennsylvania Station. I can't remember exactly, but he'd just come back from India, and nobody knew who the traveler was and he lay there a long time before they could identify and then reclaim the body from the morgue. This great American architect, maybe the greatest of them all, and he's lying in a men's room where some passerby rolled him and took away his wallet . . ."

"Why are you telling me this?"

"Because I'm not planning to die," said Lawrence. "It may be a new blockage, it may be the old stent's occluded."

A nurse appeared.

"My new best friend," he said. "Meet Hermia."

"Pleased to meet you," said the nurse. "This one's a talker, isn't he?"

"It's all those drugs you've been giving me. Valium? I'm usually the silent type, strong and silent—ask Hermia here. I've been silent forty years."

The women smiled at each other, and a fat man with enormous arms came in and mopped the floor. Then an orderly arrived and maneuvered Lawrence in his hospital bed out the door and down the hall. She walked with him and watched the elevator open and waited while they wheeled the gurney in. He lifted his hand to her, valedictory, and then he disappeared.

HERMIA MOVED THROUGH THE NEXT HOURS, days, with a strange doubling sense of what was happening, had happened, as though the migraine which was not so much a migraine as the aftermath of terror had brought with it alertness and an equivalent lack of alertness. Everything mattered immensely and nothing mattered at all. The details to attend to—her car needing gas, the clothes she changed, a bowl of chicken noodle soup, the messages offering assistance from the Banners and Wilsons, the telephone numbers Lawrence provided and the calls she made to Vail and Phoenix and a long conversation with his daughter in Chicago, the Monday night alone in the house, trying and failing to and then finally falling asleep at three—were unimportant and important, consequential and inconsequential both at the same time.

It was, she told herself, shock. It was minute by hour and hour by day and all she wanted, needed, was for Lawrence to get well. He had mattered to her long ago and then he had not mattered much and now he mattered to her very much indeed. The space by his side was the only thing visible, all she could see of the world.

Except the space kept changing, was the cubicle he lay in, first, with a blue curtain on an oblong rail they could use for privacy, and then the semiprivate room with a man from Barnstable in the next bed, who coughed and coughed, and then—when the procedure was over and the smiling doctor from

Pakistan informed them that indeed we found a blockage and removed it, inserting one more Cypher stent, this one a ninety-five percent occlusion but in a secondary artery, you can consider it related to and a kind of sequel, really, to what they didn't deal with before—a private room. The doctor was elegant, doe-eyed, and he seemed to assume she was married to Lawrence, because he spoke to her with the deferential attentiveness reserved for family members when a patient has been at risk. The doctor was a baby, they all were babies, really; how did it happen, she wondered, that doctors and lawyers and presidents all were infants now? Your medical team in Michigan, he said, and we of course have been in touch, decided—correctly, in my opinion, correctly—the left anterior descending was a good deal more important; a lot of this, madam, is luck of the draw and where the plaque decides to lodge, so if there was an earthquake in July you can think of this as a December aftershock, and if we had to do it all over again, if we'd had the entire picture we might have considered a bypass, but anyhow it's over now and you did the right thing coming in . . .

She sat with Lawrence. He slept. She held his hand and listened to him breathing, and when he was discharged next day she brought him back to Truro. The pots she'd left for cleaning an eternity ago were waiting for her, in the sink, and the pans and unwashed glasses on the counter. Lawrence lay on the living room couch, beneath a blanket, while she set the house to rights.

He watched. He was weak, and sentimental, and told her he was grateful and loved her very much.

"Don't say that," said Hermia.

"Why? Why not?"

"Unless you mean it."

"I do," he said. "I *told* you . . ."

"We sound just like children."

"No. No we don't."

"Remember what you called it, the school of second chances?"

"It was you who said that."

"No."

"It was."

"Just listen to us arguing. We do sound like children."

"I love you very much."

XII

H E STAYED. SHE NURSED HIM CAREFULLY. HE SAID
she did not need to, but Hermia insisted; she made him
take his pills and tea and brought him breakfast in bed. "You're
spoiling me," he said, and she agreed. "I'm fine," Lawrence assured her, "truly," and she told him to lie down.

The weather remained cold and clear. He walked a half
mile daily, and then a mile, then more. As the month of December progressed he found himself imagining the holidays in
Truro and wondering if he should leave, or if they might travel
together. The radio commenced with Christmas music, Bach
and Christmas carols; the announcer for Cape Cod Classical
listed bake sales and charity drives.

Catherine called and kept in touch; so did the boys. She
would be willing, his daughter proposed, to fly one-way to
Providence or Boston and meet him there and share the drive

back to Ann Arbor. "I'm planning to stay," said Lawrence, "a little longer, maybe. If the lady of the house will let me . . ."

Across the room Hermia smiled. The telephone was in the living room, and while he talked he watched her: the severity of features softened by increasing age and the patrician nose and neck blurred by firelight. Her hair was gray. Her earrings and her necklace were a matched set of pearls. She wore her reading glasses and a cable-knit black sweater, and they were having their six o'clock drink; he told his daughter he was getting better, getting stronger, feeling fine.

And this was true. At times—walking with Hermia down to the beach, or driving back from Provincetown, or setting the kitchen table for two—he felt as though each minute of each day was a reprieve. He might, he thought, have died. He should not, he told himself, exaggerate; he had never been in danger, and would soon be well. His heart had not been damaged, and Lawrence tried to make a point of this: his heart was whole. Yet the whiff of mortality hovered and—walking together in the cold wind, or unpacking groceries—he asked himself if what he felt was hope or hopelessness, if the two of them had a shared future or only the present and past.

"It's day by day."

"You sound"—he smiled at her—"like an inspirational video. Some guru of the cherished moment."

"It's always day by day. Only, sometimes we're more *conscious* of it."

"I love you," Lawrence said.

He said this to her often, as though trying the phrase on for size. It fit. He could not remember the first time he'd used it, the occasion he first spoke the words, but the episode in Cape Cod Hospital had loosened something in him, and sentiment poured out. Love was unstoppably with him, it seemed: he told Hermia he *loved* the house, the smell of her hair on his shoulder, oysters, Handel's *Messiah*, the feel of her forearm and hand. Often he wanted to cry. He *loved* the *St. Matthew's Passion*, the fading light at Pilgrim Spring, the scent of fresh-crushed mint. She reminded him that he had been more self-protective, chary once, and he said, "That was then. This is now."

"You sound"—teasingly she repeated the phrase—"like an inspirational video."

He nodded. "Tonight let's have pasta and scallops. I'm cooking. There was a special on scallops at the Fish Market."

"Oh, *excellent*."

"And Scotty assured me these were actual scallops, not bottom fish or sea skate cut to shape."

"Sea skate?"

"Right: they have the same consistency. Some vendors cut up sea skate into what they sell as scallop chunks for maybe five times the price . . ."

"But that's illegal," Hermia said.

"*Caveat emptor.* What was that slogan—what were they advertising? You know, 'accept no substitutes.'"

"Butter, I think."

"I love you," Lawrence said.

THE BANNERS VISITED. The Wilsons visited. One evening they went to the movies, a comic film called *Sideways,* and watched the actors cavort. One afternoon they attended a concert, a benefit for Outer Cape Emergency Services, and the performers were good; they played Mozart and Schubert and then something atonal by a Russian. "I smell like fish," said Lawrence, "I promised to be gone by now."

"Oh?"

"I said I'd be leaving two weeks ago, and you should kick me out."

"I will," she said, "I promise. Just as soon as you begin to stink. It hasn't happened yet."

He was conscious of his children and grandchildren and therefore all the more keenly of Hermia's isolation. Although she did not speak of it, he sensed a grieving absence, a privacy surrounding her he could not share. She was, he told himself, both the girl he'd desired in college and the sixty-three-year-old he visited, and this juxtaposition of strange and familiar confused him: which Hermia was spooning soup, which woman shared his bed? Lawrence bought presents for his relatives—fishermen's sweaters in Provincetown, a ceramic tea set from a gallery in Wellfleet, a compass and a set of paints for Andrew's children, Jack and Elizabeth—and sent them almost furtively, as though this evidence of family might wound her, and his attachments elsewhere were unfair.

She was conscious of his restlessness, his sense that he should be at work and that his work felt less important now than earlier he'd hoped. He had dreamed of consequence, an enduring reputation, and as a Fellow of the American Institute of Architects had wanted greater recognition of his buildings and his writings. But this was not forthcoming and she knew it bothered Lawrence to watch identity fade. Often he doodled—on napkins or scrap sheets—crosshatching buildings in perspective and drawing elevations of houses on the shore. Some mornings he worked on his sequence of lectures—the "Arcadian," "Deconstructionist" and Koolhaasian "junk-space" of contemporary urbanism—for the course he would offer next term.

They were conscious of adjustment, the way rough edges fit. He took an afternoon nap. She thought dawn the best time of the day. Each sunrise is chock-full of promise, said Hermia, with everything opening up. You *are* an optimist, he said, and she said only in the mornings, not by night. They talked about their shared journey to Pompeii and how long ago it seemed, how far in the receding past; can you believe, asked Lawrence, we met just three months ago? Or, depending how you choose to count it, more than forty years. If I'd jumped ship, she said to him—I thought about it, did I tell you?—and simply finished up the trip in Rome, we would have missed each other; is that, he asked, our plain dumb luck or fate?

Their pleasures were quiet ones, cooking and reading and watching TV. In December, darkness fell by five o'clock, and the nights were long. They watched Jim Lehrer's newscast nightly, on Channel 2 from Boston, and when at program's end the screen displayed, in silence, the faces of soldiers—the names and hometowns and ages of those reported killed in Iraq—Lawrence stood at attention, his shoulders squared and hands against his thighs.

He hated the war, as she hated the war, but that did not prevent their mourning the young dead. They talked about how much had changed, and also how little had changed, since their own period of protest—Vietnam, then Watergate—and how there'd been a crisis in the availability of oil thirty years before; all this had been foreseen. It's not so much a question, they agreed, of *whether* but *when* the bill for oil comes due; they spoke of their parents and classmates and the inexorable forward march and then the triumph of time.

His sister telephoned. "How are you?"

"Fine."

"That's not what I've been hearing."

"I'm fine."

"And where *is* this anyhow, Larry; what sort of area code's 508?"

"Truro. On the Outer Cape. I'm here with an old friend."

"Which one?"

"You never knew her. Hermia."

"*That* Hermia? *The* Hermia?"

"Happy holidays. And thanks for having tracked me down; you spoke to Catherine?"

"She's worried about you. *I'm* worried about you. An old dog performing his favorite trick."

"What a pleasant way to put it, Allie."

"Well, you haven't exactly been brilliant at this, have you?"

"At what?"

"At figuring out who to live with, or visit. At making romantic decisions."

"And you've been such an expert?"

"No. But promise me you're being careful."

"I am, I promise," Lawrence said—and wondered was that true?

EACH NIGHT, in front of the fire, they talked. "I want to know everything," he said, "*everything* about our years apart. I hate not knowing where you were in 1969. Or 1996."

"Or 1986."

"Or 1991."

They tried for five-year intervals but these were difficult to manage: one memory led to another, one scene bled into another and could not be confined. The house he built near Lake Champlain, for instance, and her home in Arlington were hard to keep distinct. The structures themselves were dissimilar, but the time frame was the same, and he had flown to Burlington and Albany while she was living nearby. His time lying ill on the island of Rhodes and hers in Nova Scotia seemed somehow the same journey, and her work at Harry Abrams and his at SOM belonged to the same past. Once, he referred to Interlochen and the arts school at Cranbrook, and she asked him which was closer to Ann Arbor. Lawrence smiled. You're being, he said, a typical easterner; not everything across the Hudson River is in another country, and you should visit me there. They talked about the seventies and eighties and nineties, how they had felt about the new millennium and what they did that night. Remember the millennium bug, asked Hermia, how everyone was certain the computers and the banking system would go haywire and the world was coming to an end? It is, he said, it was, it will, except not the way we imagined.

Continuity was their subject: things that last. She spoke about her friend Anne Martineau and how the Prospect School had grown famous; the school itself shut down for lack of financial support, but they'd kept extensive records, and the archive proved a resource for educators everywhere. So nobody's enrolled at Prospect now but everyone studies the children, the drawings and maps they produced. You can't predict it, Lawrence said, the law of unintended consequence is not the exception but the rule.

They talked about retention, what stays or fails to stay. He spoke about his grandson, Jack, the way he loved to chart the stars, and wondered if there could be such a thing as a born astronomer, a person fascinated from the start by outer space. Galileo, Tycho Brahe and the rest; I'm not comparing Jack to Isaac Newton, said Lawrence, it's just that everything about the night sky *speaks* to him. I've been looking all my life and can barely identify the Big Dipper, but this kid *knows* the constellations and his favorite toy's a telescope and I wonder if an obsession like that will stay with him in professional life or be like other hobbies and one day disappear. Some things remain, said Hermia, they don't just fade away.

"It's short-term memory that goes." He reached for her hand. "I can remember everything about you, say, in April 1962, but who I met and what I did last year is hazy by comparison."

"Our waiter's name?"

"I meant, before that. Darko. I mean, before we met again.

It's like the world was black- and-white and now it's Technicolor."

"You're spoiling me," said Hermia.

"I feel like everything went out of focus and now again it's clear."

They reminisced about Cambridge. When he returned in 1964 for architecture school, said Lawrence, he missed her on a daily basis but had failed to understand it at the time. Let's not rewrite history, Hermia said, and he admitted you're right, that's what I'm doing, but it could use some revision, my personal history could be improved. Together the two of them wondered if they might have stayed together, or if it was inevitable that they broke apart. There had been no single reason, no one thing that went wrong. They were not ready to marry, and then they were ready for marriage but with the wrong person. Do you want a refill, Lawrence asked, and she shook her head.

The woodbox was empty; he carried in logs from the stacked wood outside. She talked about her marriage and he talked about his marriages, and they agreed they might have chosen better, might have made fewer mistakes. They tried to speak of happiness in the same vein as sorrow—to deal with it as seriously and to make it last. I'm sorry I was jealous of Charette, offered Hermia, it was irrational really, but I never knew how truly crazy jealousy could make a person till I married Paul. What happened to him, Lawrence asked, and she said I heard he made a life in Thailand but was killed in Sarajevo in the war. Was he covering it, asked Lawrence, and she said yes, he went back to work for Reuters and got in the way of a bomb.

It's strange, said Hermia, I had forgotten all about him, or at least I thought I had, but when the news arrived I found myself dreaming all over again, unable to shake it, remembering everything, *everything.* You think you've closed the book, he said, but then it opens up. In my case, though, whenever I run into Janet—it's a small enough town so that happens—I think, Good Christ, how is it possible I shared a life with her; what did we have in common but a house and bank account?

Two sons, she reminded him, and Lawrence said that's true. I loved and love them very much, but it's still as if I produced them with a nearly total stranger. And now they're grown-up strangers, and I see myself standing in the kitchen: making breakfast, making lunch for school, putting training wheels on bicycles or wiring the transformer for the train set in the basement, and I think the person in that picture is impersonating *me.* I must have been there, must have done the things I can remember having done with, *for* the children, but it's like another life. Or dream of existence. You know . . .

I do, she said, I know. Most of the time I'm sleepwalking, he said, but with you I'm wide awake. It's as though the rest of life has been, well, just the rest of life. She spoke of how Arturo drew his dead wife's face obsessively, and modeled it, how Irene had been memorialized everywhere inside the house. There are stacks and stacks of paintings, Hermia said, and plaster casts and maquettes made of clay and it's as though she's still alive, alive to him at any rate, when you walk into the room. It's like that picture, Lawrence said: you're sixty-three and six at the same time. Not really, said Hermia, not like Irene; my father only noticed me for the duration of the portrait, but she was the point of her husband's career, the face he drew over and over. You've been that way for me, he said, for all these years I've kept you in a safe place in my heart.

She smiled. "The left ventricle."

"Right mitral valve."

"I want the whole chamber," she said.

ON THE MORNING of the winter solstice the front doorbell rang. The day was cold and gray. Hermia was doing errands at the hardware store in Wellfleet, then mailing a package at the post office, and therefore he answered the door. It was rare, he understood, for someone to use the front entrance, or ring; most of those who knew the house entered through the kitchen, and so Lawrence expected a stranger.

A woman stood on the stoop. She was tall and black-haired, slender, somehow familiar; he wondered if he knew her or had seen her somewhere in Truro but knew he would remember so striking a young presence and that they had not met.

"Can I help you?"

"Good morning. Are you the man of the house?" She held, he could see, a petition: there was a clipboard, a sheet of paper with some signatures on it, a pen.

"Not really, no. I'm visiting."

"Are you a registered voter in Massachusetts?"

Lawrence shook his head.

"Is this"—she consulted her sheet, then gave Hermia's name—"her residence? Is she the person living here?"

"Yes."

"And can I speak to her?"

"She's not at home. She should be back in an hour, maybe less."

"Oh, I'm sorry." Her disappointment was palpable, but there was also—he saw it in the canvasser's face—relief. Her face was pale. She was wearing mittens and a bright red scarf.

"You could come back."

She shook her head. "Excuse me . . ."

"You're lobbying for something, right?"

Again she shook her head. Then, stamping her foot, she stepped away and he remembered where he had seen her: at the poetry slam in Ann Arbor, years before. But this seemed so improbable he could not credit it; he told himself that Hermia would not welcome a petition, and he should let her go.

The visitor withdrew. Her car had its lights on, idling, its exhaust an additional billowing thickness against the wintry gray. The car was an old Subaru, a battered Outback station wagon with a roof rack: white. There was no one in the driver's seat or passenger seat; she'd come alone. Lawrence watched while the car disappeared.

Oddly unsettled, he finished the *Times.* The news was bad. There were suicide bombers and scandals over prisoner abuse. Social Security was, the president warned, in trouble; it would be a disaster for our children unless we invest in private accounts. Others disagreed. Lawrence folded the page for the crossword, then put the paper down. He noticed a crack in the left lower pane of the six-over-six-pane living room window and went to examine it, tracing the line of the break. Had it been there earlier, and had he failed to notice, or was the fissure new?

He heard a car engine, then saw it. The Subaru was returning up the driveway, with Hermia behind; they must have met near the entrance and, unable to negotiate the single lane, the visitor was backing up. Then the two women emerged, and they stood together a moment, face-to-face.

She did not believe it. She could not believe it. It was everything she'd hoped for, dreamed of, the daughter she'd despaired of standing at her side. Hermia's voice changed, broke, but it was not a question—or, rather, in the asking the question was answered: *Patricia?*

It was not, could not be, possible; it wouldn't happen like this. A light snow was falling, breeze-eddied, and she was shocked and shivering and holding her car keys and purse; she had been to Nickersons and then the post office, waiting in line, and decided not to fill the tank but do so with Lawrence later, since there was a quarter tank remaining and she was anxious to return to him and uneasy now alone. On the Pamet Road she'd felt a strange—what was the word?—premonition, a sense of something happening or about to happen, hovering, a shift in the sound of the engine or slight recalibration of the pressure in her ear. She cracked the window open, and the sound changed pitch. These days all change was threatful, and she was feeling anxious and accelerated down the driveway and nearly hit the car oncoming, then braked while the stranger backed up.

Her first reaction was anger: this was *her* house, *her* drive. Her visitors were few, and rare, and this was not a car she knew, or delivery truck, so maybe it was just somebody rubbernecking in Truro, or using the drive as a turn-around, lost, and she assumed that once she'd passed it in the parking circle the car would go away. It did not. It stopped. It was not a meter reader, not a service call. A woman emerged from the driver's side, tall, black-haired, in a black woolen coat and red scarf, and stood and waited for her, shifting her weight on her feet. Her mittens too were red. She peeled them off, uncertain, inattentive, and the way she peeled them off—finger by finger, in sequence— was her daughter's, smiling . . .

"Patricia?"

"How *are* you, Mom?"

"Are you all right?"

"I'm fine. I should have called, I know. Or given you some warning . . ."

"Let me look at you. How is this possible?"

"Possible?"

"That you're standing here, I mean."

Her daughter held out both hands. In the crook of her arm she was holding a clipboard. "Could I come in? It's cold."

WHAT FOLLOWED WAS DAY AFTER NIGHT. The two of them did enter, and Lawrence said, "Hello, again," and Hermia said, "You've met?" Not really, Lawrence said, and introduced himself, and Patricia explained to her mother that she'd arrived a bit before, and had just been leaving. She was deciding not to stay, or not this morning anyhow, which is why they'd almost crashed into each other at the mouth of Hermia's driveway, for she had nearly lost her nerve, and driven off, and had only been pretending to be mounting a petition drive and asking for a signature. Because what if her mother had sold this house also, or moved, and after all these years some total stranger answered; how would, *could* she have explained herself and what other reason offered for her presence at the door?

"Take off your coat," said Hermia.

"Yes."

"Do you want coffee," Lawrence asked, "tea?" and they all pretended that the visit was a normal one, a reunion after time away that did not entail disappearance and had not lasted for years. They behaved as though the child and parent had some catching up to do but not a total realignment of the daily round. "Tea, please," said Patricia, and sat down.

She told her tale. It emerged haltingly, little by little, but it did emerge. It had adventures in it, and people who were kind to her, and people who were less than kind, and dangers she alluded to but did not describe. That would come next. That came over time. Over time she did describe the places she had gone to and the people she had lived with and the farms she worked on—an orange grove in Florida, a cherry farm in northern Michigan—not as a day laborer, because she didn't have the hands or back for it, the stamina, but because she admired the migrant workers and had helped them organize—cooking, doing bookkeeping, laboring side by side and in a kind of solidarity with the unions and the workers—because the life of privilege and world of art and commerce from which she'd come seemed somehow to have been, *become,* the enemy and very far away.

That had been the point, of course, the starting point at least, this anger she'd been harboring in Arlington in the picturesque house with a trust fund and prospect of college and marriage and all those things the upper middle class can take for granted but our neighbors up in Woodford or Sandgate couldn't dream of, much less take for granted. Her friends in Arlington had been the children of the rich, the country gentlepersons—remember, Mom, that's what you used to call them?—and then there were the others, the dropouts and the inbred and the ones with walleyes and a hundred-pound sack of potatoes in a trailer for the winter: two worlds so separate that when she tried to bridge them she felt she was doing the split.

Rueful, Patricia smiled. Her teeth were good. It's one of the marks of distinction, she told Hermia and Lawrence, one of the ways we could tell which was which: what side of the orthodontics tracks you come from or if someone took care of your teeth. I thought of pulling them, you know, as an act of solidarity; Rain did, remember Rain? She used to say the difference between us and the locals is only cavities, is crooked teeth, and so she had hers pulled. The last I heard she was on welfare, living with a shell-shocked vet, but nobody who knew him knew if what went wrong was Desert Storm or something else inside his head, and Rain and Ryan and the others are ancient history now.

She spread her hands. She was wearing a diamond ring. There had been, she said, a sense of adventure, a belief that we were making up a whole new set of rules. And we were all so certain everything would work out fine: munitions manufacturers and gasoline cartels would come to see the light. When I left I felt a kind of desperation, Patricia was saying—*banishment, exile*—and of course I know and knew that it was self-imposed.

Except there was pride in it too. I'm twenty-nine by now, she said, old enough to know much better, but back then I was seventeen and with the kind of ignorance a teenager can wallow in: you close your eyes, it's night. You laugh, the world laughs with you. Give me your poor, your huddled masses, your weary was our theme song: the Statuettes of Liberty just yearning to be free. It's what we called ourselves, remember? The Radical G-String Quartet. There was all this music in my head, this certainty that everyone would start to sing and everybody join the universal melody, putting down their briefcases and Uzis and chorusing *Joy to the World* . . .

It didn't work, said Hermia, there isn't much joy in the world. Not a lot of music anyhow, her daughter said, sometimes I think that what I missed most was the music, not the guitar but piano, that silence in our living room I used to love to fill. And sometimes, on some dinky little mattress in the hallway of some boarded-up apartment I'd sing myself to sleep with *Kinderscenen*—you remember *Kinderscenen*?—or a phrase from *Für Elise* or the pages from the notebooks of Anna Magdalena Bach. You don't have a piano here, do you? and Hermia said, No. I didn't want to be reminded, didn't want one in the house.

"I'm sorry," said Patricia. "I deserved that, didn't I?"

"Yes."

Lawrence watched. He did not feel unwelcome or intrusive in their presence but the two women were focused on each other, completely absorbed in each other. The girl kicked off her shoes. Her toenails were dark red. Hermia wore glasses, as if her child's face was a small-print text and she needed to read every word. Mother and daughter sat close together on the couch, and it was as though the adult and her youthful self had been conjured into being by a kind of stagecraft: two halves of the one whole.

From time to time he left the room—to tend to the kettle, offering tea or replenishing olives and nuts. That afternoon he went walking alone, and when he returned at three o'clock it was clear his presence in the house had been explained. We knew each other long ago, Hermia was saying, and met again—it's embarrassing to admit this—on a cruise. A *cruise?* Patricia asked. At least it wasn't a college reunion or some sort of dating service, Lawrence said; at least it wasn't the Internet, with Google playing Cupid.

Next the girl described her history of doing nothing special, of being nowhere special, and how all that time—a dozen years!—you tell yourself that in fact it *is* special and the people you are with or not with matter, and the town you stay in or the road you travel is the only town and road. She spoke about Anne Martineau, the memory of her failed commune in the Pownal Valley, a place Anne had talked about often, not romanticizing it but making it seem like a life choice. And therefore she herself had joined one for eight months in Oregon, but it wasn't a success—the men

discussing how to build a teepee, or who would fix the tractor, and the women performing the actual work. We were always, she said, a bonfire away from freezing, and laundry
was a project, and the apples were blighted that season; you
raised a farm girl, Mama, but I wasn't any good at it and
wasn't all that interested in the end.

"You should have called," said Hermia. "And let me know
you planned to come. You could have written to tell me . . ."

"I know. I *should* have. I do know."

There were old scores to settle and explain. There was the
question of her silence, her telephone calls that left no sort of
message and letters that weren't really letters; do you have the
slightest idea, asked Hermia, how long I waited and how hard
I searched for you and how much it horrified me that you disappeared? Her face was stone. I know, I know, her daughter
said, it's inexcusable and I'm not making excuses, but the only
way I could continue was by forgetting everything, forgetting
you were waiting. Then little by little I *did* escape, I *did* forget,
and it seemed harder and harder and then finally impossible to
come back home; I never left the country, but the places I was
living in did feel like different countries, and the only way to
keep on keeping on was, can you forgive me, denial: not dead,
but dead to you.

She talked about hunger, then anger, the way you think a
safety net is waiting until you end up on the floor and find the
net has shredded and there's no one left to shelter you or offer
up a hand. There had been music to start with, and protest
songs, but it wasn't possible, or possible for *her* at least, to make
people listen or to pay attention. And when she did get a foot

in the door, what they wanted—mirthlessly she smiled again—were the other parts of her, not feet.

Then when the music failed she did poetry slams, a year or two of summer stock: disaster in the Poconos and, for one brutal winter, Minneapolis. There were towns she couldn't name and others she'd as soon forget where what she lived in were motels on the outskirts by abandoned mills or railroad tracks, and what flourished were crazies and rats. This thing called poverty, she said, is not as picturesque as I believed; I know it sounds ridiculous, ridiculously innocent, but the vow of poverty did seem attractive once. Sometimes I tried to blame you, Mom, for having failed to bring me home; sometimes I thought you should have tried, oh, *harder*, and then I tried to punish you for quitting hide-and-seek. Oh, it's a very long story, she said, and Hermia said we've got years of catching up to do; will you stay tonight at least? Patricia said if you want me to, I'd like that. Of course I do, Hermia said.

For the anger and suspicion and old scores to settle were less important, finally, than the pleasure of renewal and the grief assuaged. She had driven to the Cape from Boston, not with any conscious plan, but not on a whim either—or, rather, if it *was* a whim, it was one she'd planned. She had thought about writing, or calling, of course, but every time she tried to call there'd been too much to say. She had arrived without a suitcase and could always turn around and had been half expecting to, but this was better, this was best, the meeting she had dreamed of and imagined now for years . . .

Lawrence watched. The girl borrowed her mother's gray sweater. The dusk arrived, then dark. When Patricia shook her long hair loose, it was with Hermia's old insouciance, and at the base of her neck there was a butterfly tattoo. Something *my* mother used to say, said Hermia, your grandmother: every single winter solstice she declared the winter over now, this is the shortest day of all and they're getting longer and soon it will be spring. So why have you come back today, what made you change your mind?

Frank, she said, my prince. I've met the man, my prince at last, the one I plan to marry. He has this way about him, this *certainty* that right is right, wrong's wrong. Black's black for him, white's white. We were at this Fund-Raiser for Children of Africa, children with AIDS—well, *he* was there as an invited guest and I was working the concession stand, you know, dispensing beer and spring water and T-shirts. And he bought a pair of candied apples and offered me one of them, handed one back, and I said I couldn't accept that, and Frank said yes I could. So we argued a little and talked and walked and, when my shift ended, left the fund-raiser together—because I knew, and he did too, from the very first minute I saw him, *this* was the real thing.

Her face was radiant: it *is*, she repeated, it *is*. I knew it right away. We've been together now for months, and this is his engagement ring and of course I want you all to meet, but I think—*he* thinks, *we* thought—I needed to do this alone. One night I told him who I was, and where I came from when I wasn't playing hooky, and he told me I should settle up, declare myself, and what's totally amazing, Mom, is his father *knew* you way back when. His father, asked Hermia: who, what's his name? Patricia said, Will, he knew you back at Radcliffe, when he was living in Cambridge, and said he admired you while you were still in school. *Will,* said Lawrence, what's his last name, and when the girl offered it Hermia laughed; they talked about coincidence and how the three of them were friends, the *best* of friends, said Lawrence, but then we all lost touch, and what's he doing now? Now he's retired, said the girl; he was an entertainment lawyer and a big success at it; he told me how he played the guitar and wanted to play for a living, but wasn't good, or good enough, and so he went to law school and ended up dealing with music from what he called the corporate side, the making of deals, not CDs. He was, I think, almost embarrassed to have made a lot of money and run a kind of empire; he said he thought of it as selling out. But he's the *sweetest* man, the kindest man, and once I finally met him—when Frank took me out to Malibu—I understood, it's what I *felt,* I could come home. When I told him who you were and when he made the connection, he gave me—it sounds so old-fashioned saying it—his blessing. He sends you his best.

It was as though, thought Lawrence, the story was being enacted again, but this time in the younger generation: the girl and boy repeating what their parents once had done or failed to do. In the morning when he took his pills he heard their visitor breathing softly in the room beside the bathroom, and he told himself he ought to leave and let the child and mother celebrate alone. Alone together, Lawrence thought, and once again his eyes went wet, and he was overcome by how much and how often he'd been self-absorbed, king of his own little island, the self, and how the gift to make to Hermia would be his own departure. He might have lived his life with her but had not been prepared for it, was careless and unready . . .

Therefore he packed his bag. It did not take him long. Hermia came into his room and watched; she was wearing her dressing gown and slippers and asked, What are you doing? He said I thought it would be better for you, the two of you, if I just left, if I leave you alone. Not forever, I mean, for a while. You're used to this, said Hermia, you've done this sort of thing before, and he said it's different now. He could be home for Christmas; he could see Catherine, or Andrew, or John. Don't go, she said, I'm happy at last, don't just go and wreck it, okay?

Do you remember, Lawrence asked, those arguments we used to have—I don't mean the two of us, I mean *everybody* used to have—about coincidence and conscious choice: free will and determinism?

Yes, she said, and sat.

Well, I've been asking myself, he said, all night and morning I've been wondering if this is an example of one or the other or somehow a mixture of both; I feel, I mean, as if we're playing out a set of parts that someone else has written, I feel like a character in an old play and trying to remember what to say.

She smiled. " 'My lord, I do repent me . . .' "

"No."

" 'My liege, I did deny no prisoners . . .' "

"Not that one either. But you're the English major."

"Don't leave me," Hermia said. "It's only a few days to Christmas, and I need you to come down the chimney. They have a life, she'll go away. Not disappear, but leave again."

"It's wonderful to see you happy. So complete."

She looked at him. He smiled at her. His dear face shone. "Please stay."

Acknowledgments

Chapter 2 of this novel was published as "Spring and Fall" in the *Southern Review*, Summer 2006.

For details of and expertise on an architect's career, the author wishes to thank Douglas Kelbaugh, Dean of the A. Alfred Taubman College of Architecture and Urban Planning at the University of Michigan, as well as Margaret McCurry and Stanley Tigerman of the Chicago architectural firm of Tigerman McCurry. Thanks also to my colleagues at and the staff of the Institute for the Humanities at the University of Michigan—particularly its director, Daniel Herwitz—for making me so welcome during academic year 2004–5; it proved a safe haven and splendid place to work.

For permission to reprint Samuel Beckett's "Gnome" (1934) the author is grateful to Grove/Atlantic, Inc.

About the Author

Nicholas Delbanco is the Robert Frost Distinguished University Professor of English Language and Literature at the University of Michigan, where he directs the Hopwood Awards Program. He is the award-winning author of twenty-three books, including his most recently published novel, *The Vagabonds*.